RINGO'S TOMBSTONE

Center Point
Large Print

Also by W. R. Garwood and available from
Center Point Large Print:

Kill Him, Again

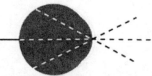

**This Large Print Book carries the
Seal of Approval of N.A.V.H.**

RINGO'S TOMBSTONE

W. R. Garwood

CENTER POINT LARGE PRINT
THORNDIKE, MAINE

This Center Point Large Print edition
is published in the year 2022 by arrangement with
Golden West Inc.

Originally published in the US by Bath Street Press.

The text of this Large Print edition is unabridged.
In other aspects, this book may vary
from the original edition.
Printed in the United States of America
on permanent paper sourced using
environmentally responsible foresting methods.
Set in 16-point Times New Roman type.

ISBN 978-1-63808-460-0 (hardcover)
ISBN 978-1-63808-464-8 (paperback)

The Library of Congress has cataloged this record
under Library of Congress Control Number: 2022938342

To
That True Blue
Lady
My Wife
Arlene

RINGO'S
TOMBSTONE

1 Rider from Texas

He rolled out of his damp blankets with first light. Poking up the remaining embers of the fire, he added some semi-dry grease wood, and finally got a pot of coffee going with water obtained from the nearby Whitewater Creek.

After shaking out the last of the grain, purchased at Steins Pass on the Arizona–New Mexico line, he filled Blackbird's morral and slung the fibre nose-bag over the horse's head. When the great, black horse had finished, he watered him in the sparkling stream, then staked him down again.

Out of food, except for the last of the coffee, he stood over the welcome warmth of the fire, tin cup in one hand and the Adjutant General's letter in the other.

Once more he re-read the single sheet of copperplate script, put down by some anonymous clerk at Austin:

"February 15, 1881
Sergeant John Ringold:
Pursuant to these orders, you are to immediately leave the State of Texas and proceed to Tombstone, Arizona Territory.

There you will assume a different identity and await further instructions. These are to be picked up at General Delivery four weeks hence at Benson, A.T.
Signed, William A. King,
    Adjutant General, Texas"

There was a lengthy note, scribbled in another hand on the back of the dispatch:

"John,
I don't know who was at fault in the shooting at Lampassas on February Twelfth. But blood-feuds have about run their course in this State. Your intrusion into the Higgins and Horrell troubles might be condoned as a relative, as I know you to be kin to the Horrells, but never while wearing the Ranger Badge.
    If I were not a longtime friend of your father, Colonel Ringold, you would this minute be jailed tight! So, keep out of Texas until I sort this over. Consider yourself on a half-pay while in A.T. At least you might be of some use to the Wells Fargo Company!"

There was no signature, but Sergeant "on half-pay" of the Texas Rangers, John Ringold, recognized the fiery voice of Uncle Bill King, and was certain the Adjutant General meant every hen-track.

Wells Fargo? What had that firm of freight agents to do with himself? It was a question he'd posed, more than once, on the journey from Brownwood, Texas.

The sun, now standing at about seven o'clock, was burning the last shreds of river mist into flat, floating tatters of crimson flame—like that fire at Horrell's—when he rode away from the river, heading on the last weary miles toward the mining camp with the ominous name—Tombstone!

And as he rode, he found his mind back-trailing—to the events that had stampeded, one after the other, forcing him out of the Rangers—and two territories and a half a state away from home and family.

Like magic-lantern slides the scenes flashed on the screen of his memory.

There had been six men in the scout from Captain Spark's Ranger camp on the Gabriel River, ten miles east of Burnett, in north-central Texas. He'd been in charge of them and pushing the detail at a good trot, despite the time of night. A new moon, pared down to a pale sliver, flared and faded behind the shifting, ragged overcast, allowing momentary glimpses of water-soaked road.

Their guide, Old Buford, a black stablehand from the Horrell Ranch, had come clattering into camp about dark, chattering out a tale of night-riding, fence-cutters due at the Horrell spread. The old fellow had been overjoyed to find Marse Johnny Ringold in camp, and ready to ride back with him.

After listening to Buford's tale that Horrell had, somehow, got wind of a raid on his new barbed-wire fencing, Captain Sparks detailed Sergeant John Ringold and a party of six to hustle the twenty miles back to that ranch—but with an iron-clad order to refrain from any gunplay.

"This whole area is one powder keg right now, Sergeant. These damned fence wars seem to keep breaking out all over. It's got to the point where just about everybody is either a Fence Man or a Free Grass Man, and this looks like another flare-up at Horrell's—though, for the life of me, I can't think but what those blamed Horrell boys had seen enough trouble in the past ten years, without taking up with bobwire."

Ringold had nodded silently, collected his men and headed out of camp, wondering if Sparks knew he was a second-cousin to the forever-feuding Horrells.

They passed through the village of Burnett at six o'clock, and turned north onto the San Antone-Lampassas Road, following the constant urging of their guide, who clung to the saddle horn of his piebald mule, mumbling. "Foh Gawd, I ain't suh if'n we be able to get dar in time . . . but I wuz mighty glad to find out t'was you, Marse Johnny . . . knows you won't let them fence busters bring harm onto our ole place . . . knows you'd fight foh th' place wheah you and them boys had sich happy times."

Old Buford was right. Those had been happy times out at the Horrell spread. His father, Colonel Ringold, first cousin to old Sam Horrell, was a lawyer, and had been ever since the end of the war. And it was as a town youngun', visiting his country cousins that he, Johnny Ringold, got his first taste of riding bareback, playing at Comanche fighting, hunting Santa Anna, and the rest of the delights of outdoor life.

But that was all nearly ten years past. There'd been two years of schooling at Texas College, and six years with the Ranger force between that carefree time and now. He hadn't even seen any of the Horrells for a year or so—just about the time that the Horrell-Higgins troubles petered out due to the many deaths on both sides—and the unceasing efforts of the Ranger office to get both parties to sign, what amounted to, a final peace pact.

"Fence-cutters just ain't all, Marse Johnny," the negro went on. "Marse Sam Horrell also tell me dat some of de Higgins been makin' fight talk again in Lampassas . . . sayin' dey wuz put off two years back . . . dat the Rangers forced 'em into a yaller-coward truce. But no moh!"

"Don't sound like any Higgins. Sounds more like some barfly trying to stir up trouble," he told his second-in-command, Corporal Jennings.

"Guess we'll get to see," Jennings dryly commented. "Here, you Buford, keep down that caterwaulin'. We ought to be durn close to th' Horrell place, hadn't we?"

Jennings was right. They'd crossed the Sulphur Creek bottoms, and half a mile beyond the brush-choked thickets an enormous pecan tree marked a rise of ground. He and the Horrell youngun's had camped out there years ago, before that troubled family had packed bag-and-baggage and jaunted over to New Mexico Territory—to get away from some fight over land rights—or possibly from their old foes, the Higginses. But the Horrells had come back in time for Mart and Tom to be shot down by night-riders. And now only young Sam was left—and calling for the Rangers.

"Stretch out!" He turned in his saddle and waved his little party into a looser group. "Corporal Jennings, you and Siekert ride ahead with Buford, but keep him quiet. Thompson and Brown, and the rest of you—fifty feet apart." He'd caught sight of the pecan tree again, now towering tall and gaunt againt the late winter skyline.

14

As he rode forward, the moon clotted over with a clabber of dirty silver wool, and it began to look like snow, but the light ahead grew—glaring with scarlet intensity, until the fleeting cloud wrack sailed in a sea of floating flame. The waving branches and trunk of the pecan were burnished crimson as they galloped past.

"Fire! Hell of a fire over there," Jennings shouted back, and as they crested the rise, a towering orange and black plume billowed up from an outbuilding.

Taking the old rail fence, south of the house, he led his bunch pounding up to the door of the rambling, two-storied, white-frame building.

"Gawd! Gawd! Deys killed 'em all—killed 'em all. Killed poh ole Spoht dah." The negro tumbled from his heaving mule and stood, wringing gnarled hands over the lifeless body of a Horrell hound. "Spoht! Oh dem devils—killed de best coon dog in Buhnett County."

"That Rangers, Buford?" A voice echoed from behind a shuttered window on the upper floor.

"Yes, this is John. Is that you, Sam? What the hell is going on?"

"We lost our hound and our barn out there, with my two best riding horses. The rest are out in the back eighty, if they ain't gone off where the bobwire was ripped down. I saw them polecats through my night glasses while they cut out a heap." Horrell pushed the shutters open and leaned out, Winchester in hand. Behind, the shadowy forms of women and children peered down.

"Marse Sam, wheah dem debbils? Ain't heard no shootin'." The old man rose from the still body of the animal and wiped his eyes.

Horrell emerged onto the long, wooden porch. "Hasn't been anyone around since right after dark, when about a dozen rode up and opened fire from the road," he said, clasping Ringold by the hand. "When I got the folks all into the house, about half of that trash went down and set a fire to the barn. The rest went out back after the bob-wire. Never said a word any of 'em, with their damned flour sacks over their heads. I didn't dare come out—someone's got to stay alive to run this place."

Ringold and his men stood around, staring at the smoldering, orange heap of the barn, talking to the Horrell clan, when the sound of hoofbeats grew on the Lampassas road.

"Inside, everyone." Ringold shoved women and children back into the building, and stationed his men behind the corners of the house. "Get the horses out of sight around back."

He crouched down behind the picket fence, facing the road with Horrell, and Privates Siekert and Brown, as a cluster of horsemen swept into the drive, pulling up scant yards from the silent house.

16

"Rangers! Get those hands up and sit still," Ringold shouted at the suddenly frozen group of riders.

"Johnny Ringold, sure as Moses," rang out a rasping voice.

He recognized the man as Jake Ryan, a distant relation of the Higginses, and a known bar-room loafer and small-time thief, who'd done time for some stolen mules a year or so back.

"Barn burning night-riders!" yelled Sam Horrell, standing up with his rifle glittering at the silent horsemen.

"You're under arrest, every mother's son of you! Pile off those mounts!" Ringold, backed by Siekert and Brown, advanced. "Where's your flour sacks?"

As he approached the group, he spotted several other familiar figures from around Lampassas. There was Bob Moore and Jesse Vineyard, in addition to Ryan, who seemed half-drunk. But the one who stopped him in his tracks was Rufe Higgins, a cousin of Pink Higgins, who ranched a small spread about twenty miles to the east.

"Damn it," Ringold cursed. "I was thinking it was just some fool barn burners . . . not you and that damned Jake Ryan. What are you trying to do, using a torch to start up a hell of a trouble again?" He peered at the hulking Higgins, trying to read his expression.

"Flour sacks and torches? What in hell are

you rantin' about?" Higgins shoved his big belly at Ringold. "See this badge?" He poked a thumb at his sheepskin coat. "Horse's head, right? Anti-horsethief patrol . . . and I head it for th' hull county. That's just what we're a'doin' here. Got word in town that night-riders or horsethiefs was about this way . . . and we come out, th' boys and me." He stared off at the smoldering barn. "Looks like they got here, all right."

"They did, or you and your gang did," Sam Horrell growled.

"Shut your damned mouth, Horrell," another of the silent riders spoke up. "Here we come out to give you a hand and find your place full of Rangers, and one of 'em a tin-star of a Horrell, eh, John Ringold?" The man stared at him in the gloom, hand near his holster.

He knew the speaker, and it was like looking at himself in a clouded mirror. It was Jim Rush, a boyhood chum who'd camped out at the old pecan tree with the Horrell boys and himself, when both had been town kids. Jim later had taken up with a fast saloon bunch, becoming a rounder and so-called sport, just about the time that he, Ringold, had joined the Rangers. In the old days, the two had been nearly inseparable— and were even known as the Lampassas Twins. Then his parents had moved on to Brownwood, where his father had taken over a law firm, when the old attorney, who'd founded it in the Fifties, had passed on.

Even now, Ringold knew the resemblance to Rush was mighty close. Both were the same height of about six-feet-one in their boots. Both were rangy and, he supposed, that they could be accounted passable looking—at least their features were both rather thin, with a good straight nose, and firm mouth and jaw, while their eyes, as the Beadle Dime Books would say, were wide-set and piercing. And that was where the resemblance went astray. Ringold's eyes were dark brown, like both his and Jim's hair, but Rush's were tiger-cat green.

"Forget what I look like, Johnny?" Rush chuckled sardonically. "Maybe you think you've seen my face on one of your fool fugitive posters?"

"No, Jim. I was just thinking it's been a long time since we kids . . . well, come on, get back to the rest of your bunch, and let's try to get this straight."

He turned to Higgins. "I hear someone has been making a lot of fight talk in town about running out the Horrells. Anything to do with that?" He motioned old Buford over, from where he'd been lurking in a fence corner. "Buford, here, said such nonsense was going on."

"Hell . . . I ain't got time to argue about a fool darky," Higgins blustered. "And I don't take it kindly gettin' shoved about fer doin' our duty comin' out here to ketch some damned night-ridin' rascals . . . and gittin' lied about by some nigger."

"That's right, Johnny Ringold." Jake Ryan swaggered forward. "Two barns burnt last night, not ten miles from here . . . and we'll ketch'm yet, and don't need any Horrell kinfolk to help us," he gritted. "And you, Buford, what right you got telling tales . . . 'cause some of us boys was pokin' fun at you?"

"Close up, Buford," Ringold commanded. "It's plain some wrong talk went on . . . from the wrong kind of folks." He was about to order Ryan, Jim Rush and the bunch with Higgins to remount and head for town—when, without warning, Ryan grabbed a knife out of his boot, and went for the old negro, slashing at him murderously.

Ringold pulled his Colt Frontier and slammed its long barrel against Ryan's head, pole-axing him before the knife could do any damage.

But in drawing the pistol from its holster, it had been an involuntary act to cock the weapon—and it discharged from the blow. Its explosion ripped through the night air and Higgins folded up in the middle, and tumbled headlong beside Ryan.

The Rangers surrounded the remaining men, disarming them, including Jim Rush, who struggled between Siekert and Brown. "You heard Higgins! We're deputized County Officers to uphold the law. You, Johnny Ringold sure played hell this time! We ride in here trying to get our hands on those night-riders . . . you tell us we set that fire. You and your Rangers are sure . . ." He broke off as Corporal Jennings got a hammer lock, wrestling him to the ground beside the two prone figures.

"Sergeant! Higgins here got himself a clincher." Jennings looked up from the motionless Chief of the Anti-Horsethief Patrol.

Sam Horrell squatted down beside Jennings. "Yep, John, looks like that stray shot got him right in the middle of his brisket. He's about as dead as he'll ever be." He rose, leaning on his Winchester, and shook his head. "Sure hope this doesn't start things up all over again . . . there just ain't enough Horrells and Higgins left."

There was nothing more to do. The barn-burning, barb busters were untraceable in the dark, and it was snowing enough now to cover their tracks. And with a corpse on his hands, dead from Ringold's own pistol, he ordered the bunch back to Lampassas, under guard of Corporal Jennings and two of the privates.

Ryan, who'd come around with a sore head, was trussed up in his saddle as was Rush, who muttered threats and curses under his breath. Higgins was lashed face down over his horse's back, and cinched tight with a picket rope. The rest went along quietly in the descending snow-squalls.

Leaving Brown to give Sam Horrell a hand in watching the place, in case of more trouble, Ringold rode the twenty-odd miles back to camp, arriving there in a driving snow storm around midnight.

The interview with Captain Sparks, in the commanding officer's wind-battered tent was as chilly as the blustering, snowy night outside.

"That Higgins was some sort of a peace officer in pursuance of his duty? Am I right, Sergeant?

"But . . . he was also a Higgins riding up to a Horrell place at the wrong time and hour. Is that what you are saying?" The testy, little Ranger Chief sat on the edge of his cot, wrapped in a pair of saddle blankets, poking irritably at a stubborn sheet-iron stove that refused to fire up. "Damned Yankee Government-Issue stoves . . . about as worthless as your own promises!"

"Sir!" Ringold stiffened. The events of the past eight hours had placed a heavy load upon nerves and temper. "That ranch had been hit hard when we arrived, as I've reported . . . burned barn, destroyed stock, terrorized women and children . . . and cut wire. And you want me to treat Higgins and his rascals with kid-gloves and rose-water!"

"Higgins!" The Captain leaped up, forgetting

the sluggish stove, shedding his blankets, to stand like a feisty, little fighting cock in his buckskin-top boots and red flannels. "It's exactly because you up and shot a Higgins that we could have an outbreak of another damned feud between those fire-eaters . . . worse trouble than dozen barb-busting fights. And all because you couldn't subdue a man without blowing a hole in him!"

"Captain . . ."

"Sergeant, you are dismissed. Get that report in writing tomorrow. I'm sending another patrol to the Horrell place to relieve those men. And in the meantime, take a week's furlough. Go visit your folks. You surely need a change of scenery!"

It was at his parents' old, two-story, stone house, with its wooden gallery running across front and ends, standing back at the end of a lane on the northern edge of Brownwood, that the Adjutant General of Texas caught up with him.

They were sitting down to a late Saturday breakfast in the long, white-plastered dining room, with its oak-beamed ceiling, when the local mail carrier arrived with an "official" State of Texas envelope.

"Well, John?" Colonel Ringold paused, coffee cup halfway to his mouth.

"Uncle William sends his regards and . . .

thinks it would be better if I take up traveling for a spell."

"Oh, Johnny? What does he mean . . . traveling?" His mother's gentle, aristocratic face was touched with anxiety as she rose from the immaculately spread table.

"Actually it's a reassignment. Just a temporary thing, Mother. With all the thunder and lightning after that affair at Horrell's, the Adjutant General feels that as I am kinfolk to Horrell, I should absent myself for the time being."

"Run away? He orders you to turn tail and skedaddle? By Harry, that doesn't sound like the man who rode stirrup to stirrup with me from Sixty to Sixty-Five, while we thrashed Yanks over half our poor country!" Colonel Baylor slammed his coffee cup down in its delicate English bone china saucer to the detriment of both. "Well," he mopped at the shards and moisture with an Irish linen napkin, jerking a thumb at an attentive black servant for another refill. "Well . . . I suppose Bill could have had something in mind."

"Yes, like the beginning of more troublesome times," Mrs. Ringold joined her tall son at the crackling fire. "It's not that John is any more a coward than ever you were, Colonel Randolph Ringold. But orders are orders, as you certainly know." She clasped her son's hand and smiled up at him. "I suppose I am relieved now that you never took up with one of our young ladies, though enough have kept setting their caps for you. Now, you can leave for a spell and have no ties to pull you back . . . until matters work out. Where do these orders take you?"

"Arizona Territory."

"Arizona? My, that is a good long piece. But I should like to see it, myself. They say it's beautiful in a wild and vast way, especially in the spring." A daughter of pioneers, she had married the son of a man who had helped to establish the Lone Star State, half a century before. "Just think, Randolph! John will be riding through that lovely, lonely land while you sit in your office and hunt for torts or whatever you are perpetually looking for in those dusty, old, calfskin books." Like a young girl, she sometimes sought to tease her successful attorney husband. But she was ever aware of being the wife of an ex-soldier and the mother of a Ranger. "Colonel, why don't you go over the maps with John, while I see to his clothing and provisions."

The semi-arid wastelands of western New Mexico Territory lay well behind. Turning north toward Tombstone, he now rode through an area that seemed more fitted for stock-grazing than for the giving up of its mineral wealth. Over to his left, a line of meandering willows marked a

25

good-sized watercourse, the San Pedro, which gave its name to the lush valley through which he traveled.

The road soon swung more to the northeast, and he began to catch glimpses of the black, bristling super-structure of mineshafts. And, in the intensifying sunlight, the mountains loomed up on all four corners of the horizon—two-dimensional as pale blue, cardboard cutouts—Dragoons to the northeast, Mule Mountains to the southeast, Huachucas to the southwest, and Whetstones to the northwest.

He met his first human, three miles from town, as he was threading through the upthrust, rolling Tombstone Hills. This was a wagoner, stolidly lashing at the indifferent backs of his nine teams of mules, as they pulled three, immense loaded ore wagons southward. At Ringold's friendly wave, the man gave a short jerk of his head and spat a rippling stream of amber on the offside of his craft.

Ringold sat on his black horse, in the middle of the road, and watched the rumbling, inexorable progress of the freighter on out of sight over a hill. He'd meant to inquire as to a good place to put up, and where to board his mount, Blackbird, upon arriving in Tombstone.

Though it was just March 8, the warmth from the noon-high sun had driven any lingering cold from the crisp, dry air. It was a far cry from the

26

snowy-chill of central Texas. That Arizona sun surely had a bite of its own.

He spurred on his horse, racking him along as the roadway eased down into a gulch and up onto Tombstone Flats. Here he met his second Arizonian, and this one had no difficulty in holding speech.

"Wait up there, stranger, and I'll ride with you . . . if you want some company." The speaker was a medium-sized fellow, dressed in dark, checkered coat and pants, shiny black boots, and topped off with a dark brown, narrow-brim sombrero. He stood beside a beautiful paint mare, tightening a cinch.

"Sure enough." Ringold reined in and waited as the young man swung up in to a very elegant, hand-tooled saddle, displaying a long barreled pistol on his hip.

"From Texas, ain't you?" The man's wide, blue eyes twinkled with good-will. "Could tell from that old saddle. Steal it off'n a Ranger?"

"Well," Ringold was a bit nonplussed by such a question, "to tell the truth, you pretty near hit the mark. I did come from Texas, but the saddle's been mine for quite a few years." He kicked up Blackbird to keep even with the Paint's cantering gait. "You some sort of expert on saddles?"

They were approaching the outskirts of Tombstone, and riding past the first miners' cabins. "Turn in here," the stranger indicated a sandy

27

lane running off at right angles to the stage road. "This is Tough Nut Street. Leads right down to Fourth, where you can put up your plug at th' Pioneer Livery. Y'see I deal in horses. That answer your quiz on bein' a saddle expert? I use Pioneer most of th' time when I don't go over to th' O.K."

When they dismounted at the livery and had turned their mounts in to the pot-bellied stable-owner, the stranger led Ringold over to the nearest saloon—Hafford's Corner Five, at Allen and Fourth, adjacent to a very presentable hostelry, the Cosmopolitan Hotel.

"My name's Deal . . . Pony Deal. Got that handle from th' business I sort of pursue when I ain't playin' cards."

Ringold lifted his brimming schooner of beer in a salute. "This is one unusual town. Damned good beer, and really first-rate buildings. Yet it's way to hell-and-gone out in this back pasture of Satan." He took a long pull at the beer, and glanced over at Deal. "Hope you don't take offense."

Pony Deal leaned back against the long, polished mahogany, while he killed his drink and signaled the efficient Mexican barkeep for refills. "Hell, I'm not one of the city fathers. And you'd be surprised the folks that find Tombstone a great place to hole up . . . ah . . . y'never said your name?"

"No, I guess I never did. Well, you can call me . . . Ringold." He'd spoken before thinking, and now he cursed silently to himself. Off on the wrong foot before he'd got the trail dust out of his throat. Uncle Bill had most definitely ordered him to use an alias in Arizona Territory.

"Ringo? Sounds Mex or Eyetalian? But you sure look just plain Anglo to me." Deal pushed over a refilled glass.

He took it silently and downed about half, while his mind revolved swiftly. This nosey, young barfly had misunderstood. *Ringo?* It wasn't much of an alias, in fact damned close to his real name—but what about it? He didn't feel like a man on the dodge, yet it appeared that this Pony Deal suspected him of being just that.

"There a front name to that Ringo?"

"Name is John." He shifted a foot on the brass bar-rail, and slowly adjusted his ivory-handled Colt in its well-worn scabbard. If Deal accepted him as being on the scout, why not play it that way? But he wasn't going to change his first name—it would have to stay plain John. He emptied his schooner and stared into the bottom of the glass.

"Here, let's have one more round before I go check in to that hotel, and catch up on some back-sleep. And *John Ringo* is buying!"

2 Ringo Meets the Clantons

He had arrived in Tombstone on Saturday, March 8, and for the three days remained in his second story room at the Cosmopolitan, coming down for meals in the spick-and-span dining room and only wandering out around the streets in the evenings. Pony Deal had seemingly vanished after their whistle-wetting in the saloon—and no one else paid any attention to him. That was the way he wanted it, until he got his bearings, for he still had some days before picking up his orders at Benson.

Without frequenting the dozen or so saloons too often, he still got a strong impression of the liveliness of the place, particularly at night. Most of the evening roisterers were not cowmen, but miners, intent on washing the shaft dust from their hairy throats and bucking the tiger—and up until midnight they made Tombstone howl. Strangely, there were few discharges of weapons, even though there seemed no ordinance against packing firearms on the streets.

In the daytime, the commercial and social face of Tombstone was in evidence. Elegantly dressed women, mainly wives of mine-owners and merchants, were to be seen at the northside of town as they paraded from store to store, carrying sunshades and beaded handbags. Women of another variety were also on the streets; demimondaines and saloon girls. But these be-feathered and furbelowed females seemed to keep to such south Tombstone avenues as Tough Nut, and Allen Streets, leaving Fremont and Safford to "the ladies."

Wondering where Pony might have got to, he inquired at the livery stable only to be met with a shrug. After lunch that day he went up to his room and dug out a well-thumbed copy of "Fugitives From Justice"—kept in his saddle bags along with other trivia.

This *Book of Rogues*, printed at Austin, was an official publication circulated to Rangers and State officers each half year. His copy was dated 1880, making it a year old, but he vaguely recalled a wanted listing from Deaf Smith County, over near the Texas–New Mexico line. The information was there on page eight:

"DEIHL, CHARLEY—Theft of horse. Age 26; height 5 feet 8 inches; weight 135 pounds; color white, complexion light; eyes blue, hair sandy; is quick spoken, one gold tooth; thought to have come into state from Nebraska where he is supposed to have been a member of the Doc Middleton band of horse thieves. Believed to have left Texas."

So that was probably where Pony had got to—off scouting for stock—and not his own. He wondered if the gruff livery man was in on the game. But it was really not any of his business. He was on the run out of Texas, himself. Hadn't Pony spotted him as a possible fellow fugitive?

With the end of the week approaching, and both the Tombstone Nugget and the Tombstone Epitaph read from stem to stern, he grew more and more restless. Taking Blackbird from the livery, he rode west out of town to the flats beyond Comstock Hill. Here he was beyond the clatter of the boardwalks and the chuff and clink of the steam engines at the mine shafts that ringed the outskirts of the town.

He dismounted and sat on a large, flat rock letting the golden warmth of the late February sun ease through his red, woolen shirt. Off to the north rose the saw-toothed blue scallops of the Dragoons, reputed stronghold of Cochise. But Cochise was long gone, and the main burr under the Army's saddle blanket now was old Nana, who'd taken over as the Apache scourge of God after Victorio had been ambushed by Mexican Regulars down in the Tres Castillos Mountains.

According to the Tombstone papers, Nana this minute was rampaging through southwest New Mexico, with all the New Mexican troops hot after his ever-cold trail. Tombstone papers, the Nugget in particular, had pointed out that the

Indian War wasn't over yet, and the mountain ranges surrounding the town offered a perfect avenue of attack for wild warriors—mountain corridors capable of spewing out sudden death from the four corners of the compass.

It was little wonder that everyone riding out of Tombstone, or in, went heeled for trouble.

He looked to the south, in the direction of the nearest Army Post, Fort Huachuca, on the northern slope of the Huachuca Mountains. It was a good twenty-five miles away, yet the air was so crystal clear he could easily see the ground-glass glitter of the Fort's heliograph, a minute sun-spark that winked and blinked its message to some unseen troop out on the prowl for Apaches—or renegades—or horsethieves!

That post was scant miles from the Mexican Border, and reputed to be as strong a deterrent to smugglers out of Mexico as it was to Apaches, according to the Tombstone Epitaph. Those free-booters, who chose not to pay revenue, despite the Fort, were said to bring in everything from sterling silver, for the fine ladies of the town, to number one Hong Kong opium for the pipe-dreaming crowd in Hop Town, the Chinese section at Second and Allen Streets. And the export merchandise "midnight trans-shipped" through those same Huachucas, often consisted of good Spencer Carbines and Winchester 76s—bound for vainglorious Mexican revolutionaries and just plain bandits. So said the Nugget.

Yet it wasn't to chase smugglers, or Indians or even people like Charley "Pony" Deihl—alias Deal, that he'd been ordered to Arizona Territory. It was to work, in some manner, with the folks at Wells Fargo—and he'd damned better find out on Saturday.

Vagrant thoughts concerning those murderous Apache warriors, from the pages of the Nugget and the Epitaph, got under his hide and he could feel the skin along his shoulders chill and crawl, despite the growing glare of sunlight. He shook his head with a grunt and pulled off his dusty hat, running his fingers through his thatch of black hair. If there was one thing that got him it was the stealthy way redskins had of slipping up on some poor bastard—and then the death stroke. He recalled tales his father had passed on from his father of the battles and twilight attacks of the Comanches back before the war.

And his friend of those childhood days, Jim Rush, as just a sprout, had sat beside him listening to those bloody tales. He'd bet Jim would sing a different tune now, if he were out here on this frontier. He wondered what Jim and the rest of that Higgins crowd were up to. Probably under peace bonds to watch their step—that is, if the Higgins-Horrell trouble hadn't broken out again. But that would be because Uncle Bill

King didn't have the know-how or firepower to keep the peace with his Corps of Rangers. He'd probably assign one Ranger to watch the whole crowd. It was just like him. "One Ranger, one riot," he'd said before, had Uncle Bill, but it worked.

He gave a brittle laugh and swung up into Blackbird's saddle. Unbeknownst to the Territorial Governor of Arizona, Adjutant General William King of Texas had assigned one Ranger to Wells Fargo.

He rode back toward Tombstone noticing the round clusters of hedgehog cactus beginning to break out in blossoms of pale orange, and patches of rattleweed along the roadway sporting their own yellow buds. Spring was on its way to Southern Arizona.

After he put up his horse at the Pioneer, he tugged off his stained sombrero again, and looked it over, then stared down at his battered boots. If the rest of his rig seemed as poor as that, he'd play thunder close-herding with the sporting crowd.

Though he'd stopped by the Corner Five several times for a beer, he'd stayed out of the more elegant dives—such as the Oriental and the Alhambra, where most of the big games went on. He knew he could hold his own with a deck. There were several members of Captain Sparks's company who still owed him some months pay.

So, now was the time to start looking like a gent of leisure—not too prosperous yet enough to sit in on some games.

But there was no use in investing in over-expensive duds—if that Wells Fargo assignment turned out to be some shotgun messenger's job, or perhaps driving some damned stage.

One of the better establishments dealing in men's clothing was Sydow and Kicke's Emporium on Allen. Stepping up to the door he collided with a man just coming out.

As the stranger bent to retrieve a shiny plug hat, before it rolled into the dusty street, his velveteen-trimmed cutaway flapped open to display a brace of pearl-handled pistols. "Dammit! Why don't you cowpokes watch your feet?"

Ringold caught the runaway lid on the bottom step, brushing it off as he handed it back to the pale-faced gambler. For gambler he must be with long, white fingers, expressionless face and drooping blond mustache.

The man planted his hat back on his yellow hair and stared at him, with eyes that reminded Ringold of a cougar's—grey-green and deadly.

Here was the first dyed-in-the-wool killer he'd ever met, every sense sharpened by years in the Rangers told him so. He'd come up against cow-thieves and outlaws in his time, but they were generally just men who'd taken a wrong turn in the trail. Compared with this one, the Higgins crowd and even Pony Deal were all just so many Sunday school kids.

"That's a fancy hat. Mind if I go on in and buy myself one?"

"Stranger, it just isn't your style." The man's voice was as expressionless as his face.

Ringold held the door for the fellow, wondering a bit at his side-wise descent of the steps, like a sidewinder. The gambler kept his cutaway open, with a pair of transparent fingers, like some elegant lady lifting her skirts slightly to allow for a safe passage. But it was evident that he was allowing easy access to his pistols.

Once on the wooden sidewalk, the man removed his hat, gave it another brush and then glancing back at Ringold in the doorway, gave him a chilled smile. "No harm done to the old tile, I guess. A hat is a hell of a thing to row about anyway. If you've got any money left after those bandits in there get through with you, come on down to the Crystal Palace for a friendly game."

By the time he'd made the last of his purchases, he was pretty well parted from most of his wallet's contents. It was, he told himself, in a good cause. Those old trail clothes had seen their last days, and he'd really needed fresh duds.

With the plump and balding Herman Sydow hovering at his side, he gave a last glance into the gilt, gingerbread-framed mirror and decided that, while plug hats might not be just his style, he did cut a pretty decent figure in his black, broadcloth suit. He stood in a pair of the best boots in the place—Cowboy's Pride, black calfskin stunners, going for a steep five dollars. What topped off the "ensemble" as far as he was concerned was a Crescent sombrero in dark grey felt, with a gold star and a silk cord around the band. That went for a whacking four dollars—damned near half the price of the suit.

Leaving the bowing merchant, he stopped off at a barber midway in the block, took himself a bath in a tin tub in the back room, and had a hair trim and a close shave out front.

The fly-specked calendar on the barber shop wall told him that tomorrow was Saturday, March 15, and the day he was due in Benson.

He went by the hotel, left his range clothes in a bundle on his bed and going back out sauntered down to the Crystal Palace Saloon. He felt like celebrating a bit, because after tomorrow—who knew? He might be pitching hay in some Wells Fargo feed lot. That was one reason he'd saved his old clothes.

At first he didn't spot the cold-eyed sport in the saloon, but hearing the crash of overturned chairs at the far end of the place, he peered thru the rifts of drifting blue tobacco smoke, and saw a knot of men breaking apart from one of the tables, scattering like a covey of quail.

They left a gambler sitting, shiny new hat on the table beside him, along with a pile of chips. One of his pearl-handled pistols rested on the green baize table cover, near a motionless right hand.

Standing across the table was a young cowhand, as motionless as that deadly right hand on the table. The youngster stood frozen—staring like a blundering bird, charmed by a king snake, gaze locked on the grey-green eyes of the man in the velveteen-fronted frock coat.

The young puncher's hand hesitated, halfway to his pistol butt, also frozen for the long, tension-jammed moment.

Ringold felt the moment imperceptibly moving to a showdown. He'd seen too much gun play not to recognize the impending finale.

This young kid hadn't the chance of a hailstone on a red-hot stove. Noting the tensing of the youngster's arm, the beginning of the downward swing—he moved, flipping back his coat with a thumb, grasping his Colt, and whipping it up—barrel a scant foot from the gambler's patrician nose. "Hold it!"

The man, never moving a fiber, merely gave him that chilled grimace, and slowly shrugged, while the air whistled from the puncher's clenched lips in a sigh. "Make your play," he murmured, slowly pulling his hand back from the tabled pistol, "that is if you want stiffer action." Still moving in delayed motion, he drew a long, slim, twisted cigar from his vest, and breaking the tiny red point of a lucifer, with polished thumbnail, he lit up.

The room still vibrated with unseen tensions. Customers shifted uneasily along the edges of the room—waiting.

The young cowhand beside him cleared a hoarse throat. "Mister . . . is it o.k. if'n I . . ." Here he was interrupted by the bustle of two men elbowing through the batwings and making a noisy way toward them. One, a stocky, red-faced man in nondescript dark pants and shirt, crisscrossed with a wide pair of yellow suspenders, decorated with an enormous, nickel-plated star, and armed with a calvary-length Colt, shoved his larger companion out of the way. "Keep back, Ike, till we see what this is all about!" Turning on Ringold, "You put up that weapon, and you . . . Doc," whirling back to the gambler, "keep those lily-white hands of yours in plain sight!"

The gambler, hailed as Doc, smiled his most frigid grimace and, leaning back, puffed leisurely on his cheroot. "Easy does it there, Mister Sheriff Johnny Behan. I like my Gold Coast Twister too well to waste my breath on any fussin'."

"You, Mister, put away that weapon right now," the Sheriff barked at Ringold, who had hesitated to put up his Colt. "Right now!" Behan's black chin-whiskers poked aggressively at him.

Ringold shrugged and jammed the six-gun back into its scuffed holster, keeping his hand easily at his side.

"Now, by gobs, what is all this?" Behan bustled back to the gambler, Doc, and the still immobile young puncher, while the big man at his back began to chuckle deep in his vest-clad barrel chest.

"Hell there, Sheriff, I can see plain what's happened. Same as last week when I let this young rooster come in here and perch on the wrong roost. This young pup just cain't stay away from Doc's game. An' the two on 'em just strike sparks." He cuffed at the young puncher, sending him staggering toward the door. "Damn you, Billy Clanton! Git out front and up on th' wagon . . . and drive back to th' ranch. Old Pa will skin you for sure this time. I'll ride your buckskin."

"Right, Clanton." The gambler blew a ripple of smoke from his peculiar cheroot at the ceiling, and leaned back in his chair. Reaching out, he took the pearl-handled six-gun, and, giving all a slight grimace, holstered the weapon. "Sit down, Mister . . . , never got the name?"

"Ah, *Ringo*. Think I'll hold on our game. One brace a day is about enough for me." He gave the man Doc a short nod, and turning made his way through the gathering crowd. For some reason that cold-eyed sport had chosen to back off, just why he couldn't say—for he was dead-sure that it didn't happen too often.

He stood on the sidewalk outside the Crystal Palace for a moment, idly watching the movement in the street—drays and hacks, as well as saddle horses passing along the way. Well, if he had wanted to advertise himself as a quick-trigger man, always a topic of interest among the sporting crowd, he couldn't have pulled it off any better. From the talk inside and the feeling he'd had in his bones, this Doc was plenty bad medicine—and one of the town's real hardcases.

Thinking it over, he wasn't sure how he'd got away with it. He'd never been a practicing *pistolero*, like some of the boys back in the Company, such as Jennings and Seikert. Both those Rangers were always ready to slap leather, as they called it, to see which was the faster in getting his pistol into action—as if that had much to do with it. He'd seen a lightning artist, called Wilson, try to fight it out with a gunman named Ben Thompson back in Austin. He, Ringold, had been on leave at the time in Austin, and was standing not twenty feet away when Wilson beat Thompson to the draw—only to wind up on the floor with three bullet holes in himself. Wilson had been fast, but Thompson had been steady, thumbing back the hammer of his six-shooter and letting the other have it—one, two, three, while Wilson missed both shots.

"Mister Ringo, can I get in a word with you?" And the big man, Ike Clanton, was beside him, a splay-toothed smile stretching his face. The very opposite of the gambler Doc's frosty grin. "Sure did save that fool kid brother of mine, throwin' down on Holliday th' way you done."

Ringold, jolted out of his thoughts, smiled back at the big, burly fellow, but declined an invitation to cross the street to the Oriental for a drink. "Maybe next time, Mister Clanton. But could you tell me just why your brother and that Doc were at such loggerheads?"

"Oh, Doc's been havin' a hell of a lot of bad luck for th' past three weeks, ever since his friends, th' Earps, left town on one of their huntin' trips. Seems they're Doc's luck. Anyways, Billy got on Doc's nerves. Was winnin' again today, and Doc, who's meaner than a turpentined coyote, was tryin' to rattle Billy."

"That Sheriff, Behan, broke it up mighty fast."

"Don't fool yourself, Mister Ringo. If you hadn't stopped Doc, he'd a'plugged Billy sure. He was goadin' him to draw, and then . . . bango! Goodbye, Billy Clanton."

Always uneasy with any sort of gratitude, he nodded to Clanton and set off down the boardwalk toward the stage office at Allen and Third. He'd decided to leave Blackbird at the livery and take the stage over to Benson in the morning.

Might as well let the driver show him the way the first time.

As he was going into the office to buy his ticket, a buckskin pony loped past in a cloud of dust, and a voice hailed him. "Got yourself some friends! We stick tight as burrs, ever you need us." And Ike Clanton was gone, heading south toward the Clanton Ranch.

3 The Benson Stage

He rode Blackbird into Benson in the early afternoon, having left Tombstone at ten. He'd had second thoughts about waiting for a coach that didn't leave until four—but retained his ticket for the return stage that evening, planning on tying his mount behind.

The entire twenty-eight miles had been uneventful, with the only activity along the trek being a runaway ore wagon. This had broken loose with its evil-tempered mules while the driver was visiting one of the two dilapidated saloons at the crossroad hamlet of Contention that lay halfway between the two larger towns.

It proved to be a good thing that he had not waited for the later stage when he picked up a letter addressed to Boxholder Number Nine at the window of the small post office on Colorado Street.

The envelope, bearing an ordinary two-cent stamp, with a bad portrait of Benjamin Franklin, and no return address, was postmarked from Tucson, A.T. two weeks before. The message inside was as brief as its one line of crabbed script would permit—but it spurred him to prompt action: *See Thorne at Wells Fargo in Benson and lose no time.*

The Wells Fargo office was over on the next street. Two clerks, equipped with green eye-shades and paper cuffs, were at their desks, thumbing through bills of lading, while a third was involved with a pile of ledgers. As this one was nearest the door, Ringold rapped a knuckle on the railing in front of his desk.

"Yes?" A pair of blue eyes darted a quick glance upward from over steel-bowed spectacles. The mouth was nearly invisible under a bushy mustache of sandy red.

"Like to talk to Mister Thorne."

"And, you are?"

"Name's John Ringo . . . Ringold."

The sharp blue eyes glinted behind thick lenses as the man arose from his ledgers, pulling down his vest and removing his set of paper cuffs. "I'm Thorne . . . Benjamin Thorne. And you are very welcome, Mister . . . Ringold. And promptly on time, I might say."

"Thanks."

"Come back to my private office." Thorne indicated a door at the end of the room. Two office workers never gave them a glance as they dug away at their paper work.

Once inside the small, neat room, with the door closed, Thorne waved him to a seat in a wooden, slat-backed armchair and took another behind the desk. "Well, Mister Ringold, we can speak a lot easier here not that the boys out there would ever let anything go beyond our walls." He removed his glasses, polishing them up on the end of his red sateen tie. Replacing them, he leaned back and looked quizzically at his visitor.

As Thorne seemed to be waiting for him to begin the conversation, Ringold stretched out his legs, and adjusted his gun belt under his new black coat. "You probably know more about me than I do you . . . and what this is all about."

"You are correct." Thorne hesitated for a moment, and unlocking his desk, drew out a telegram. "We received this more than a month ago. I'll read it. It may fill you in a bit." Placing the yellow flimsy on his desk, he removed his glasses again, and holding them up in the shaft of afternoon sunlight, streaming in from the alley window, polished them on a bandana. He raised them and squinted through the thick lenses at a door to the right of his desk.

Despite his relaxed position, Ringold was ready for whatever was coming. After all, he'd ridden many hundreds of miles to this meeting—and if Thorne wanted to take his time, that was all right. But he found the delay a bit queer.

Was that a sound of a door opening and closing? Had it come from behind the wall at Thorne's right? Whatever Thorne had been listening for, he seemed satisfied and cleared his throat, stuck the glasses back on his nose and began, "Leaving out the stops and inserting a word or so, it reads:

'Sergeant John Ringold of Captain Sparks's Company has been dispatched to your area as requested by Chief Special Officer Hume . . . and the Governor of Arizona Territory." Thorne cocked an eyebrow, rubbed his luxuriant red mustache, and concluded, "It's signed . . ."

"King!"

Thorne smiled slowly, replaced the message in the drawer of the desk and turned the key. "So, I suppose I'd best remember to call you, ah, you said?"

"I've already taken the moniker of *Ringo,* since coming to Tombstone. It was wished on me by a fellow I met at a bar." He laughed shortly. "Not much of a switch in names, but I guess it will have to do."

"Well, as you say, it will have to suffice. I'll remember to address you by that name, and I might say that, according to the telegram, your efforts seem to be known in the highest of places."

He straightened in his chair. "It's mighty flattering, I suppose, to know that the head of the Rangers and the top man of a territory are in cahoots . . . or what's the word, cognizant of my efforts . . . whatever they're supposed to be. So, I've got a question for you."

"Yes?" Thorne sat with his head cocked toward the side door.

Ringold opened his coat and let his hand rest easily on the arm of his chair—just in case.

"What was all the rip about me getting here. That's what the letter read that I just picked up at your post office . . . *'See Thorne and lose no time!'*"

"And here you are."

"Yes, but it was mailed over two weeks ago in Tucson, and it seems folks here aren't in one bit of a hurry."

"Ah, you're politely telling me that I'm slow in getting down to cases?" Thorne got up and stepping to the side door, stood smiling deeply into his red mustache, eyes twinkling sharply behind thick glasses.

"Yes." He also arose, keeping his hand near his holster. "That's another question. What's the business this Chief Hume . . . whoever he is, is talking about?"

"I think the man to tell you that had best tell you, himself. I guess you caught me listening for him." Thorne held a well-groomed hand high in a peace gesture, and turned the green door knob with the other, while Ringold watched narrowly—ready for whatever might be on the other side of that door.

Thorne flung the door open, which let onto another smaller office. "Chief Special Officer Hume, please to meet Sergeant . . . Ringold."

Ringold stood watchfully beside his chair while a medium-sized man in a plain black suit entered with hand outstretched.

He took the firm handclasp of the Chief of Wells Fargo's detective force. "Sit down, Sergeant, we've a lot to talk over." Turning to Thorne, "Benjamin, sit back at your desk, and I'll take the other chair here."

For the next two hours Ringold listened to the hefty statistics of crimes committed against Wells Fargo—not only in Arizona but in California, and other states and territories. The total number of successful and attempted holdups was surprising—many not having ever been covered in the press.

Hume ran a hand through his bushy, grey hair as he read from a publication, circulated within the organization, and authored by himself and the man behind the desk. Its full title was very impressive: *Report of Jas. B. Hume and Benj. Thorne, Special Officers Wells Fargo & Co's. Express, Covering a Period of Eleven Years. Giving Losses by Train Robbers, Stage Robbers, and Burglaries Since November 5th, 1870.*

There were, Hume said, smiling wryly, 242 stage robberies, and 24 that had misfired. There were only 6 train holdups, half of which failed. But that staggering total of 242 stage robberies was enough to turn the hair grey on the head of each member of the Board of Wells Fargo.

In addition to the theft of a box of gold bullion, worth over $2,000, that had vanished from the Benson Depot platform within the past month, there'd been two attempts on the Benson Stage in the last 60 days. One above Benson and one down near Tombstone.

"I can pretty well name the culprits, myself," gritted Hume, lighting up a twisted cheroot. "And I will!"

"Oh, no need—we're fairly certain they include Harry Head, Jim Crane, Zwing Hunt . . . and, probably, that cussed sagebrush dentist . . . Doc Holliday," replied Thorne.

"Holliday?" Ringold sat up in his chair. "That Tombstone gambler?"

"The same." Hume puffed a pair of wavering smoke rings at the westering light coming in the alley window. "The very same sharper and rascal who lit in Tombstone back in February of last year, along with that bunch of Earps. Sweepings of Las Vegas, New Mexico Territory . . . and Dodge City up in Kansas, if I don't mistake their ports of departure."

"This Holliday, is he any shakes with a pistol?" Ringold inquired.

"Fast and not the devil of a bit afraid to use one when he has to . . . but I hear he'd rather haul off and fire a scatter-gun. At least, I've been told he used one at Las Vegas," replied Hume.

"Well, you've one thing in common," said Ringold.

"Yes?" Hume scowled through his cigar smoke.

"You both seem to like Gold Coast Twisters."

Hume regarded his cheroot with veiled distaste. "Ah, it does cost a pretty penny to smoke 'em. I know where my spare cash comes . . . but with Holliday, I'm not so damned positive."

"Gambling?"

"That and rambling. I'm certain he's been in on at least one of the attempts on the stage, as Thorne mentioned." Hume puffed his cigar down to the nub and ground it out on the floor with a boot heel.

"Fred Dodge, our gumshoe in Tombstone, seems positive Doc was in on that last try in December," said Thorne.

"Fred Dodge? I thought you were short-handed here?"

"You might say we still are," growled Hume looking at his watch. "Oh, Dodge is a good man. He got onto Doc without much trouble. But he can't seem to see through those Earps. Tells us they're bastions of law-and-order. And mainly because both Wyatt and Virgil have been busting their galluses for a year since they come to Tombstone . . . trying to grab onto a lawman's job. Wyatt made two tries for Sheriff of Pima County, but Johnny Behan beat him out. And Virgil, who seems a cut above his brothers, was defeated this January for a bid at town marshal."

"But we still feel they're just rounders . . . no worse than a lot of folks crowding into Tombstone," said Thorne.

"I guess you can see that you've got your work cut out for you, Sergeant." Hume walked over to the side door. "The way you come recommended from your Adjutant General, it seems you know how to use your head . . . or your gun." He opened the door, then turned and extended his hand. "You'll get your orders, for the time being, from Thorne here. I've got to hustle to catch the up-train for Tucson. She's due in twenty minutes. Goodbye, Ben. I'll be in touch." The door closed, and he was gone.

Thorne stood looking out at the fading light in the alley. Clouds were rolling in from the west. "Looks like the weather's in for a change. Might get a bit of snow tonight." He absently pulled a poker chip from his pocket, flipped it a few times, then replaced it.

Ringold buttoned his coat. "Thought I'd left that back in Texas."

"Oh, it won't last. We're really knee-deep toward spring." He removed his specs and polished them on his vest. "By the way, you would probably like to hear your orders?"

"Yes, it could make me easier in my mind. And I hope it's not riding shotgun or pitching hay, or sitting out there." He jerked his head toward the front of the building. "Thumbing through papers."

"No. It won't be anything like that."

"If you've got this Dodge watching things in

Tombstone, I'm wondering if you've anyone else?"

Thorne came around the desk and gave him a sly poke in the ribs. "Actually we do have someone else . . . in fact he's waiting for you up at the Royal Queen on First Street."

"Who would that be?"

"A fellow called Pony Deal."

"Pony?" He had to laugh, in spite of himself. "Why that scoundrel was the first person I met at Tombstone. And he was out at the end of town, waiting for me then?"

"Yes, come on this way." Thorne reopened the door Hume had used. "Take this way out to the alley and up to the corner. He's been with us, ever since he left Texas. Seems to know all the right . . . or wrong people. Valuable in his way."

With the back door opened, Ringold turned up his coat collar. A brisk March wind was whipping pieces of straw and twigs up the alley. "So Pony watches Fred Dodge. Who watches Pony?"

"That's part of your job, but don't be obvious about it. He'll get your orders to you . . . whenever we have something." Standing in the doorway Thorne polished his glasses once more. "You could lounge around for months doing little, and then all at once we could need you badly. In the meantime pick up your wages in an envelope marked 'Boxholder Number Nine' at our Post Office . . . on the first of the month."

Replacing his glasses, he shook hands. "You won't need to come over to the office . . . unless something's doing. And don't make yourself known to Fred Dodge, either." The door shut.

He went up the darkening alley toward Pony at the Royal Queen.

Pony was easy to spot as he sat facing the door, playing two-hand poker with a shabby-looking young fellow in puncher get-up.

"Well, if it isn't my old friend from Texas. Ringo, wasn't that th' name?"

"Howdy, Pony. Heard you were in here running one of your slick-deck games."

"Right as rhubarb. Here's Harry Head. I guess old Harry's taken all he can off'n me. Y'might take his seat if you can stand th' gaff." Pony's gold tooth sparkled a welcome.

The young puncher indicated as Harry Head smiled shortly, and pushing back his chair, nodded to them and walked up to the bar, joined by another rather down-at-the-heels cowhand. Both ordered drinks and began a guarded conversation.

"Well, sit down. Y'can keep an eye on that pair if you wanta, but I wouldn't worry about 'em."

"Who was worrying? I don't care who you skin at cards."

"Well, I see you been in to pow-wow with th' big chiefs, and they must'a told you about me

. . . and what we're supposed to be up to." He grinned slyly, tooth sparkling. "I know you're on th' dodge out'a th' old Lone Star . . . same as me . . . and ready to turn your hand to helpin' Wells Fargo put th' kibosh on certain parties. But Thorne says you're straight, as far as that goes. And so am I . . . with them." He sighed virtuously. "I can play a straight game, when I wanter."

"Glad to hear it," Ringold caught the waiter's eye and ordered a couple of beers. "I wondered about your game when you braced me as I was coming into Tombstone that first day."

"Oh," Pony chuckled as he downed the last of his glass. "I was out there, on orders from Thorne, to give you a welcome. We'd expected you for three days . . . and I sure killed a lot of time waitin' for you."

"Sorry to put you to all that effort." Ringo re-ordered.

"That's o.k., just part of th' job of bein' a horse-back gumshoe. Just like now, when I was tryin' to pump Harry Head some while waitin' for you. Y'see," and Pony leaned forward. "Harry and old Bill Leonard over there just don't smell like a couple roses." Pony swelled up a bit as he lit a short-six cigar. "We figger they might try somethin' on th' money box sometime. Old Bill, if you can believe it, was a sort of drummer for some company that went busted back east. So he got him a job with th' Box-O as a third-rate cowhand and hay pitcher . . . and that Harry Head ain't never done nothin' but gamble and steal horses. Uh, he ain't no kind of judge of good horseflesh, and that makes real trouble for himself . . . only if he does grab off just Greaser mounts."

"So, you figure they could be up to something . . . tonight?" Ringold felt the old thrill of the chase sweep up his backbone—like the Ranger days now gone, for who knew how long?

"Naw. Not really. I know Mister Thorne could be suspicious of such saddle bums as that pair . . . but they'd have to have a whale of a lot more sand and fight than they got." Pony stared out at the gloomy night, now filled with wind and rain. "Besides, I don't think anyone's goin' very far in such stuff as that tonight."

Two-and-one-half hours later Pony turned out to be a poor weather—and crime prophet when the Benson-Tombstone stage came slopping and lurching into Benson.

Ringold, sitting over a good supper at the town's best restaurant on Boulder Street, had dismissed the two shabby punchers from his mind on Pony's say-so, and was lingering over his second cup of Arbuckle's when the *explosion* hit town.

Gunshots split the rainy night, which vibrated with Comanche-like war whoops and barking dogs. Somewhere near the railway depot someone had tied down the whistle of a sidetracked freight engine.

Tossing down his money, Ringold got outside and heard from dozens of hurrying Bensonites that the stage had been shot up, and was already unloading its casualties over at the Wells Fargo Office on Parker.

When he arrived, half the population of the town seemed to be clustered around the Concord. He noticed Pony standing near the coach with his mouth open—and maintaining a good distance between himself and Benjamin Thorne.

Thorne stood like a man carved from rock, with the raindrops smearing his glasses, while several muscular roustabouts were in the act of lugging in the green strong-box.

But it was the burly driver, who stood, calmly spitting gouts of tobacco juice downwind and leaning on his shotgun, who was the center of the immense crowd and the several frantically scribbling newspapermen.

"And then what occurred, Mister Paul?"

"And then what ercurred? Well, by hell . . . I'll tell you what ercurred! I'd jest traded seats with poor durned Bud Philpot, givin' him a breather up by Drew's Station . . . that little crossroad. It was good moonlight, with jest a smidge of rain in th' air as we come easin' up th' grade. All of a sudden like, someone sings out in th' mesquite: 'Whoa boys!' And before we could do a thing there was a shot from a big bore gun, and then a riglar dumned volley! Well sir, pore Bud keeled over, and after I grabbed him up and put him stiddy on th' seat, I got th' hosses under control. Then damned if Pete Roerig didn't git it too . . . so I brung th' stage in . . . but those killer bastards didn't git nuthin' . . . not a peso!"

Thorne jerked his head at Ringold, and the two sauntered around to the side of the Wells Fargo building, unnoticed by the milling mob. Pony spotted them, but stuck close to Bob Paul, the shotgun messenger, who seemed to have plenty left to say.

"Well . . . it came sooner than I would have guessed," murmured Thorne, squinting through rain-smeared spectacles. "But even though they missed getting at the strong-box . . . and I don't mind telling you there was close to thirty-thousand in it . . . it's made Wells Fargo look mighty bad."

"Not to mention the way it made the driver and passenger look . . . *plain dead!*"

"Yes, that's most tragic. We'll have trouble with both bullion freight, and the regular passenger traffic. Yes, it's all mighty tragic." Thorne finally became aware that his glasses were also in tragic shape, and yanking them off, stuffed them in his vest pocket. Squinting more than ever at Ringold, he pulled him closer by the lapel, and dropped his voice, though they were the only ones on the sidewalk.

"Fred Dodge came in here about five minutes behind the coach. Seems he got wind that there was bullion on the coach . . . we don't even tell him sometimes. He was trailing the coach, on a hunch, when it was stopped, but was too far back to do anything about the killings." Thorne paused and glanced around at the empty sidewalk. The noise all came from out front. "Anyway, he high-tailed back to Tombstone to alert the law there, and then split the wind on back here to Benson. Damned near killed his horse. So, there's a hell of a posse out by now from Tombstone . . . Sheriff Behan and his sawed-off deputy, Billy Breakenridge, as well as that bunch of high-rollers from the Oriental Saloon . . . Wyatt, Morgan and Virgil Earp, and that little gambler of a Bat Masterson."

"With that many out pawing over the ground, they'll probably trample down every hoof mark and anything else those killers left."

"Dodge went up to Doctor Gruber's with the bodies from the coach, but he'll be back in a little spell, so I want you to clear out . . . back to the hotel, or wherever you plan to spend the night. There's a couple of good boarding houses over on Front Street. In the morning you ride out early to Drew's and inspect the site of the robbery." Thorne hauled his glasses back out, rubbed them on his sleeve, and replaced them on his nose. "This little rain squall is about over, and you'd best get going before Dodge returns. No use in him knowing anything about you. Not that we don't trust him. He's a good man, but he's around the Earps and Holliday, and he might just let something slip. The least people who know your real identity the better."

Ringold, who had remained silent during Thorne's instructions, nodded, knocked the water from the brim of his crescent sombrero, turned his coat collar down and stepped off the board sidewalk. "Do I let Pony know if I find anything?"

"Yes," came the voice of Thorne from the shadows. "Pony's straight enough. Look over the ground and see what you can see . . . then tell him to get the information up to me on the double. He'll stay in town and ride out with you in the morning. Tell him I said so."

"All right. I'll give him the tip-off before I go over to Front."

The crowd was drifting away from the stage as Ringold walked past. The keyed-up shotgun messenger had gone into the office—still talking, while Pony and a good dozen townsfolk were out on the boardwalk, still rehashing the details of the robbery.

He jogged Pony in the ribs with his elbow as he threaded his way through the group. "Have

61

a night-cap with me, friend. It'll help keep you from having nightmares about . . . whoever your friends Leonard and Head found with enough sand to give them a hand tonight."

Pony glanced hurriedly around, but none had caught Ringold's undertone.

"Sure, why not?" His voice sank as they walked away from the place. "Y'don't think it *was* them? Why, they hardly had time to get down there to Drew's Station."

"You said . . . *hardly?*"

"Well, yeah, I guess they could've, but it's mighty hard to swallow. They just ain't bully boys."

"Somebody else was, though, and with brass enough to kill . . . even if he was too fast on the trigger to get at the strong-box."

They stopped at one of the bars next to the Front Street Hotel, and after a couple of beers decided that he would leave town at ten a.m., with Pony trailing along about half-an-hour later. Both would meet at Drew's Station—by chance, in case anyone was lying out in the brush.

He was astride Blackbird, and riding past the Wells Fargo office at quarter to ten. Glancing at the building in the glittering sunshine he saw the blinds were up and it seemed to be business as usual for Thorne.

He pulled rein at Drew's Station, where the

rickety little El Paso and Southwestern crossed the stage line and looked the place over. There were a couple of houses, a cigar-box of a depot on the newly constructed rail-line, but no one was in sight.

Tying the horse by the side of the little general store, he went inside to discover most of the inhabitants congregated around the pot-bellied stove. After purchasing a couple of Tampa Belles at five cents a pair, he sat in a corner of the store on a cracker-barrel, listening to locals giving their views of the crime. When, each in turn, had aired his supposition and calculated guess, the store-keeper turned to Ringold. "And what d'ye figger, Mister?"

"I'd say the posses from Tombstone should turn up something, before long."

"Say . . . ain't that another of them snoopers out there right now, and ridin' along th' railway?" observed a member of the Drew's Station elite.

"That sure ain't no lawman," the fat store-keeper responded. "That's that dumned Pony Deal . . . horsesharper from Tombstone."

Ringold left the cracker-barrel hastily, and bidding goodbye to general store assemblage, went out, untied Blackbird and joined Pony.

"Last night's bunch done tramped five thousand hoof marks into this ground," Pony grumbled.

"Spread out and let's quarter the area. You start

63

west of the depot, and I'll work out through the brush along both sides of the road."

"Well, we got a little, but I don't know how far it'ud go in any court of law," Pony growled as he dusted off the knees of his checkered trousers. "Also, a sort'a funny thing!"

"Let's be thankful for anything . . . even funny things."

"I spotted most of the shoes around here. Lot of them come from Behan and his bunch . . . and them damned Earps." He paused and dusted his hands. "And as hard as it prods me to say it, I got to admit that I recognized two sets of prints that I'm certain belong to Head and Leonard. Also, two plain sets of livery barn shoes . . . but I can't say where from."

"We might check the Benson and Tombstone liveries as to who took out horses last night," mused Ringold. "And now what about that funny thing?"

"Just here," and Pony unclasped his hand, displaying a brass cartridge, of at least .50 calibre. "This here little foxy-face is from a big old Henry rifle. They use 'em for buffaler shootin'. Th' skunk shootin' that off was aimin' to kill."

"Where'd you find it?"

"Over by that big quartzite boulder, half a dozen yards north of the railway crossing."

"Then you should have looked a mite closer on

the south-side of the crossing as well," Ringold smiled as he opened his own hand to display a pair of half-smoked Gold Coast Twisters.

"Meanin' what?" Pony handed over the shell casing for Ringold's collection.

"That there's just one man I've seen smoke such a weed around these parts, other than Mister James B. Hume of San Francisco . . . and I don't think he was hiding out in the chapparal last night with Leonard, Head and Company."

4 The Earps Meet Ringo

Ringold arrived back at Tombstone that morning in time to find everyone discussing the story that had appeared upon the front page of The Tombstone Nugget. It was boxed in on the front page in bold type, but had not been featured by John Clum's rival Tombstone Epitaph.

"Positive proof exists that four men took part in the attack on the Benson Stage. The fourth is now in Tombstone. He is suspected for the following reasons: Yesterday afternoon he engaged a horse at a local livery stable, stating that he might be gone for seven or eight days or might return that night. He left town about 4 o'clock armed with a big Henry rifle and a six-shooter. He started toward Charleston, and about a mile below Tombstone cut across to Contention. When next seen, it was between 10 and 1 o'clock at night, riding back into the livery at Tombstone, his horse fagged out. He at once called for another horse, which he hitched in the street for some hours, but he did not again leave town. Statements attributed to him, if true, look very bad, and if proved, are most conclusive as to his guilt as a principal or an accessory after the fact."

He tossed the paper in a barrel in the alley and sauntered into the Oriental, where he'd discovered he could obtain a decent lunch and a schooner of really outstanding beer. He might also, he thought, hear what the "fourth man" had to say.

"So, I'm a stage robber?" Holliday, sitting back toward the rear of the room, his flat, metallic voice cutting through the hazy smoke like an Arkansas Toothpick through cheese, addressed the bevy of rounders, cappers and plain suckers. "That damned, silly paper oughta watch what it prints."

The bartender, with grey slits for eyes, a tawny, waxed mustache and wearing a buckskin jacket, dexteriously slipped in another round of drinks at Doc's table—and a comment: "It seems, Doc, that Johnny Behan thinks you went out lookin' for a small battle, with that big Henry and your six-shooter."

"Listen, Buckskin! I don't know why you feel you have to poke your nose into a pleasant little talk, or, for that matter, just why you up and quit that posse you say you were out with. Still out there lookin', ain't they?"

Ringold didn't catch the short answer from the hard-looking barman, but it seemed to momentarily jolt Holliday from out of his nonchalant repartee. "Any time, Buckskin, you think you'd like to try to pull off a citizen's arrest, just come ahead and try your luck." He sank back in his chair while the admiring crowd continued to throng about, and josh the gambler.

"Some folks seem to think that being armed with a rifle and a six-gun make the case against me look bad," Doc observed genially. He held his glass of rye, squinting through its amber brilliance. "Hell, next time I ride out into the country that could be bristling with renegade injuns, I'll just wear me some kid gloves, and tote along a batch of Sunday School tracts."

"And you just might carry along an extra handful of twenty-five cent Gold Coast Twisters to keep 'em pacified." Ringold walked over and tossed one of the cold cigar butts onto Holliday's table. He wasn't sure, at the moment, just why he'd done that, but the cards were on the table now!

Doc was on his feet swiftly, right hand on pistol handle before he seemed to realize what he'd done. He then uncoiled slowly, smiled his usual frosty grimace, and keeping his hands carefully in sight, sat back down, nodding with unconcern at the group surrounding the gaming table— until they also relaxed and moved back to take seats opposite Holliday. Over in the corner, the bartender, called Buckskin, was redepositing a sawed-off shotgun under the bar.

"Hell!" Doc wagged his head slowly and then downed the entire glass of whisky. "Folks, I guess this jay of a Ringo here must think he's another self-appointed posse man. But, like Buckskin

Leslie over there at the bar, he finds it a hell of a lot easier to ride the old trail in a comfortable saloon."

Ringold turned, without a word, and passing out of the Oriental, walked down a block and established himself at a table in the Can Can Restaurant. As he worked his way through a plate of steak and eggs, the subdued jingle in his pockets told him he was just about to tumble into a "financial hole"—like that Eastern moneybags, Jay Gould.

If that calendar on the wall of the restaurant was correct, he had just about two weeks to wait for his Wells Fargo pay. And then, of course, his "half-pay" should be coming from the State of Texas. It could all go toward making a pretty good down-payment on a fine little cow spread down around the Panhandle some day—if he lived to collect.

After a second cup of coffee, he began mulling over a trip back to the Oriental to try his luck with Doc. But the more he thought about it, the more he hesitated to drop the rest of his roll. And besides, he didn't think Doc would prove too cordial.

He knew now that his attempt to brace Holliday was just plain Ranger tactics—trying to smoke a culprit out into the open. But, though Doc almost went for it, he'd been too savvy to really tip his hand.

What Thorne would say, he hadn't any idea. He'd sent Pony on to Benson to report to Thorne what they'd uncovered at the robbery site—and ask for instructions.

While he was polishing off a slab of berry pie, the piece de resistance, according to an over-enthusiastic menu, Pony ambled in and seated himself at an adjacent table.

"What's good today?" Pony flashed his gold tooth at the apparent stranger across from him.

"Don't try the pie," Ringold answered as he arose to pay his bill. Pony tipped his sombrero at the scowling proprietor and followed the paying customer onto the sidewalk.

"Mister Thorne don't figger we got enough on any of 'em to call in th' law."

"Call in the law? Well, what about your pair of no-goods, or that cold-deck artist of a Holliday? He's spread all over the front page of the Nugget!"

"Yeah, but what you gotta learn is that th' Nugget's solid Dimmycrat and th' Epitaph's rock-solid Republican. Everybody knows th' Dimmycrats are out to nail Doc Holliday's hide to th' barn door . . . seeing he side-kicks with th' Earps, who're dyed-in-the-wool Republicans."

"You mean we have to tread easy around a damned bunch of politicians to lay our hands on Doc?"

"Yeah, and from what I hear over to th'

Oriental, you just about got yourself on th' fancy end of one of Doc's six-shooters."

"They tell you why?"

"Yep! Buckskin Frank Leslie said you up and socked the great doctor in the mush with an old cigar butt. I wonder if it was one of them you picked up at Drews?"

"If I did, I still have one left, plus that Henry cartridge case!"

Walking as they talked, they brought up at the Pioneer Livery on Tough Nut Street. "I left my Brandy mare here when I come in a while ago, but I'm gonna propose a way out of you gettin' into any more rows with Doc or his friends," said Pony. "Mister Thorne thought you might stay out to Joe Hill's and my little spread over near Galeyville. T'ain't far, 'bout two hours' ride from town here, and only three over to Benson. Y'can roost there for damned little. Joe is sort'a pardner of mine and a right good feller. Fact, we both keep a bunch of tradin' stock out there. I come out couple times a week and can keep you filled in on th' Wells Fargo dealin's."

They rode out of town up Fourth and through several blocks of quite pleasant-looking homes. Most of the lots were surrounded by picket fences and shaded by cottonwood and willow.

"Them's where th' store-keepers and big bugs from th' mines live. Old Tombstone's comin' along all right. She's County Seat of Cochise

County, though I never could hold with puttin' dumned injun names on such things."

They passed several small, busy mines, but Ringold could see that most of the mining activity, that gave life, itself, to Tombstone, was situated to the south and west areas bordering the town. A large rise of ground over to the west was labeled Comstock Hill by Pony. "Not much in th' way of minin' goes on over there." His gold tooth twinkled in the afternoon light. "They up and plant 'em feet first there." And Ringold looked upon Tombstone's personal Boot Hill.

Ahead lay the purplish-blue glory of the Dragoons, washing across the northern horizon in wave upon frozen wave. "Now them's mountains! And I heard tell when that old devil Cochise could send out two hundred savages from there to raise Hail Columbia . . . but they're all gone . . . or leastwise most. Times keep changin'. Country gettin' sorta civilized."

Ringold felt a vague sense of unease—the kind that had visited him before whenever he'd thought of those renegades. It would always pay to be on the ready out in these wild stretches. He didn't figure to wind up with his toes to the sun like some of Arizona's population. And then another vague shape drifted coldly across his mind—that sure-thing killer of a Holliday. That pay from Wells Fargo was not going to come easy.

About three in the afternoon they rode across a broad mesa, down a half-dozen washes, and coming up on the other side, found themselves traversing an immense bed of hedgehog cactus, many already brave with their bright pink blossoms. A half mile beyond, nestled against a towering outcropping of orange sandstone, stood the Hill and Deal Horse Ranch. According to Pony, Galeyville, with its one hundred and ten souls, lay about three miles to the west.

Coming up to the ranch, itself, they were loudly greeted by a half-dozen dogs of about a full dozen varieties per animal. All seemed noisy, but friendly.

"Let me do th' talkin'." Pony scratched his chin and nodded toward an unpainted log barn. "Y'see, Joe over there always is a bit jumpy 'bout strangers. He got into a little trouble back in Texas, and had to leave there on th' lope."

"Guess Arizona's full of ex-Texans." Ringold dismounted slowly and stood rubbing his hand over Blackbird's flank. The Winchester poking out of a knothole in the barn door remained unwavering. But it finally was drawn back in, and almost immediately a short, burly little man came rolling toward them. "Hully damn! Guess I'll go to takin' tickets fer admission to this hyar shebang." The voice had a squeak in it like a door hinge sorely in need of oiling.

"This here's a good friend of mine, named John

Ringo. John's all right. And I told him he could roost here as long as he'd like'ta." Pony was rattling along as fast as if he were pressing the good points of some pudding-footed buzzard-bait.

"Awh, I ain't talkin' 'bout your friend," squeaked Hill. "I'm talkin' 'bout that damned posse ridin' in here from over Galeyville way. And after I tole 'em there ain't been nobody around in a week or so save some coyotes and a couple big lobo wolves, damned if they didn't up and disbelieve me . . . and say they'd be comin' back."

"Well let'm, Joe. What'do we care a rap about 'em! Was it that goat-whiskered Johnny Behan and his little horn-toad depooty, Billy Breakenridge, or them other sidewinders?"

"Here, let's put up yore hosses." Hill led both mounts toward the barn, Ringold and Pony walking along with him. "Naw, it was Behan and his little shadder. And y'know I don't like th' way they was sizen' up our stock. By grabs, if here they don't come back again!"

Ringold could see three horsemen loping in from the northwest. He had no trouble in recognizing Behan, but the other two were new to him.

"Little cuss is Breakenridge, and that big jasper's Fred Dodge," Pony observed, loosening his Colt in its holster.

With the little deputy leading in a well-supplied

74

pack mule, the trio looked capable of spending a month out on the man-hunt. Sheriff John H. Behan of Cochise County, black goatee wavering in the breeze, was resplendent in a pair of suspenders of extraordinary width and the color of a fireman's shirt. The rest of his garb was pure Sunday-go-to-meeting. The big man, pointed out as Fred Dodge, with his walrus mustache, looked like a banker who'd tied his dingy grey coat behind his saddle and left the bank for a jaunt around the block. He was armed, but only with a saddle-gun, as were Behan and Breakenridge. But that pair also packed six-guns on their hips.

Looking them over carefully, as the threesome dismounted, Ringold thought he could spot a hold-out gun's bulge under Dodge's yellow vest. Here was a cautious man—what they called a detective.

There was an argument going on between the three as they tied their horses to the corral rail, near the barn. The big, hefty Dodge and the little red-headed deputy, Breakenridge, were going at it hot and heavy, voices raised in dispute.

Leaving Joe Hill to take their own horses down to the barn, Pony and Ringold sauntered up to the squabbling lawmen.

"I certainly can't see any justice in the way you both have determinedly thwarted Marshal Virgil Earp and his men in their operation as a posse!" huffed Dodge.

"Hell, outside of Virge they ain't an Earp worth a plugged peso. And their saddle tramp of a Bat Masterson's just a damned trouble maker," scowled Breakenridge. "You know th' whole gang is out to throw dust in our eyes . . . whether you realize it or not. You may be on Wells Fargo's payroll, Dodge, but I wisht you'd go back there and ride with yore friends and let th' Sheriff and me try to find them dry-gulchers." Breakenridge's blue eyes snapped.

Commencing to swell up like a horned toad, Dodge was silenced by Behan's raised hand. "Hold it, you two! Let's talk a moment to these folks and then get on our way. It's a durned long haul up to old man Hughes' Double Adobe in the San Simon." He swung around to Ringold. "You a new man in Tombstone?"

"One of the new ones, Sheriff. But I suppose you do get a few other pilgrims into your hole in the road once in a while . . . stages and railway . . . as well as horseback?"

"Now I remember you from that little fracas at th' Palace. Seems you somehow backed down Holliday when he was threatenin' to plug that fool Clanton kid." Behan thoughtfully stroked his chin whiskers.

Ringold said nothing, but winked at Pony, who had been leaning against the corral rail, with the placid air of a choir boy.

"This is Mister Ringo, I think it was," Behan

introduced Ringold to Breakenridge. "And this is Fred Dodge of Wells Fargo."

Ringo shook hands all around.

"You folks still lookin' fer stage robbers?" squeaked Hill, coming back from the barn. "Y'won't find any stuck around here, and that's a fact."

"No, Joe, we just wanted to make it plain to you and Pony . . . that if you should happen to see anything funny out this way . . . to be sure and get word to us. After today we'll probably head back into Tombstone, before riding elsewhere." Behan untied his big bay from the corral rail and swung up into the saddle.

"Well, I can tell you all that I sure do see somethin' damned funny . . . and right now." Hill threw a thumb over his shoulder to the northeast. "I'd say that bunch on them crowbaits comin' down th' slope over there is 'bout as funny a sight as I seen lately. That's gotta be them Earps, ain't it?"

Breakenridge and Dodge hastily mounted, though Dodge acted as if he would hold back, if he dared, and within a minute all members of Behan's group, including the pack-mule were hitting a good clip off across the mesa in the direction of Galeyville.

The four horsemen, slowly riding up to the ranch, seemed as bushed as their mounts. Three had the look of kinsmen. A big, burly fellow, blond like his brothers, was in the lead upon a blaze-faced black. The other two blond men and the medium-sized fellow were all mounted upon dun horses. All were carrying arms, and with the exception of the young man, who was dressed in a dusty suit and wore a derby hat cocked over one eye, all packed saddle-guns.

"That damned rascal of a Behan just won't cooperate," the tallest and thinnest of the brothers rasped from a dust-dry throat. "And just because we left town in a hurry. Well, there'll come a time when Mister John Behan won't carry it so cock-of-the-walk!"

"Oh let up, Wyatt. You know him and Billy are the only lawmen with authority out on this here hunt," said the largest man, dismounting from his black horse.

"Yeah, Wyatt." The young man in the business suit and derby piled off and dusted himself, then straightening his incongruous head-gear, "Virgil's the nearest to a lawman right now and even he ain't got a bit of weight when it comes to any jurisdiction."

"Gettin' to be a real lawyer, ain't you, Bat?"

"Wyatt, you gotta recognize that when they peel your badge because the citizens want a change of faces on the force, it ain't the end of the world. Virge almost come in ahead this last election, and maybe you can ride in on his coat-tail next time."

"And in the meantime, Wyatt, if you can stop thinking about Johnny Behan's badge for a minute and how Virge lost out as City Marshal to Ben Sippy, maybe Joe here'll let us water up and do some swappin' if we can." The other brother batted the dust from his sombrero and looked hopefully at Hill.

"Not a chance, fellers," Hill cleared his voice, but it still squeaked. "If you'd come by next week I expect some mighty good remounts . . . but right now . . . well, ask Pony here."

"Pony? I wouldn't ask Pony th' time of day," gritted the Earp called Wyatt. "And so far as this other short-trigger man. He don't look like he'd tell anyone if the sun was up."

"Oh, forget it, Wyatt." The man called Virge turned back to Hill. "Say, Joe, can we water up good and maybe get us some grub? We're tryin' to keep up with Behan, because Wyatt and Bat have some idea he's ridin' in circles to throw us off. And then he'll go on and grab them Wells Fargo holdup men."

"Then why in Tophet don't you all stay off his neck and let him do his duty?" Ringold felt like flustering the sour-faced Wyatt.

"Well, for one thing, Mister . . . ?" The largest Earp raised his eyebrows.

"Name's John . . . Ringo."

"That so? Heard you had some words with Doc Holliday some days back. I'm Virge Earp. Was City Marshal, like you heard, until last election. That one there's Morgan. And th' little fashion-

79

plate is Bart Masterson. We call him Bat. He's an old friend from Kansas."

"Now if you think this pilgrim can keep that straight, why in hell don't you tell him why we particularly are out after those thieving bastards?" Wyatt grumbled.

"Oh, you go ahead," grinned Masterson, as Virge shrugged and he and the rest led their weary mounts down to the barn, where Joe waited with feed and grain as well as water.

"Well, Mister Wyatt," Ringold smiled at the glowering Earp as he yanked his mount toward Joe Hill's barn corral. "I hope you all catch your men . . . because, if you don't . . ." He left his sentence unfinished, watching the man's expression change.

"Meaning just what, *Mister?*" Wyatt drawled the last word, as he began to water his thin bay mare.

"Meaning, if your posse can't produce results, or Behan's, for that matter, why there's an old saying back in Texas that goes . . . 'shoot the nearest sheep-killing dog you can catch and his blood'll fetch the rest of the pack.'"

"Never heard such fool nonsense." Wyatt jerked his horse away from trough, and within half an hour, equipped with half a gunny sack of canned grub, the foursome were riding into the red-streaked sunset after Sheriff Johnny Behan and his posse.

"And now you've met th' Earp Gang. But I forgot you already know th' boss . . . Doc," Pony grinned as they sauntered up to the ranch house for supper.

Pony set off for Benson the next morning. If there was going to be any action develop from the slim bits of evidence unearthed at the robbery site, it was decided that Pony would return promptly and so inform Ringold. If there was a wait for the posses to turn up something on their own, he'd ride on south on a horse-buying expedition, for he and Joe had wangled themselves a contract, of sorts, for remounts down to Fort Huachuca, and it needed attention.

Ringold stuck tight to the horse ranch—waiting. There was little doubt but that Doc's big Henry rifle was tarp-wrapped and buried out in the desert, beyond the reach of half-pay Rangers, like himself, or any pompous detectives such as Fred Dodge. And as to Behan and his man, Breakenridge, he doubted their ability to run down the bandits, though he was convinced they were absolutely straight.

The Earps were another cut of cloth. They had the look of sharpers, of men consistently on the make, and anyway they could bring it off. Big Virge seemed a half-decent sort, but one that would still bear watching. Morgan Earp and their little gun-fighter friend, Bart Masterson, were likeable enough, but Ringold had known likeable killers before—rattle-snake deadly when the smiling stopped and the shooting began. And that Wyatt! He seemed to pack around all the grudges he could find.

Both Hill and himself kept expecting Pony to return, but the week went by and the days continued to follow each other, becoming more sunny blue and spangled with hours of mellow warmth that foretold the coming of golden Arizona spring—to be followed by blazing Arizona summer.

Joe Hill rode over to Charleston, in the middle of the second week of Pony Deal's absence, to fetch back some grub. When he had gone, Ringold took his field glasses and inched his way up the towering outcropping of orange sandstone that reared itself into a small mountain behind the barn to dominate the nearby countryside.

Working his way until he found a horizontal surface that was just right for "perching," he estimated his elevation at about one hundred and twenty feet above the barn roof. His view in three directions was comparable to the free-ranging vision of some circling hawks.

He could see as far to the west as the infinitesimal cubes and oblongs that were the actual shacks, cabins and houses of Galeyville. And there was the pyramidal upthrust of Galeyville's single smelter. Southward the framework of several of the larger Tombstone mines came into view, in particular the Lucky Cuss Shaft, the Vizna Hoist, as well as the massive, but unfinished red bulk of the Cochise County Court House.

Over to the east there was only rolling table-land, sparkling in the bright crystaline air all the way to the New Mexican line. Swinging his glasses toward the southwest he caught a smudge of dust inching in his direction. A minor adjustment brought into view several horsemen racing toward the ranch.

Keeping his glasses on them, he discovered there were two members in the pursuing party. One had been hidden, for a time, traveling parallel to the others up a dry wash.

Before the rider out front was within a hundred yards of the ranch, the pursuer who'd emerged from the dry wash, rode up the last embankment and brought down the man's horse with two shots from a heavy saddle-gun.

The downed stranger hit the ground running and kept on in a broken pattern until hidden behind the barn.

Though both pursuers were out of range, Ringold squeezed off a shot from his Colt and halted the pair. The two horsemen wheeled away, as if expecting more return fire from the ranch, and rode at a gallop toward Tombstone.

"Hey, down there!" Ringold yelled at the barn.

There was no answer for a long minute, then a man's head poked out.

"Come on out and show yourself! If I was after your scalp, Mister, I'd be mighty able to take it from here!"

"Don't shoot . . . fore Gawd . . . don't shoot!" The stranger eased out of the barn, hands held high.

"That you, Ike Clanton?"

"Yeah, Ike Clanton all right. And that damned Doc Holliday's pure careless with his blamed buffalo gun." Clanton shaded his eyes with his hand as he peered up at the rock face watching Ringold clambering down. "That you, Mister Ringo?"

"Yes, Ike. And what was all that ruckus about?"

"Well, you see word's out that I . . . ah . . . saw what I wasn't supposed to th' night th' Benson Stage was robbed."

"You say, the word got out that you saw the robbery?" Ringold leaped down the last six feet to land in the sand by a disheveled Clanton. Here was a rock-solid lead if there ever was one.

"Yep, and made th' mistake of talkin' to Earp."

"Earp? Wyatt Earp?"

"That's th' huckleberry."

"So, how'd they get after you out this way?"

"Was ridin' over to Galeyville about sellin' some cattle. Guess Wyatt and Doc must'a follered me on purpose."

"Well, come on up to the ranch house. Joe Hill's due back from Galeyville, and I guess he can bunk you with no trouble. I may ride back with you tomorrow down to Tombstone." He'd pump Ike casually about his statement regarding the robbery while they ate dinner.

"Mister Ringo, that'd be fine . . . but I'm gonna stay out of Tombstone for a spell. Like they say, 'It's safer to pull freight than a gun.'"

5 South of the Border

Ringold and Ike Clanton were skirting the western fringes of Tombstone as noontime whistles at the various mines were saluting the lunch hour. Ike pointed out several of the largest operations while they rode past the West Side, and the Lucky Cuss—the first of Ed Schieffelin's big strikes, and the one that brought Tombstone into being—a community more mining town than cattle camp.

"That Joe Hill sure puts out a dandy meal," Ike grinned reminiscently as he recalled the previous evening's supper. "You just don't run into many sour doughs like him."

"Maybe we should have invited Doc and that Wyatt to stay for supper," mused Ringold, pulling out cigars and offering one to Ike.

"Still don't know how to thank you for savin' my old red neck," replied Ike, lighting up. "And it's sure a plain fact that you did th' same for my kid brother. Sure owe you a heap!"

Ringold had held back, so far, discussing Ike's astounding confession at being a witness to the stage robbery of the Benson Coach. Just why, he wasn't certain, possibly because Joe Hill had arrived back soon after Holliday and Earp's thwarted attack on Ike—and that was the main item of discussion until bedtime—reinforced by a bottle of Old Crow.

They were about to split up, and it was now or never. "Ike, we talked about a lot of things last night, but never got around to how you happened to get in the middle of that Benson Stage robbery."

"Yeah, I guess I didn't want Joe Hill squawkin' around about that as well as Doc's tryin' to shoot me full of holes." Ike took off his battered, black sombrero and swatted at an early horse fly. "No reason my friends shouldn't know, though. Well, I was ramblin' down th' stage road from a game of cards with some fellers I knew. Fact is, my kid brother, Billy, was also with me . . . taggin' along as usual. Anyhow, the both of us had rid down nearly all th' way from Contention to Drew's when . . . rap! rap! rap! There was firin' and we see them rapscallions pullin' triggers . . . and though they was all back in th' bresh somewhat . . . I couldn't help recognizin' 'em. I tell you that old stage damned nigh up and run over some of 'em. But from what I hear with th' driver gettin' it, and grabbed from topplin' off by Bob Paul, they was all too bamboozled to see straight." Ike chewed hard on the remains of his cigar. "Good night, and here she come, so I pulled quiet-like, along with Billy, off th' road and there we waited till everyone'd rid off. And then, let me tell you, we split some breeze for our home ranch!"

"But how did this Wyatt Earp tumble to the fact you were a witness?"

"Like I've said before, I got a big mouth. And I was blowin' around in one of th' saloons about my suspicions, and all that. And here comes Wyatt, sidlin' up to me. And about wore out with all th' posse ridin' he'd been on . . . without catchin' nobody." Ike puffed on the damp remains of his stogie. "Guess he was just about as techy as a teased snake because Johnny Behan finally caught himself one of th' bunch. 'Course I didn't see that one, Lute King, th' hoss-holder. Guess he was scootched down in th' bresh with th' bridles, so I didn't count him."

"So, they got one after all." For having a big mouth, Ike could keep things to himself if he'd a mind to, it seemed. So Behan and Breakenridge must have had some luck after they were at Joe Hill's.

"Yep. And with my big mouth, I up and said they didn't get th' right ones . . . th' ones that did all th' shootin'."

"Then Wyatt blew up?"

"Naw, and that was what fooled me, I guess. Right away he says 'we know that there was Bill Leonard, Jim Crane and Harry the Kid Head!' "

"He named names?"

"Yes, and then he told me that he could put me

88

in the way of gettin' some of that Wells Fargo reward money."

"And where was he going to get Wells Fargo money?" Ringold was so intent that he didn't notice a rider coming toward them from the east.

"Said it was all open-and-above-board for legitimate information leadin' to death or capture. Said he wanted to kill th' three of 'em . . . just like that! And just for th' glory of it, he said." Ike winked slowly. "Somehow Wyatt got it into his thick head that I knew where them pony boys would be hid out. Hell, I don't get off'n the ranch more'n twice a week . . . so how'd I know?" He spat out the shredded remains of the cigar stump. "Wouldn't I be a great one to sing out for blood money? And him killin' jest fer th' glory of it . . . ugh!"

"That wasn't what set the pair of them after you yesterday?"

"Naw, it was another fool thing I said."

"Yes?"

"I said, 'Hell, Wyatt, as long as you're goin' after 'em, why not nail th' big lobo, hisself . . . Doc Holliday?'" Ike took up his reins. "Well, Mister Ringo, don't want to hold you out here any longer. Thanks fer your company this far. Guess I'll jest learn to keep my eyes open, and my mouth shet a bit more often. *Adiós*!" And Ike Clanton was cantering down the side road to his ranch, leaving Ringold sitting with narrowed eyes and dangling cigar.

Clanton's hoofbeats had barely dwindled into the sandy silence when there came the sound of another horseman's approach. Still bemused, Ringold turned to behold Pony Deal racking toward him from the east.

"Hold up there, stranger, I got some news that'll knock th' spots off'n anything you ever heard of," Pony shouted as he drew within earshot. He was travel-stained and riding a dark brown gelding.

"Where's your riding stock?"

"Delivered twenty head over to Huachuca this mornin' early. If I hadn't been in such a rip to get back, I'd have got more for 'em. Driv 'em pretty hard and had to take less from that old devil of a Commandant. My paint pulled up lame, and I had to leave her at th' fort."

Despite the fact the two horsemen were sitting in the middle of the Tucson Road, six miles from Tombstone, Pony kept craning his neck around as if expecting company.

"What about your news?" Ringold shied his cigar at a big, red tarantula that sprang back into its burrow at the base of a small yucca.

"That Ike Clanton who just rid off?"

"Yes. I rode down here to keep Holliday and that Wyatt Earp off his neck." And Ringold recounted the events of the previous day, as well

90

as the positive identification of the four stage robbers.

"Ike's got a big mouth and th' day's comin' when, I bet, th' Earps and Holliday are gonna raise a hell of a commotion . . . beside these damned stage jobs."

"That may be, but what about that news?"

Pony swiveled his head again. "Oh yeah, I near forgot, wondrin' about Ike." He guided the gelding nearer to Ringold. "Got a line on two of them Benson robbers. Ain't no doubt, now you say they know th' hull bunch."

"Who are they, and where are they?" Ringold felt like giving Pony a swift kick. And he also wondered a bit at Pony's apparent unease.

"Why it's nobody but my pals Leonard and Head. And they're coolin' their heels over at Owl City, New Mexico Territory, right this minute as calm as choir boys. Don't know where th' others are . . . but I bet those two could tell."

"You left them there?"

"Yeah, and I was ridin' in to get th' word to Behan, but when I see you sittin' out here like a duck on a rock . . . damn, said I, Ringo ought to steal a march on old John . . . and certainly on th' Earps and their sore-tail posses."

"But if I bring them in or get into a fight and the word gets out, wouldn't that blow the lid off my Wells Fargo job?"

Pony yanked his sombrero off and ran fingers

through his red hair. "Say you got word from someone, never mind who, and as you were over that way . . . you pulled th' old citizen's arrest. Sort of a one man posse. And you steal th' Earps' glory. Besides Thorne will back you all th' way."

"That's half-way sensible. And I do know what Head looks like."

"Yeah, but don't forget he knows you. Remember I introduced you in Benson."

"Yes, just before he helped Holliday kill two men."

"That's so." Pony dismounted and adjusted his saddle girth while he informed Ringold as to the most direct route to Owl City—a played-out mining camp fifteen miles southeast along the Tucson stage route.

"Looks like you're in for some rain. I run into several storms coming up." Pony unstrapped a bright green slicker from behind his saddle and handed it up to Ringold. "Here take it. I'm goin' on into Tombstone and won't need this."

Wasn't it just like Pony to sport a kelly-green slicker when most folks kept off the rain with yellow waterproofs? With an eye on the sweeping cloud formations, Ringold tugged on the slicker and set out in the direction of Owl City.

"Good luck," Pony called, "and if you should bump into anyone askin' about me in particular, tell 'em you ain't seen me lately."

Ringold pulled up and watched Pony loping

through the splattering raindrops toward Tombstone on the brown gelding. What had he been up to now? There was possibility he'd got himself into some shenanigans over horses at the fort.

Three hours later he was crossing a rickety plank bridge over the swift-running Sweetwater as the rain was letting up. Shortly thereafter the road curved to the southeast, and he came upon a small hamlet of eight buildings, including a saloon and hotel that appeared to house a small restaurant. The entire metropolis rejoiced in the name of Pirtleville.

Making inquiries of the bald-headed bartender and hotel-keeper, he found Owl City to be about five miles eastward in the Pedregosa foothills, just over the line in New Mexico territory.

"Owl City is about as good a handle for th' place as you'll find. Sure t'ain't much awake daytimes at least," offered his bartender-host, smiling benevolently as Ringold ordered a shot of the best whisky in the house and invited him to have one.

"Not much going on there?" He ordered himself a plate of steak and eggs.

"Nope, ain't more'n a couple-dozen folks over there. Just a fizzled mine they still try to work sometimes . . . also a sorta saloon and store. But that's New Mexico fer you. Derned slim pickin's." He shook his head as if in wonder that such an insignificant place as Owl City should even exist.

"Say now!" The gratis drink seemed to have stirred up other memories under the bartender's shiny scalp. "Wonder if you heard anythin' about that gang of horsethiefs that raided a *rancho* down below th' border nigh Agua Prieta . . . and run off twenty head. Wounded two of th' *rancho*'s Greasers to boot! Happened nigh on to a week back. Was even in th' Douglas News."

"No. I'm from over west and don't get to see many papers." So that was what Pony had been looking over his shoulder about. He must have laid up in Owl City for a few days before pushing his stolen horses on to the fort.

Thanking the barkeep for his explicit directions, he went out and mounted Blackbird for the last miles to the old mining camp.

Guiding his horse around scattered boulders, washed-down into the vague track that was the main road to Owl City, Ringold kept a sharp lookout for any possible ambushes, but saw nothing live save for a horned toad sitting damply upon a large rock, pessimistically watching the progress of horse and rider.

The shimmering yellow band of the rainbow's arch, still blazing northward over the blue-grey mountain bulk, was repeated in the many patches of desert marigolds threading the road and clinging to the rocky hillside. The cheering sight of such early flowers raised his spirits for a moment. But he somehow grew depressed as he rode around an outcropping of red sandstone to look upon the scattered shacks and battered buildings of Owl City, strewn along a barren hill a mile east.

He noticed the unpainted general store and saloon on down the road about one-hundred yards from the main group of buildings, none of which seemed occupied. It was a dispirited view that plainly proclaimed: "Here came men, filled with hope, who strove to make those hopes into golden realities, and yet, somehow, all failed." The mine went busted, and the men with hope moved on—those without hope remained.

And somewhere in this half-dead, little mining camp were two such men, without any actual hope—Head and Leonard—abandoned by their treacherous leader, Doc Holliday, and now being hunted down by that murderous Wyatt Earp—and by himself!

He rode up to the saloon-store, which bore the regal title of "The Golconda," and tied Blackbird to the hitching rail beside three other rain-damp mounts.

Unbuttoning Pony's green slicker, and keeping his hand close to his pistol, he walked up the rickety steps and into the building. There were about half-a-dozen men in the dimly-lit interior. Several appeared to be old, hard-rock miners, possibly some of the die-hards working the petered-out mine. These sat around a poker table with a pair of seedy cowpunchers, while another, also in range clothes, stood at the bar, back to the door, in conversation with the bartender.

All this Ringold took in at a glance as he stepped into the smoky room.

The group at the table looked up incuriously, while the man at the bar turned his head. For an instant there was silence—and before Ringold could make a move, the man at the bar tossed off his drink. "Well, Pony? Decide to come back and lay low with us for another spell?"

Ringold, in his bright green slicker stood, watching Harry Head at the bar, waiting for the bandit's move when he discovered his error.

"Come on up." Head was still unaware of his mistake in the dim light of the flickering yellow lamps. "Have a shot before old Leonard gets back here. The damned fool rode down the Bernadino Trail this mornin' to see if he couldn't pick up a few strays from that bunch you rousted th' other day . . . thought some might still be on the loose. Gotta get us some sort of travelin' stake." He turned to the barkeep. "Two more."

Ringold slowly pushed back the slicker flap from against his gun butt and stood his ground. "Head!" His voice rang against the saloon walls.

Harry Head spun around, took two steps forward, and saw the man in the green slicker wasn't Pony. For a moment, the young man's handsome, dissipated face was blank—then he suddenly seemed to recognize Ringold. "I don't like this, Mister. Move out!"

"Hold on. I don't want . . ." But before Ringold could complete his sentence, Harry Head made a frantic grab for his pistol, while Ringold's six-shooter boomed out a shattering blast of fire and lead.

Just one shot, and Head crumpled against the bar—and lay motionless.

Ringold held the smoking six-shooter on the suddenly rigid gamblers, and bartender, who were reaching for the ceiling. "Hold on everyone! This is a lawful action." He motioned for the miners and cowpunchers to settle back down at their table. "You, Mister," he called to the barkeep over to where Head lay. "Take a look. Is he still alive?"

"This here man is plumb dead." And the barkeep, kneeling solemnly at Head's side, raised a hand as if taking an oath. "That's my findin's as Coroner of Owl City . . . and as Town Marshal, I say he made his move fust . . . and got what was comin' to him." He rose stiffly and stood staring at Ringold. "It's a pure open and shut case of self-pertection, on yore part . . . and th' damn fool deceased should'a known better . . . though why he thought you wuz Pony Deal's beyond me. Yore a good foot taller." He squinted

97

at Ringold for a moment and then nodded. "Ah, probably th' green slicker yore wearin'. We wuz joshing a little rounder named Pony about such a get-up."

As Ringold said nothing, the man looked at him more narrowly. "You just happen to come by this way . . . lookin' fer Head?"

Ringold holstered his pistol and turning his slicker and coat back, displayed what no one else around Tombstone, including Pony, had viewed—his Ranger's Star pinned near his left armpit. "Texas Ranger, working on a stagecoach robbery." He decided to say nothing about Wells Fargo unless forced into it.

"That does it then." The Barkeep-Marshal went back of the bar, rummaged around and drew out a cigar box packed with papers and tattered documents. "Here we be." He slapped a printed form on the bar and, producing pen and ink, invited Ringold to make his official report for the township records. "You fill that out and as Township Coroner, I'll wind her up ship-shape."

While Ringold tersely indented the particulars, the cowpunchers came over and, picking up Harry Head by the shoulders and boots, carried him across to a battered pool table by the door and laid him out.

"That's nice, boys, but keep yore hands off'n his effects. That's official prop'ety now." The Barkeep-Coroner-Marshal, whose name, appearing at the bottom of Ringold's completed report, seemed to be Samuel Cheatham, took the paper and filed it back in the cigar box.

"Well sir, Sergeant, I won't say that young hellion hadn't got it comin' to him . . . and as pretty a piece of dead-center shootin' I ever did see!"

"I'd rather have taken him in on his feet." Ringold glanced at the small crowd staring at the dead man. "I'll have to take his papers for proper identification." He paused. "And, of course, you as the proper official are entitled to the deceased's, ah . . . effects to compensate for handling the funeral arrangements."

Marshal-Coroner Cheatham became the smiling host. "Here, have one!" And running a calculating eye over the group at the makeshift bier, "Drinks on th' house, gents. Hate to say it, but that there corpse wuz a bad'un." He raised his eyes virtuously. "And we just don't cotton to such likes around here. So, belly up and drink to his sad obsiquees . . . which will take place in th' mornin'."

While the group, with many a side-glance at Ringold, clustered along the bar, he approached the dead man. Head lay with hands at his sides, eyes staring at the ceiling with the surprised look on his pallid face of a youngun' caught bare-handed at the cookie jar.

Ringold closed the man's eyes, trying not to

look at the big hole the .44 had made in Head's chest. He went through the pockets, noting that the bandit's cash in hand wasn't more than enough to buy a couple more rounds for the "mourners." But the barkeep would realize a fair piece of change from the sale of Head's gun, horse and equipment.

There was a letter and couple of clippings from the local papers, referring to the stage holdup. There was also a fairly expensive watch, whether Head's or stolen. He'd leave that up to the Owl City official.

He went back to the bar, and calling Cheatham down to the end of the long, zinc-topped "watering trough," explained exactly what he had taken, turning over the timepiece and thin roll of bills.

"It seems you've had several hardcases in here lately, including Head there, and Leonard," Ringold observed.

"Yes, that's so," Cheatham replied, busily looking over the watch.

"If you knew they were fugitives from a robbery attempt, and a double killing, why did you let them camp here for?"

The barkeep pulled at his greying, handlebar mustache. "This here's a mighty small place, and we got ourselves a live-'n'-let-live motter. Ain't only about thirty folks in th' hull place, and if them what ride in don't pull any rough stuff

". . . and spend their sponduliks peaceful-like . . . well . . . ," he shrugged.

"This Pony . . . Deal must have spent some time here too, according to Head."

"Yeh, he did, all right. Had some horses that, I guess, he grabbed off'n some Mexican bandits . . . least wise he claimed they was sorta prizes of war. He wuz here about three days. Pretty good spender." Cheatham looked over at the corpse. "Guess I better send somebody up to Olafson's cabin and have him come down to measure that one for a wooden overcoat."

Meditating over his drink, Ringold's thoughts were drifting back to Texas and the shooting that had catapulted him into the present killing, when a man came through the front door.

The newcomer, a lanky, raw-boned fellow of around forty, with a long jaw and scrubby, sandy beard, was pulling off his slicker, when he caught sight of the immobile figure of Head stretched out on the pool table.

"Hey there, Leonard!" The bartender, suddenly metamorphosized into Marshal, yanked a shotgun out from under the bar, while the customers scattered.

"Hell, Cheatham! What happened to Harry?" Leonard made a dive back out the batwings just ahead of the shotgun's thundering blast.

"Why'd you pull that?" Ringold, blazing with anger, ran for the door in time to hear the sound of hoofbeats rattling off into the echoing darkness.

"Jest tryin' to back you up." Cheatham stood beside Ringold, peering out into the rainy evening.

Ringold swallowed his original reply, and informed the Barkeep-Official of his sudden decision to ride back to Pirtleville and spend the night. "And thanks for the . . . backing up . . . ! Where'd you think Leonard will go now?"

"No way of tellin', but I guess he'll travel back down below th' border. Him and Head claimed to have been there a couple of times around Agua Prieta. That's about twenty miles south of that dinky, little Pirtleville."

While they stood at the doorway, the rain-drizzle let up and a silvery, late-March moon broke through the dwindling clouds.

"Good luck on your hunt, Sergeant. Don't worry. That kid in there'll get a good send-off in th' mornin'."

"Thanks, but you keep a lookout for Leonard that he doesn't double back and come to *your* funeral." Ringold swung up into a wet saddle and rode away from Owl City and toward a bed for the night at the Pirtleville House.

6 Agua Prieta

Following an early breakfast, Ringold left the Pirtleville Hotel-Saloon where the rising sun ignited the hulking Animas Range, eastward, into waves of frozen flame. It had stopped raining sometime in the night, and for the first hour of his travels, little gusts of fine snow fell like white powder over yucca and sage, as the morning sun wandered in and out of the clouds.

The total distance of the jaunt to his target of Agua Prieta, in old Mexico, had been something over twenty miles—and now, arriving just southwest of Douglas, he neared the International Border, with less than seven miles to go.

If he'd been equipped with the necessary papers, he would have passed through the custom station at Douglas—but that was out of the question and so he rode toward the International Fence with no intention of having any truck with any guards or custom officers.

His talkative host at Pirtleville had passed on the information that there was considerable trouble in Mexico at the present time, for with Benito Juarez dead just five years, Mexico's Presidente, Porfiro Diaz, was still having trouble with rebels and with swarms of outlaws claiming to be rebels. And, said the landlord, they cast a hard eye upon all travelers, particularly those with the air of drifters—which Ringold took as a not too subtle comment on his own appearance.

It wouldn't do, he thought, to flash that Ranger badge too often, for wasn't he under direct orders to work only as a representative of Wells Fargo? And Wells Fargo, itself, would not welcome any undue publicity regarding the robberies of their coaches, or the bitter medicine doled out to the guilty—even if they did post rewards "leading to conviction . . ."

Reaching the barrier of the International Fence, he could see the taller structures and chimneys of Douglas to the west, interspersed amongst upthrust organ-pipe cactus and cholla. He was near enough.

Dismounting, he opened his saddle bag and, extracting a pair of wire cutters, purchased, with no questions asked, at Pirtleville's general store, went to work on the heavy fencing with all the gusto of a Texas "barb buster." When he'd cut enough for a good opening, he rolled the wire aside and led the horse through, then pulled it back into shape and wired it together with pieces clipped for that purpose.

Riding on southward, he glanced back and could barely make out the marks of his passage.

For a spell the sun shone down all golden and warm, melting the scattered patches of snow, and evaporating the small puddles of last night's downpour. Then it began to rain, all over again. This had to be one of the rainiest years on record.

Ringold had kept the grass-green slicker on, and now he buttoned it up to his chin and with a curse gave Blackbird the spurs. Mexican weather was as changeable as Arizona's, which wasn't strange—as he was only about four miles below the line.

The land, sandy and scattered with the ever-present sage, cholla and clumps of *pinon* pine, presently gave way to long, swelling waves of grass-covered mesa, where small herds of cattle—mainly longhorns, along with some of the new white-faces, were browsing in the gently falling rain. These animals lifted their heads as he passed, looking him over, but made no attempt to hit for the brush as Texas cattle would have done.

Others took note of his passing, for as he rode around a small herd, a pair of Mexican wranglers trotted cow ponies out of a grove of *pinon* pine.

Ringold started to rein in to determine if he were on the right line for Agua Prieta, when the larger of the two Mexicans leaned down, yanked out a Winchester rifle from his saddle sheath and fired. The other herder, minus such heavy artillery, pulled a six-shooter and sent three bullets after the saddle-gun's "blue whistler."

Both spurred up and came hell-for-breakfast after him.

He didn't stop to exchange words or shot, but

put the steel to his own mount. Blackbird, unused to such treatment, gave a great bound and raced away over the grassy mesa. What was it the pair had shouted upon catching sight of him? Was it *bandido*? Did they think him a outlaw? That was possible with such thieves as Leonard and Head taking cover below the line. Another rifle ball whizzed over his shoulder.

The broad reaches of the grassy mesa began to gradually slant downward into a valley, whose walls, hundreds of yards apart, thrust up their rocky faces as he thundered onward.

In the distance there was a good-sized *rancho*, surrounded by leafless cottonwoods, with white outbuildings hedged in by both wooden and adobe fencing. The ranch house veranda was swarming with running figures, hurrying toward a string of mounts, tied along the fences.

Over his shoulder he could see his two pursuers were no more than fifty yards behind, tall, flopping hats jammed down over their eyes. Again came the crack, crack of their pistols. They were driving him headlong down the funnelling valley—straight at that bunch of horsemen at the rancho.

Bottled in, he felt a blaze of anger at being rough-herded, the way Clanton had been hustled by Holliday and Earp. But, at least, Ike had someone waiting to give him cover. And Ike could have split away in any direction, but he,

Ringold, was being forced into a desperate box!

The sides of the mesa now were tilting until they were too steep to allow any divergence of flight—just one direction—straight at the ominous *rancho*!

Now close enough to the place, he could see the *rancho* was alive with some sort of military personnel, in big sombreros, and crossed cartridge belts slung over chests peppered with brass buttons.

A single rider loped out ahead of the milling band, mounted upon a superb palomino, and halted to await the finale of Ringold's rushing descent. His gold-laced jacket and trousers set him off as an officer.

When they hit the bottom of the valley, the pair behind let up on their fusillades but continued to rend the air with curses and shouts, in broken English.

Ringold thought their blustering a waste, for he didn't intend to ride through that patrol of hard-faced Mexicans just ahead.

Yanking Blackbird to a sudden halt, just in front of the gaudy officer figure, he turned to see the two pursuing *vaqueros* both sitting their saddles meek as sucking-calves.

"You travel in much hurry, *Señor*." The man on the palimino spoke pleasantly enough, but continued to stare at Ringold, while he tugged away thoughtfully upon his long, black mustache.

Ringold glanced from the officer to the scowling bunch in front of the ranch house, carbines at the ready. "And you speak mighty good English for a damned bandit chief!"

"Bandit—!" The man leaned back and roared with laughter, then shouted something in Spanish to his companions. The only word Ringold caught was "ruffians." The knot of men shouted back in apparent amusement. Even Ringold's recent "escort," busily engaged in peeling off their slickers and shaking water from their enormous sombreros, howled with gleeful amusement.

"You are a mighty bold one, sir." The chieftain, certainly not Mexican, with his light skin and big roman nose, held up a hand at several well-dressed men, emerging from the ranch house, motioning them back.

"Yes," he continued, as Ringold sat sweltering in that damned green slicker. "Yes, mighty bold . . . and I'm bound to say, unobservant." He gave his enormous mustacheos a decisive tug. "You Yanks should be aware of Mexico's new Federal Police . . . the Ruales, and even more so . . . what a full Colonel of the Ruales looks like!"

"Sorry." Ringold leisurely unbuttoned the green slicker, for the rain had quit, again, and the sun beamed down upon the *rancho*. He kept his hands carefully in sight of the thirteen armed men as he proceeded to divest himself of the rain-wear. "I'd heard, somewhere, about Ruales, but didn't know they were operating so close to the border."

"Close to the border? What have borders to do with anything?" The Colonel rode his horse directly up to Ringold. "Those loco Rangers of Texas never halt at borders and neither do we . . . that is, when we track Apache animals!"

"Apaches?" Ringold felt a cold finger momentarily touch his spine.

"Yes, they are on the move, again. Some of the renegades have been crossing the border, both ways, for the past month. But I, Colonel Emilio Kosterlitzky, will settle their hash sooner or later!"

"*Si*, and *bandidos* like that Gringo pig!" One of the *vaqueros* shouted.

Ringold, who'd removed the green slicker as they talked, shook it out to dry, and saw two bullet holes in its skirt. "*Bandidos*? Why . . . if I'd known you'd come that close, there'd be two mighty dead bastards up on the hill . . . you . . . !" Words failed him as he turned back to the Colonel, who'd been watching every move.

The pair of *vaqueros* broke into rapid Spanish, urging their little cow ponies up beside the Colonel and Ringold.

Kosterlitzky listened attentively for a moment, and then spoke to Ringold. "These are both good men, Juan and Pedro Cabronne. They are brothers who ride for old Don Ortiz back there in the yard." He indicated a tall, old Mexican, who stood with folded arms, taking in all the commotion at his *rancho*. Other *vaqueros* and ranch hands gathered nearby, watching, along with the hard-faced Ruales.

"Yes, they're sure good at shooting." Ringold, seeing the completely contrite look on the brothers' faces, had to smile. "Well, maybe they aren't any too good, but what was the ambush all about?"

"It was all a natural mistake. There were tracks of a broken-shoed horse near the herd a day ago, where the ground was soft by a water hole, though there were no animals missing. Also, some days back, a Yankee horsethief single-handedly fought Don Ortiz's men at dusk one evening, wounded two of their compadres and took a herd of twenty mounts straight north through the border fence, and escaped. A devil of a fellow!"

"Yeah, a devil of a fellow." Ringold grinned tightly, mentally giving that devil of a Pony Deal hell.

"The other thing that made the Brothers Cabronne attack you was your appearance," Kosterlitzky went on. "That slippery Americano, of the twenty stolen horses, wore a raincoat of the same frightful green, and rode a big black gelding . . . so you see their natural error?"

"When did you say that rascal ran off those horses?"

Kosterlitzky smiled benevolently and waved off the Cabronnes, who gave the Colonel and his "guest" several bows and polite flourishes of their huge sombreros before riding around the Ruales and on up to the *rancho*. "If you are not some Yank horsethief, yourself, disclose your identity and reason for being here, and then, perhaps, I may tell you. Your papers, if you please!"

"No reason to hide anything, but I've been too much in a hurry for papers. I'm Ringo . . . John Ringo . . . and seeing you're a law officer, and won't let it go further, I'm working on running down a stage robber for Wells Fargo, out of Tombstone."

"And you calmly cross the border without any papers, I wager, and without contacting the custom station at Douglas."

"I figured that if the Ruales and Rangers could ignore boundaries, when in a hurry, why not myself? I've a good idea that man riding the horse with the broken shoe could be the one I'm after."

The Colonel barked an order in Spanish at his men. They relaxed and shoved their murderous little carbines back into the saddle scabbards. Some dismounted and rolled their inevitable corn-husk cigarettes, while others merely slumped in their big, embossed saddles, taking a brief *siesta*.

"Back to my question, Colonel. How long ago

did that fellow, in the green slicker, run off *Señor* Ortiz's horses?"

"I admire your attitude, *Señor* Ringo . . . most resolute. But in answer, ten days ago."

That damned Pony! He was certain now. But why had Deal lent him that raincoat? It had nearly cost him his neck, and yet it gave him the edge when he caught up with Head. Rolling it up and tying it behind his saddle, he took another look at those bullet holes. Well, he'd try for Bill Leonard now, and then when he got back to Tombstone, he'd have a talk with Pony.

"You muse, *Señor*?" Kosterlitzky cleared his throat and commanded his men to mount and make ready to ride.

"Just thinking about someone."

"Which way do you head in this hunt for the man with the broken-shoed horse?"

"Thought I'd ride on in to Agua Prieta and look around some."

"Good! We have quarters there and are stationed in this area for the time while the Apache is loose. You may have an idea, for there are always plenty of riff-raff about, in the cantinas. Rogues a'plenty ride into Agua Prieta from time to time . . . and your man may be among them."

The Ruales headed down a well-kept road, running at right angles to the *rancho*. Ringo rode beside the Colonel. He was told that several renegade Indians, presumably Apache had been in the vicinity of the Ortiz's *rancho*, but had done no damage other than to kill a steer and butcher the best portions to carry along with them. But the old Don had sent out a call for protection and Kosterlitzky and part of his Company had been encamped at the *rancho* for a day and a night. They had not caught sight of the rider with the broken-shoed horse during their stay.

He was a very persuasive talker, this Emilio Kosterlitzky. While they rode, as if glad to talk to a white man, again—without any apparent feeling of shame, or boasting, the Colonel spun one story after another, of the long, twisted trail that brought him from his Moscow birthplace, son of a Russian father and a German mother, to Mexico. Jumping ship from a Russian war vessel in Venezuela, he'd made his way to the United States, where he'd enlisted in the Sixth Cavalry, then got into a "fuss" with an officer. So Sergeant Kosterlitzky had crossed the border to find his military expertise highly appreciated by Presidente Diaz.

Ringold couldn't quite fathom how a Presidente of Mexico became interested in a deserting trooper from the U.S., but glancing at the hawk-faced profile, with its air of grim determination, it was pretty plain that this man, who'd deserted from two services and countries, had reached his chosen place of decisive command and unrelenting action.

Despite the Colonel's many yarns, by the time they neared the outskirts of the pleasant little town of Agua Prieta, Ringold found he'd been doing some talking, also. He'd not mentioned how he came to Tombstone, or any background outside of the fact that he was a Wells Fargo operative in pursuit of an outlaw named Bill Leonard. All this had been smoothly extracted by Kosterlitzky while discussing the activities of both red and white renegades.

But what were the odds? The Colonel had every right to know what he, Ringold, was up to. It was Kosterlitzky's bailiwick and he certainly knew it. And there was the possibility that there might be help required from the Ruales in making Leonard's arrest—if he were ever found.

For some reason the Colonel had not asked for more identification than his word that he was a Wells Fargo agent, and he was grateful for that. He could have shown Kosterlitzky the actual letter assigning him to special duty in Arizona Territory, but he didn't want to tip his hand as being a Texas Ranger, if he could help it. The Mexicans and the Texans were old antagonists, and he needed all the cooperation he could get.

"Here we part company, for the time." Kosterlitzky indicated a large, whitewashed barracks and several adobe buildings just off the road leading into the heart of town. He called for a halt, and held out his hand. "Come back tomorrow, and we will talk further. The best place for you to put up is the Tontin around the south corner of the Alameda, which is what they call their plaza. It's clean and the beds are passable. Say to old Rojaz that I sent you."

While the Ruales dismounted and led their horses into a back area of the post, Ringold rode on up the sandy street, with its guardian lines of straggling cottonwoods, into the town.

Agua Prieta was typical of the northern Mexican settlements. In some ways it was similar to towns above the border, but there were subtle differences. The houses were built directly out to the wooden sidewalks. Their tawny brick-work, flat roofs, iron-barred windows, and heavy wooden shutters gave all buildings a prison-like uniformity. All life and color of the better homes lay in the gardens and courtyards behind the adobe walls. Poorer dwellings were exposed for what they were by lack of window gratings and absence of brick floors and entrances.

There was scant activity along the street, it being close to the *siesta*, but Ringold knew that when *siesta* was over there would be little more. He'd been down into Mexico twice before. As a Ranger, he'd returned a cow-thief to a Mexican court down at Allende across the Rio from Eagle Pass. His other jaunt had been years ago as a shirt-tail youngun', traveling with his father on a brief holiday.

Few were about, but as he neared the plaza, he counted three elderly women, with black shawls drawn tightly over heads and shoulders, plus a priest in long flapping cassock, poring over his breviary as he walked. Two ambitious wood merchants in snow-white shirts and trousers and broad, felt hats, met him coming down the shady street. This pair drove eight mouse-grey, long-eared, serious little burrows. Each patient beast bore a small mountain of wood upon its back. Each animal brayed a polite good day to Blackbird as it passed.

Turning the corner, Ringold dismounted in front of the Tontin Tavern. The immediate area seemed well supplied with drinking saloons, sandwiched between small shops and eating places. But the only sound of activity came from the saloon next door to the Tontin. Lazy laughter, amiable Spanish curses, and the buzzing twang of a guitar spoke of a mere half-observed *siesta*.

Señor Rojas, who must have spent his spare time peering from his window for possible customers, bustled forth from the Tontin, tagged by a small brown-faced urchin, who immediately took charge of Blackbird, after Winchester and saddle bags were stripped from the horse. "Welcome! Welcome, your honor." Rojas, a rolly-polly Mexican, with broad Indian features, wiped beads of sweat from brown brow as he urged Ringold into the tavern. "And so our excellent Colonel of Ruales sent you to us. That is well, for we are the best house in all of Sonora. Ah!" He had craned his neck to watch Ringold fill out the tattered register. "And from Tombstone. That is well. In fact, I have a cousin in the same business as those two there." And he indicated the distant wood merchants, still visible through the plaza's leafless poplars.

"That so?"

"*Si!*" Rojas fished out the key to Ringold's room, handed it over, and picked up the saddle bags, while Ringold toted his Winchester.

"So you've a relation up at Tombstone?" Ringold made small talk as he came down the stairs on his way to one of the plaza's restaurants.

"*Si*, and the Colonel, himself, got Florentino Cajeme, my second cousin, a job at Tombstone in the wood business, after my cousin hurt his leg so bad he could no longer be of use to the Colonel as a scout. Cajeme is grandson of a famous Yaqui chief, and a noted trailer."

"This Kosterlitzky's quite a bear-cat it seems. How's he on keeping the peace around Sonora?"

Rojas wiped away at his sweat-beaded forehead, smiling broadly. "Most well, I would say. Since he has been in our area these past weeks, he has given the Jeffe, our constable, considerable help. Every bad hombre, that kicks up his heels gets the chance to become Ruale. He is still forming several companies. But, if such hombres refuse . . . then," Rojas shrugged, "it's *ley del fuga!*"

"Shot while escaping!" It was Ringold's turn to shrug as he went out to a late dinner. So that's where the Colonel recruited his hard-eyed troopers!

Despite *siesta*, he was able to obtain a passable meal of frijoles and tortillas at a small beanery across the plaza. Then he made the rounds of the saloons. By the time he'd emerged from the last tavern it was well on toward nightfall. He'd had about one drink, at each place, either tequila or iced Mexican beer, but the only Anglo he'd encountered was an elderly prospector with a red nose and a wooden leg, too drunk to do more than cadge drinks and brag about some mine he'd misplaced. "Peg Leg'll find it agin', someday. And when I do stranger, you'n me'll go halves, and that's gospel!"

Ringold bought him another drink, shook hands with solemnity, and carefully navigated out into the golden-tinged evening.

Señoras and *señoritas* brushed past, coming from the small shops, with their simple purchases, gliding along with shawls, or rebosas, wrapped about their heads until only their dark eyes, noses and foreheads were visible. Lounging citizenry leaned against walls and squatted along their walks in their snowy trousers and brilliant

118

serapes, gathered about shoulders, with the folds held over the mouth.

By stern concentration, he was able to thread his way through such placid obstacles and reach the Tontin and bed without undue incident.

When Ringold had plunged into the middle of his corn shuck mattress at night, he'd felt the room to be unseasonably warm and had slept with the window open—forgetful of the numerous belts of tequila that could have had something to do with his room's temperature.

With the coming of dawn, his open window let in all the many strident sounds of an awakening Mexican town. A series of vicious squeals rang out from a nearby yard where a townsman was feeding a quartet of superbly hungry pigs. Two back yards over, a pair of burros determinedly began to serenade the rosy-tinted sunrise, while every neighborhood cur within earshot began to yelp its accompaniment. And to put the cap-sheaf upon the whole noisy dawn, the mission bell of the large, white-washed church across the plaza began splitting the morn with its brazen cling-clanging.

He rolled out of bed, cursing, washed up in the cracked bowl on the rickety wash-stand, scraped his stubble without too many nicks, and stumping downstairs, went straight across the plaza to the restaurant where he'd dined the day before.

About ten o'clock, after a stroll about the somnolent plaza, he returned to the hotel, and settling up with Rojas, got Blackbird from the stable boy, and rode out to the edge of town for a brief confab with Kosterlitzky.

A Ruale, carbine at port, stood in front of the small adobe house that served as Kosterlitzky's headquarters. He was promptly recognized and escorted to the door with a flourish by the evil-looking fellow. Possibly one of the Colonel's *ex-bandidos*. A small detachment of Ruales sat under a barely-leafed cottonwood, playing at mumble-peg with wicked bowie knives, while their wiry, little ponies stood patiently nearby, reins sweeping the sandy ground.

"One moment, *Señor* Ringo, and we will talk." Kosterlitzky, sitting on the edge of a small table, that served as a desk, was in animated conversation with a shabby Mexican in the outfit of a *peon*—worn white trousers and jacket, ragged serape and ancient straw hat. Their speech was in some Indian dialect, unknown to Ringold.

Kosterlitzky presently dismissed the man, who slipped out with a shy, backward glance at Ringold. "Well, my friend are you still seeking for your Gringo . . . Leonard?"

"He's not around town as far as I could see, but I thought if I rode out and cut for his trail, I might run into some sign. No use in making the rounds of your dives again."

"Yes, I understand you are a good spender," Kosterlitzky laughed and waved Ringold to a chair, then sat back down behind his desk. "*Señorita* Tequila makes for a good nightcap, eh?"

"How in hell do you know what I'm up to every minute?"

The Colonel opened a drawer in the table and took out a folded paper. "Here is a map of the area that might be of service, water holes and so forth." He looked up quizzically as he handed it over. "My Russian heritage has made me very aware of the need for good intelligence, if I wished to build a truly effective force. And so, I have had you watched . . . for your own good, of course."

"Of course." Ringold took up the map and examined it, noting the roads, water courses and mountain passes. "And that would have been one of your spies that just left?"

Kosterlitzky raised a well-kept hand. "Oh, no. Just a poor *peon* who works for old man Garcia. He was sent in from the farm to complain of the theft of food from the storeroom."

Ringold stiffened and rose from his wobbly chair. "Could it have been Apaches, or do you think it was Leonard? Which way is that farm?"

"Yes, it might be your robber, as I am informed by my scouts that any of the renegades are doubtless deep into Sonora by now, at least for the present. Give me the map. So . . . here is the place, just to the west of the Raimundo River, about four miles from town. You can cross on the Faustino Bridge, here." He indicated the spot on the map. "Old Garcia will be able to tell you more, he speaks tolerable English. Perhaps you could pick up this Leonard's trail, if it were, indeed, he." He rose and shook hands. "Later I may ride out to see for myself, and now *via con Dios.*"

With a wave of his hand at the drowsy Ruales, Ringold rode off at a gallop on the road leading away from the main street of Agua Prieta. The Colonel had assured him it was the easiest way to the river.

Within half an hour, he was riding across the echoing planks of a wooden bridge over the willow-lined river, now up, rushing amber-full from the recent rains. The sky, overhead, was a vast, blue dome, devoid of clouds. The ground beyond the bridge ran in a series of gentle swells through cactus-fenced farmland. At the top of one rise, he first saw the tawny adobe walls of, what appeared to be, Garcia's farm house, with its neat cluster of outbuildings. All was surrounded by creamy-white-blossoming orange groves, flecked here and there by the deep pink of the almond trees' first fragrant blooms.

It was now earliest April, a time of growth,

helped, in part, by the use of irrigation, with water coming from the many ditches draining from the neighboring creeks that branched off from the river. Even the cactus, serving as fencing, was sending forth its flame-bright flowers.

Sitting reined-in, while looking upon all the unexpected beauty and then, in vain, at the flint-hard road surface for any sort of tracks, he caught sight of movement of a horse among some poplars in a nearby field. And in the same instant saw the briefest glint of sunlight reflecting from something near a ditch in the same field.

Then he was falling—along with Blackbird—into the roadside, as the racketing crack of a rifle echoed through his fading senses.

7 Bucking the Tiger

For a time there was nothing. Then, little by little, there was utter darkness—and somehow, he felt himself drifting through that darkness, insubstantial, yet forming into a being that dreaded the searing light sweeping in upon itself.

That blinding light, all around, filled him with a slow and sullen rage at such treatment, and shaking his head in bitter disgust, he found himself lying in the middle of a roadway, supported by someone who was speaking to him.

"A hell of a lot," he answered that someone, who, it seemed, had inquired if he were in pain. But as the road slowed its rocking, the only pain seemed to be confined to his right foot. He was, after all, in one piece, though the glaring daylight made his head ache.

"My leg . . . hurts to beat hell!" he told the man, who turned out to be the Ruales Colonel.

"Your black horse was hit by your ambusher, but only a crease on the head. Stunned, it fell with you, and upon your leg. I thought that *bandido* had done for you, *muy bueno*!"

"Leonard, it was Leonard?"

"*Was* . . . Leonard," Kosterlitzky answered, as he helped Ringold to stand on one leg, supporting him around the shoulder. "Bring over the horse," he ordered one of the Ruales, who were clustered around a big, bay mare.

"*Señor* Ringo, please to meet the late *Señor* Bill Leonard," announced the Colonel as a grinning Ruale led up the mare, with the limp body of a man draped over the horse's back. "We tried to capture him, but he would not halt, and showed fight . . . so it was, *ley del fuga*," Kosterlitzky announced dryly. "But," he smiled briefly, "let us get you and *your amigo* back to town, then attend to your injury."

After inspecting Blackbird, who'd received a nasty-looking, but superficial head wound, and a more seriously pulled tendon, Ringold was boosted aboard a spare Ruale mount and traveled back to Agua Prieta with Kosterlitzky and his unit.

On the way, the Ruale Chief told of riding out on a different route and coming upon Leonard about the time he opened upon Ringold.

Arrived back at the yellow adobe, Kosterlitzky ordered the dead bandit laid out on the rough planking of the porch, while he sent uptown for a doctor.

Ringold sat on the edge of the porch, boot off, rubbing at his paining foot, and watching Kosterlitzky go through Leonard's pockets. "Not much to help you." The Colonel, big, gold-banded sombrero pushed back, went through the hard-case's pockets expertly. "No, just a few dollars, a cheap watch . . . and this!" He tossed a folded bit of paper over.

Ringold smoothed the sheet out and read the short note, written in a crude, back-hand scrawl: *"I want you and Kid Head to absent yourself from the county for the time being. Crane knows where to go. Pick up your messages where you got this. When the next job is arranged you will be informed in time."* There was no signature, just the single letter—*S,* at the bottom of the page.

"Not much to go on, is there?" Kosterlitzky tugged at his mustache and bringing out a rickety chair from inside, sat down, ignoring the riddled body beside them.

"You've already looked at the note?"

Kosterlitzky laughed, and calling an orderly to his side, spoke to him in rapid Spanish. "I did glance at it, *Señor . . . Ranger!*"

"And you glanced over my carcass at the same time? Well, what now?" He could feel his neck burning, but held his ire as he watched a pair of Ruales advance to the porch and lug the dead bandit around to the rear.

"What now? I'd say that when your injury is attended to, you have our official permission to go about your Wells Fargo business. And you should leave promptly, as General Gomez of the Mexican Government is due to inspect this district in the next day or so. There could be difficulty if it came to his attention that a Ranger was here without papers." He motioned in the direction of town. "Ah, here comes your private physician, courtesy of the Mexican Government. Would you Texans treat a poor Ruale thus . . . if he came hunting for *bandidos* in the Lone Star?"

While the bent, white-haired doctor pried and prodded at Ringold's paining foot, Kosterlitzky carried on a casual conversation, in Spanish with the bearded physician, and in fluent English with Ringold.

"Excellent!" Kosterlitzky got up, stretched and moved back into the shade from the advancing sunlight. "The good doctor has bound up your injured ankle . . . so, and I have taken the liberty of presenting you with Leonard's mare to enable you to get back over the border."

"But, what about my own horse?" Ringold shook hands with the old physician, who stood and watched, with approval, as his patient, in a slit boot, hobbled across the porch to look over the big bay being led up from the corral behind headquarters.

"Emilio, my orderly and expert in such matters, informs me it will be a month or so before your black will be in shape to ride. Leave the horse with us and, in due time, someone will bring your mount to you . . . in Tombstone."

Thanking the Ruale Chieftan, Ringold considered for a moment. "Colonel, I've a parting question."

"Certainly, if I can answer."

"Any greetings to carry north with me, such as Florentino?"

Kosterlitzky smiled imperturbably as he helped Ringold mount the bay. "Your own saddle bags and rifle are on this horse . . . as you can see; also your vivid slicker, rolled there behind the saddle." He paused and extended his hand. "Yes, you might tell Florentino, or Cajeme, who works as woodcutter at Tombstone, to keep away from the San Rafael Valley up there. There could be retaliatory raids by some of our hot-headed *vaqueros* near the Tombstone area sometime this summer." He tugged at his drooping mustache. "I will try to see this does not happen, but we still have just so much man-power and so, *quien sabe*?"

Ringold settled down into the unfamiliar saddle, eased his throbbing ankle into the stirrup, and turned the horse.

"Bye the bye," the Colonel laid a hand on the bay's neck, "the doctor says that you should keep off that leg as much as possible for the next few weeks . . . so you will have to bide your time running down that secret *Señor S.*"

"I can wait, if I have to."

"Just so. If necessary you might be able to enlist Cajeme . . . if he isn't busy with other matters.

He is like a blood-hound, that one. He will never reveal your interests." He stepped back. "And do not fret over renegade savages. They are far to the south by now. *Adiós!*"

He took the northward course, riding up the inclined road that led toward the Ortiz *Rancho*, then veered to the left to bypass the place. He wanted no repetition of that last affair there. The land continued to swell into a continuous grassy plane as it climbed to the higher mesa. By riding far enough westward he was able to clear the narrow valley, and sunset found him back at the International Boundary.

Cutting the fence, and mending it took only minutes. Getting to be a real "barb buster," he smiled painfully to himself as he limped about his task, keeping on the lookout for any border patrols.

Within the hour, he rode out of a thicket of prickly pear, just coming into yellow blossom, and struck the Benson-Tombstone road while the new April moon arose in the purpling sky like a vast, silver Mexican bangle.

The big bay mare was steady as a rock, with a racking lope that whittled down the miles, and he arrived at the little copper-mining town of Bisbee in time for a good, filling meal at the Copper Cafe. In spite of the jarring he'd taken, and his still throbbing ankle, his appetite was mighty brisk.

Facing thirty miles and more to Tombstone, he turned the horse, he'd christened Nugget, in at Spence and Stilwell's Livery and put up for the night at the Bisbee House, a one-story affair packed with hard-rock miners.

Next morning was a blue-and-gold day, without a cloud, fashioned for traveling, and he made the best of it—loping the big bay for miles at a time. With the towering, pale-blue of Potter Mountain behind him, melting into the deeper azure of the sky, the route began to be familiar. Ten miles outside Tombstone, he struck the piece of road he'd hit when he came into the territory, just a month ago. Was it only a month? It seemed ten years. Only this time there was no Pony Deal waiting for him.

As he rode down the vast wash known as Brewery Gulch and up onto the flats outside the town, he found himself wondering just where Pony might be. He had some definite questions for him, including green slickers, stolen horses—and a person known only as *S*.

Tombstone was in fine spring fettle as he rode into town on Allen Street. Overloaded ore wagons creaked past. Ladies, fancy and proper, studiously avoided each other as they walked the wooden sidewalks on shopping trips. Off-shift miners lounged in the mellow sun in front of the many saloons, along with a handful of cowboys in from the range.

Passing the Bird Cage Theater at Sixth and Allen, he noted that "Uncle Tom's Cabin" was still playing, and the next production would be "The first appearance of the celebrated comedian . . . Eddie Foy." Foy, according to the bill, would be followed by Miss Nellie Boyd and her "Dramatic Company."

He determined to catch some of those shows—if he had the time. And it seemed he might have plenty of time by the way his ankle was acting up. No more riding out for a spell, if he could help it.

He pulled in at the O.K. Corral, it being nearer to the hotel than the livery favored by Pony. When he handed Nugget's reins to the hostler, the man cocked an eye at the big bay, but wrote out a receipt.

Carrying his Winchester and saddle bags, he hobbled over a block to the narrow, two-story Occidental Hotel, and engaged a room on the ground floor.

Stowing his gear, he limped back up the street and into Hafford's Corner Five Saloon. After a drink by himself, and seeing no one around he recognized except a sullen Buckskin Frank Leslie, he went across the block to lunch at the Can Can.

With still no sight of Pony or any of the Earp bunch, or even Behan, he got himself back to his room. Gingerly removing his boots, he piled into bed.

• • •

Came a banging and a hammering upon his locked door. Rousing himself up slowly, he stared at the bright morning light, streaming in through the single, dingy window. Fagged by the past days, he'd slept the clock around.

"Yes?"

"Open up in there! It's Pony!"

Rubbing his eyes and yawning, Ringold limped to the door and unbolted it. "Pony? Where the devil did you spring from? What's all the row?"

Pony, with a three-day growth of beard, and garbed in a plain flannel shirt and stained blue-jeans stuffed into his boots, came in batting dust from himself with a sweat-streaked sombrero. "Come from? Well, you might say I come from the devil, himself . . . that blamed Doc Holliday! He and th' Earps just rid back into town for supplies. And I tagged back with 'em. They're out on another of their wild goose chases . . . after whoever tried to halt th' up stage at Charleston last night late. I was comin' back from a trip when I run into them and hung on like a burr."

"Another robbery attempt? Who do they think tried it this time?"

"Nobody's talkin'. It couldn't have been Doc nor th' Earps though. They been sittin' tight at th' Oriental, far as I can tell. Could have been Leonard or Head . . . if you didn't run into 'em on your travels."

"But I did. Remember you put me on to Head at Owl City."

"Yeah, so I did. And . . . ?"

"They won't be coming back."

"Unhh! Mind if I sit down?" Pony planked himself down upon the creaking bed beside Ringold, who had eased back to a sitting position to favor his ankle.

"So you run into both of 'em? Well, I guess there's no use in askin' just what happened."

"But there is. You've got to report to Thorne for me. I don't think I'll be riding out much . . . even to yours and Hill's place." And Ringold went on to recount the entire string of events, starting with the shooting of young Head at Owl City, then relating his meeting with the Ruales Colonel, the ambush that failed and Leonard's death at the hands of the Mexicans. He turned over to Pony the items taken from both dead men for delivery to Thorne. But held back the letter from *S*. He'd show that to Thorne himself.

"In case you're wonderin' how quick I found you," Pony expanded, stuffing the effects into his pockets, "I had word from Sam, the hostler at the O.K. Corral, when we pulled in, that you'd come ridin' up on Bill Leonard's bay. And someone seen you hobblin' inter th' hotel here."

"I was going to ask you that."

"Hell, I'm as good a gumshoe as th' next. Was just leadin' you on about Head and Leonard.

Knew damn good and well that if you got within a country mile of either of them no-goods it was good night Katie Bar th' Door for them." He handed Ringold a sealed envelope. "By th' way, here's your Wells Fargo pay from Thorne. And also these two letters from Texas."

As Ringold did not appear too eager to read his mail, Pony got up and walked to the door. "I'll get up to Benson this afternoon. Though I might just tag th' Earps and Doc back out of town to sweat 'em. Old Behan caught himself Lute King. Found out, somehow, he was a horse-holder at th' Benson job. But King up and walked out of jail when nobody was lookin' . . . sort of took himself some leg bail. I hear he's gone outa th' territory. Crane and th' other stickup man was killed way over in New Mexico somewhere. Thorne got th' word day before yesterday."

"So that leaves just one."

"Yeah, good old Doc, and I hear tell they're gonna bring in an indictment against him again. Maybe that's why he got so virtuous and law-abidin' a posse-man." Pony went out the door. "That Bart Masterson friend of Wyatt's gone back to greener pastures back in Kansas. Guess he got enough of all of 'em. I'll send over Doctor Porter to look at your leg. If you got yourself a bad ankle bone, it could give you fits off and on for months." And Pony was gone before Ringold could get into his questions regarding the green slicker and those Mexican horses.

He opened the letters. One was from the Adjutant General's Office, short and to the point, as usual.

"April 3, 1881
Sergeant John Ringold:
I am in receipt of a report from Wells Fargo's Chief Special Officer Hume and am pleased that he feels you will be of help in weeding out the criminal element that has plagued the Company in Arizona Territory. Therefore you will continue at Tombstone for the remainder of the year, or until further notice.
Signed, William A. King
    Adjutant General, Texas"

A year! And here it was only the beginning of spring. He could have long whiskers before he got out of this affair. Cursing, he opened the other letter. It was also short, a mere hurried scribble from his father.

"Brownwood, Texas
April 2, 1881
Dear John,
Hope this missive finds you all to the good and going strong. Uncle Bill informs us that it is all right to give you this bit of

information. Your troubles could be over soon, as that young scoundrel of a Jim Rush has been found out as a fence cutter and horsethief, and sent to Huntsville Pen for five years. Ryan broke his neck in a drunken fall from a horse. So, without Rush and others stirring up trouble, and J.C. Pinckney Higgins refusing to be drawn into any law-suit over your accidental shooting of his loutish cousin, things could be ironed-out within the next month or so. Your Mother sends her best love, and so do I.

Your Father."

But if things did work out over the Higgins trouble, he seemed certain to be roped into this Wells Fargo business for months to come. Putting both letters away in his saddle bag, he went about cleaning up from the days of riding.

He was shaving off the last of his stubble when a knock at the door announced the advent of the doctor. Half-an-hour later, hefty, round-faced Doctor Porter was gone, leaving him with a rebound ankle and the advice to stay off his feet as much as possible—for an indefinite period. "And if that cracked tibia doesn't heal correctly, you could limp through life. At least you could have a shin-bone that could go out on you at any time!"

Ringold hobbled over to the Can Can for breakfast, then purchased a walking stick at the Cochise Hardware and Trading Store across the way. And for the next two weeks, with that fifty dollars pay from Wells Fargo, he camped in either the Oriental or in the more tony Alhambra, playing poker with such high-rollers as Bones Brannon and Dick Clark, along with Johnny Speck and the Dutch Kid.

But when he went over to the Crystal Palace to lock horns with Doc Holliday, who had a great reputation at five-card stud, he found Holliday still out of town after the phantom Charleston stage robbers with all the Earps, except Virgil, who was doing duty as night watchman under Johnny Behan.

"Guess old Doc's still out somewheres in th' bresh with them Earps. Play actin' I'd say. Makin' out they're runnin' down them Charleston boys, when everybody knows from th' papers that th' gang didn't get a plugged *peso* on that April twenty-first try," volunteered Buckskin Frank Leslie, coming out from behind the bar to fetch a round of drinks for the gamesters at the Dutch Kid's table.

"That and layin' low, in case th' court fetches in an indictment for th' Benson job," laughed the Dutch Kid, who had little regard for his rival at the Crystal Palace. "So cheese it with that slippery case-man, and ante up, boys! This time I take Ringo's shirt and cuffs! These pistol-packers may be a-number-one with the shootin' irons, but they just can't buck th' tiger and stay healthy."

The Dutch Kid proved to be an accurate prognosticator. By the end of April, Ringold was down to his last five-dollar gold-piece, yet he had accomplished what he'd set out to do when he'd first arrived in Tombstone. He was now accepted as a hardcase with a shady past—a man that Behan and Breakenridge, as well as the dull-eyed Fred Dodge, walked easy around when they met.

In such a set-up, Ringold would have thought to hear whisperings of the doings of the stagecoach gangs, and, perhaps, even some mention of the man, known to him as—*S*. But the grapevine in the gambling dens remained silent, and there was only bar chatter and worthless rumors a'float along the streets.

He'd hoped to look up the Indian, Florentino Cajeme, but heard he was out in the Dragoons at Pete Spence's camp, working at wood-cutting. Even Ike Clanton and his brothers never came to Tombstone.

The Earps, close-mouthed and secretive, rode back into town, along with Doc Holliday, on the morning of the first of May, without any captives or explanation of their long absence. And Pony Deal arrived that afternoon, from one of his own mysterious jaunts. He caught up with Ringold as he sat in the small lobby of the hotel, thumbing through a week-old copy of the Tombstone Nugget.

"Th' Earps ain't tumbled, but I follered them for th' past three days. Come up on 'em down around the border, west of Nogales. They could have been acrost on some sort of devilment. Say, you-all seem mighty pert again."

"I had a lot of time to sit around and rest up."

"Well, if you're feelin' that good, you'd better git that big bay out and head up to Benson. Mister Thorne's got some talkin' to do."

Ringold, minus his cane, rode for Benson before dark.

8 Trouble at Clanton's

Ringold felt himself little wiser following his meeting with Thorne at Benson. The Wells Fargo Chief had listened to the report of Ringold's, regarding the gunfight at Owl City, and Harry Head's death, as well as the ambush at Agua Prieta and the subsequent end of Bill Leonard—but was unable to hazard a guess at the identity of the secretive person—S.

Thorne had congratulated him on his efforts, telling him that his share of the reward money, a mighty hefty fifteen-hundred dollars, would be held for him until his release back to the Rangers. He was urged to favor his injured leg, but to be constantly upon the alert for any suspects.

One of Thorne's statements remained with Ringold, following that night meeting at Benson: "Whoever wrote that scribble has been partaking of too many Ned Buntline yellow-back novels. It's some sort of play-acting, I'd wager." Thorne had leaned back at his desk, chuckling and polishing his glasses. "It's got to be some half-literate saddle tramp playing at robber baron. And as for that S, what could it symbolize . . . Stealthy Sam, Slippery Slim, or, perhaps, Mister Silence? No, I tell you that such a person, or persons will outsmart themselves, and mighty soon. Then you can nab the bunch, I'm positive!"

But Ringold wasn't so positive, at all. Did Thorne suspect someone, keeping it to himself until he could play the major part and thus square himself with the home office for all the many robberies and attempted robberies within his area? It almost sounded like a case of sour grapes, but he liked Thorne and promised to keep close tabs on the Earps and Doc.

It wouldn't be particularly difficult to keep track of that foursome. With the upcoming court case hanging over Holliday's sleek, blond head, he was in evidence throughout the week as he plied his trade at the Crystal Palace. Ever since the 9th of June, Doc had been nailed down to Tombstone and vicinity by a five-thousand-dollar surety bond, issued from Judge Spicer's Court.

Ringold heard that the money was put up by Wyatt Earp. How he'd come into so much cash was the gossip of the gambling dens for days on end, and then the talk was switched from the lanky, gander-eyed Earp by the arrival of one Curly Bill Brocius.

Brocius, a Texas cowboy who'd been involved in an accidental shooting of City Marshal Fred White, the fall before Ringold arrived, but had been exonerated, walked into the Alhambra one afternoon in July. He bellied up to the bar near to where Wyatt Earp sat watching the games as a sort of combination guard and bouncer.

Ringold, who happened to be in the Alhambra, was seated in a corner, watching Wyatt and nursing a drink as he waited for Pony to come around.

Brocius, after downing several beers, pointedly ignored Wyatt, but inquired the whereabouts of Virgil Earp.

Buckskin Frank Leslie, working behind the bar, informed Brocius that Virgil was the Town Marshal, but he was out of Tombstone on business.

"So? Well, it's little to me. I'm on my way back to Texas, and I couldn't care less if Virge Earp got himself a law badge again. He surely got me in dutch when White was shot."

"Have a drink, Curly?" Wyatt, who'd stretched up to his spindling six foot two, ambled over to the bar.

"No thank you. You're Wyatt, eh?"

"Yes, Virgil's brother." Wyatt leaned grandly against the polished mahogany, ignoring Brocius's refusal. "Bartender, pour Curly here a shot!"

"Listen, Earp," Brocius, tall as Wyatt and heavier in build, shifted a boot on the rail—"I don't want to drink with any damned Earps! That chuckle-headed Virgil got Marshal White shot last fall by grabbin' at my gun when we were just funnin'. I've had my share of trouble ever since. Shot in th' neck by a tomfool drunk two months back. And now I'm leavin' th' Territory and I don't want any more trouble." His voice rose. "So, clear off!"

"I don't take such talk . . . ," Wyatt began, only to halt lamely as he found himself peering into the business end of Brocius's six-shooter.

There was a general scuffling of boots as the gamblers and beverage customers hustled to get out of the possible line of fire.

"Go get Behan. This here man's pulled a weapon on me," Earp barked at the crouching bartender. No one moved including the barkeep.

"All I want is to finish my drink and to get to hell out of this place. Too many damned fools, includin' Earps to suit me," Brocius grumbled, keeping his pistol leveled at Wyatt's belt buckle, as he hoisted the remainder of his whisky.

"No, you don't!" Ringold whipped out his Colt as Wyatt shook a derringer out of his sleeve when Brocius turned his head to pour himself another shot.

"Hey there! I ain't got no fuss with you, Mister, or anybody!" Then Brocius saw the hide-out gun in Earp's fist.

"You'll get yourself in deep trouble, interfering with a law officer in pursuit of his duty," Wyatt snarled at Ringold.

"Oh, hire a hall, Earp," Ringold grinned, stepping over and taking the deadly, little two-shot weapon from Wyatt's limp grasp. "Just because your brother's got himself appointed temporary Marshal doesn't give you a license to even catch flies!"

Brocius wiped the back of his hand across his mouth, holstered his pistol, and set his grey Stetson at an angle on his dark, straight hair. "Thanks, Mister. Like I said, I don't want no trouble. Seems to have had more'n my share ever since I got me that blamed fool handle . . . Curly Bill. Hell!" He snorted in disgust, glaring at Wyatt, who stood speechless. "Think I'd really like to let daylight into th' next yahoo who'd call me that. But that's what can happen when you have a darned Kansas dance hall gal singin' such tunes as 'Curly Bill' into your ear, and th' rest of th' trail hands hear such a fool song."

Brocius, without a backward glance at the fuming Wyatt, marched across the floor and out the door to be seen no more in Tombstone, or Arizona Territory.

"You just ain't heard th' last of this little affair," Wyatt, livid and glowering, turned away from the bar, and held out his hand for his hide-out gun.

Ringold, still grinning, broke the weapon, ejected a pair of murderous shells, and tossed it back to Earp. "If I don't miss my guess, you've a lot to be thankful for. If I hadn't stopped your play, you'd probably have started singing 'Curly Bill,' and that'd brought on your demise earlier than necessary."

The hangers-on guffawed, and reseating themselves, began to noisily discuss the events just past, as well as Wyatt's five-thousand-dollar bail bond for Holliday.

Pocketing the derringer, and ignoring the audible gossip, Wyatt stalked out of the Alhambra, for the moment forgetful of his duties as saloon gendarme.

Still laughing to himself, Ringold followed Earp, but turned back toward the livery stable.

He was no sooner astride the bay, riding up Tough Nut Street, with the intention of heading out to Hill's Ranch to look up Pony, who'd been absent for nearly a week, when he saw Doc Holliday in earnest conversation with a dark-skinned man, dressed in clean but shabby clothes, obviously some sort of an Indian. This stranger stood listening to Doc and holding the head of a wood-laden burro.

Wondering why Holliday would be purchasing firewood on such a blistering day, Ringold eased up, and pulled aside to let an empty ore wagon rumble past. In the semi-silence following the rattling vehicle's departure, he caught a word or two—"Spence had better . . . and don't know a damned thing, but you'd better . . ." Doc emphasized his remarks with a sudden shove that sent the man down into the dust, while the over-laden burro started off at a clattering gallop, scattering firewood along the way until it fetched up against a board fence at Second Street.

"Hey there, Holliday!" Ringold shouted at the gambler, as Doc yanked out a pearl-handled Colt and hit the man a vicious clout over the head.

Doc spun around, six-shooter poised, but lowered it and grinned crookedly at the sight of Ringold's Colt at the ready. "Hell Ringo, you got to keep these Siwash in their places, or they might just get th' idea they're as good as white folks."

The broad-faced native, staggering from the blow, straightened and gave Ringold a flashing, dark-eyed look.

"You feel all right, Charley?" Ringold rode nearer to the Indian, ignoring Holliday.

"*Si, Señor.*" The man wiped the blood from his eyes and shrugged slightly. "*Señor* Holliday . . . he was only upset by something he thought I had said."

"And what might that be, Doc?" Ringold kept an eye on Holliday, while he also watched the Indian padding up the street after his runaway beast, deciding he wasn't too badly injured, despite that fierce rap over the head.

Holliday, blandly ignoring Ringold's question, tucked his pistol away under his broadcloth coat, and dusted off his hands. "Get out of my way." He jostled through the knot of gawkers that were gathering along the boardwalk in front of Jordan's Feed Store.

Ringold, holstering his own pistol, touched

up the bay, and keeping pace with the striding Holliday, spoke to him again. "What a temper you get yourself into, Doc, knocking around *peon* woodcutters. Just who is that poor devil?"

Doc halted in front of the Gay Lady Saloon, with one hand on the batwings. He was no longer grinning, but coldly furious. "Ringo, I plain don't know who in hell you think you are, but ever since you showed up here in Tombstone, you've been sticking that damned long nose into things that just don't concern any fool saddle tramp at any time. You better watch your step, or . . ." The gambler hesitated and then turned on his heel and thrust his way through the saloon doors.

"Oho!" Ringold chuckled to himself as he spurred Nugget on up the street. Now he was getting somewhere. Both Wyatt and Doc were down on him plenty. They were also as jumpy as a pair of tom cats on a hot stove.

"*Señor!*" A voice hailed him as he wheeled his mount to hit out for Hill's place. It was the wood cutter, who'd rounded up his burro and was in the process of stacking back some of the jettisoned cargo.

Ringold pulled up short, and looked down at the man. "Cajeme?" As he spoke, he knew he was correct, beside Holliday had mentioned Spence in his tongue lashing.

"*Si*, my Sergeant." The Indian approached and laid a broad, brown hand on the bay's flank.

147

"You know me?"

"*Si.* I had hoped to meet with you before, but I have been away."

"Mexico?"

"*Si.*" The Yaqui's eyes, restless as dark quicksilver, took in the dusty street, with its passing horsemen, lazily rolling hacks and ambling ore wagons. "This is not so good a place to talk. I have a few things that may be of use to you."

"And some of interest to Doc and his bunch?"

"I must go now." Cajeme took up the bridle of his burro.

"All right, I'm going out to Joe Hill's Ranch . . . the one he works with Deal. Know 'em?"

"*Si,* I know both and will meet you there or out at the old Brunckow Mine ruins in three days at the first hour after sunrise."

"Let's make it the mine. I don't want to stay too long out at Hill's. I think things are getting ready to do a little popping around here."

"You may be right, my Sergeant." And with that, the Indian prodded up his beast of burden with a stray piece of kindling, heading toward the residential section of Tombstone with his wooden freight.

Ringold bunked out at Hill's for two days, waiting for Pony and Joe to make an appearance. The latch string had been out and thus he'd lazed around, cooking his own meals and thumbing through old copies of the Tombstone Nugget and Police Gazette to pass the time.

On the morning of June 23, 1881, he rode back to Tombstone, ready to meet Kosterlitzky's man, Cajeme, the following morning, only to find a good half of the town's business district in smoldering ruins.

The fire had apparently begun, from an inflammatory combination of a nearly empty barrel of whisky and a careless cigar, at the back of the Arcade Saloon. It had taken out nearly two-dozen buildings, between Fremont and Allen, but spared most structures along the main streets.

Next day, after an evening spent in wandering about the smoking ruins with most of Tombstone's populace, Ringold saddled up and rode out to the old mine as the sun glittered up into the grey-tinted east.

Cajeme, astride a buckskin mare, and wearing a sombrero and a bright yellow serape over his white canvas suit, awaited him in the shadows of the Brunckow ore crusher. The Indian greeted him with less than usual native stolidity. "*Bueno*! It is good you come, my Sergeant, and when you did."

"Hell of a fire back in town."

"*Si*, I saw it. A great excitement, and there will be plenty more excitement this morning, thanks to your Doc Holliday!"

"Excitement? And he's as much your Doc Holliday, as mine. What do you mean?"

In a rush of words, Cajeme informed Ringold of a large cattle drive coming up from the ranches of the Clantons and the McLowrys. And that, tipped off by Doc, or some of the Earps, on their last scout out of town, a bunch of border riff-raff would be mounting an attack upon that drive.

"A great cow raid," as Cajeme phrased it, as the ranchers, unaware of impending trouble, drove their herds toward Tombstone.

"It comes off this morning?"

"*Si*, and I go to Mister Joe Hill, as he is the nearest ranch to us to see if he will aid in rounding up help. I dare not go into Tombstone and ask Sheriff Behan or his men for help . . . or call on Marshal Virgil Earp."

"Yeah, it would tip off everyone, about you, including Doc and the whole gang. But I don't think Hill is around yet, both Pony and him were still off somewhere when I left the place. Just how far is that herd?"

"The Clanton herd and the rest should be halfway to Tombstone by now . . . about as far as Guadaloupe Canyon. I saw them bed down there last evening, but did not dare ride in and disclose myself to them."

"The Clanton boys with the herd?"

"No, *Señor* Ike and his brother, also the McLowrys, who ranch near them . . . all away in New Mexico to buy horses. The ranch hands, who drive this bunch of beef are just drovers under command of the one they call Old Man Clanton." Cajeme pulled his buckskin around. "The words I had to tell you are *importante* . . . but they must wait. Now I go to find who I can, even this *boracho*, Spence!"

"Hit it, and I'll get on down the canyon. Maybe they're still cooking breakfast." He put the steel to the big bay with a wave of farewell to the Yaqui. "Never met this Old Man Clanton, but I hear he's a tough old rooster!"

Cajeme saluted Ringold and spurred off in the direction of Hill's.

Ringold made straight down the Military Road toward the Animas Valley, while red mists shredded up from the nearby river bottoms. It was still early, only six by his pocket watch, as he rode over the rolling foothills that gradually elbowed in upon themselves to become the rocky faces of the towering Guadalupe Canyon. Another road forked off to the west, bypassing the ominous canyon box, but there was no time to take it.

When he emerged from the shadowy depths of the quarter-mile stretch of rocky-ribbed sandstone, the time was close on to seven. There was the camp, with the still motionless forms of the cattle bunched together, and one horse-back puncher, half-asleep at the end of his nighthawking. A cook, hunched over a small fire, near a canvas-covered chuck wagon, was rustling up breakfast, but all the rest, near a dozen figures, were still rolled up in blankets in the lee of the great upthrust hill forming the canyon end.

He was on time, at least, to warn the bunch. But they were in one bad spot—so close to the neighboring hills. And though they'd got through that damned canyon, it still looked like a mighty likely place for a proper ambush.

The puncher, circling the cattle, saw him, kicked up his roan, and came loping up to meet him. "Hey, Mister, you passin' through, or comin' in fer some breakfast?"

Ringo looked over at the looming hills and at the cowboy—a fair-haired youngster in jeans, red-flannel shirt and battered sombrero. "Where's Old Man Clanton?"

"That's him bedded down right next to th' chuck wagon. We-all was up late last night, playin' Red Dog. Ike and th' others are gone away, and th' old man . . . he's a bear for cards." The puncher broke off and stared back in the direction that Ringo had come. "Hey, two more fer breakfast?"

While Ringold watched the pair of horsemen galloping up, at least a dozen rifles roared out from the shelter of the crown of the nearest hill. Bullets spattered and kicked up sand from around

152

the horses' feet, making the animals skitter and rear.

"Get down!" Ringold shouted above the crack of the hidden rifles and the shrill keening of ricochets.

Both were off their horses and yanking out pistols as the two riders, bending low over their saddle horns, came pounding up to them.

"Gawd! Look'a there!" The cowboy grabbed Ringold's arm and pointed toward the blanket-wrapped figures by the chuck wagon. Most of the disturbed sleepers were aroused, and, along with the cook, were dashing in stockinged feet for shelter from the fusillade—but three remained motionless bundles on the ground. "Got Old Mister Clanton, I guess. See, they're hittin' 'em again and again." The blanket-wrapped bodies jerked with the brutal impact of the rifle balls.

"Hey! You-all startin' a war here," yelped Joe Hill, reining-in and leaping off his roan mare, while Pony Deal plunged from his paint like a cat, landing on all fours.

Ringold, kneeling upon the ground, and scanning the smoke-shrouded skyline, reached up and tugged his Winchester out of its saddle sheath. "How'd you find out?" he shouted at Pony.

Deal mouthed at him over the racket of the carbine and the pistols, "Injun Charley run across us as we was comin' back from Fairbank.

Said you needed plenty help! And he was sure right!"

Whack! A rifle slug struck the stock of Ringold's Winchester, scattering splinters and driving the weapon from his stinging hands.

"Hey, them Greasers are shootin' too damn close," shrilled Joe Hill, thumbing off a pair of shots at two sombreros, momentarily visible over the edge of the ridge.

Joe was deadly correct. As he cocked the Colt to throw another shot, a rifle slug slammed into his chest, knocking him over backward.

Pony's mount, struck in the same volley, reared and screamed.

"Hell! Head for that!" Ringold, hands still tingling from the rifle ball's impact on shattered carbine, led the dash for the protection of the chuck wagon. The young puncher dismounted and ran with them.

The remaining cowhands, seven in number, were flat on the ground, in the shelter of the wagon box. None offered any return fire at the Mexicans, now clearly visible along the bluff.

The fusillade had now dropped to sporadic shots. It was clear to Ringold that the enemy was meditating a charge, as each rifleman led his mount to the brink of the hill and mounted up.

The herd of cattle, through some quirk of animal nature, were not particularly spooked by the combat, but milled around slowly, bawling and pawing at the sandy soil, raising clouds of dust.

"Poor Joe. Poor old Joe," Pony squatted by Ringold at the tail of the wagon, face grief-twisted. "Dirty Greasers! Why'n hell did'ja get into this?"

"This is another Earp move. Somehow they knew this drive was coming off and, unless I miss my guess, they waited until Ike and the boys were out of the way, then got word to those bastards up there. And unless I miss another guess, there's one of the gang up there directing this fight!"

"What fight?" Pony glared over at the huddled punchers.

"This here fight, you little sidewinder!" The young cowhand poked his rifle around the corner of the chuck wagon, and drawing a bead on the most gaudily-mounted enemy, squeezed off a shot.

The big sombrero flew off the man's head as he fell sideways from his saddle, like a bag of wheat.

"Hey, you damned fool, Tom McLowry! They could'a been pullin' out!" An old cowhand raised his grizzled head, spat tobacco juice and hurriedly ducked that same grizzled head as a volley ripped down from the aroused Mexicans.

"Look out . . . they're comin' hell-fer-leather!" Pony yelped.

"Roust out, you damned cowards," the cowboy

McLowry shouted, opening up on the knot of horsemen that plunged down the slope, lashing their mounts, and firing as they came.

The old puncher and the remaining hands hurriedly scrambled up, cursing the fast-galloping foemen and young McLowry as they began banging away at the onslaught.

"Watch them cows! They're ready to run," Pony screeched at the punchers, but their sand was up, and they were gripped with the rage of battle, unmindful of everything, but Mexicans.

Their fire, more concentrated and steady, began to tell on the yelling, onrushing *vaqueros*. And as the distance rapidly narrowed, at least three riders pitched from their plunging horses.

Two cowboys suffered minor wounds, one in the arm and one in the leg. "Keep down if you don't want more bullets than you've had," Pony yelped, reloading his Colt.

The enemy was within fifty yards of the embattled punchers when the cattle, at last aroused and lashed forward by the cracking of the guns and the combatants' curses, lowered their heads and rushed forward in a massive river of horns and beef-stuffed hides—straight at the Mexicans.

There was a sudden bucking and confused plunging of the Mexican mounts as the cattle thundered at them. Then it was every man for himself. Some rode directly for the steep sides of the nearest hill, while the remainder spurred for the safety of the northern pass.

The combatants at the bullet-riddled chuck wagon, including the two wounded men, stood and hurled curses at the mad retreat. "G'wan you yellow-bellies! Hit for the cactus patch, you side-windin' frijoles! *Vamose*, you greasy polecats and hydraphoby pole-cats at that!"

Ringold looked at his watch. It was just 7:15. The whole deadly ruckus had taken place in the amazing space of just ten powder-smoked minutes.

The cattle were still rushing their bawling way through the pass toward Tombstone. Pony ran back to Joe Hill. The crushing hooves had spared the body, but not the three Mexicans. They were, literally, pounded into the sandy soil.

Ringold caught Nugget, where the animal had strayed to the edge of the hill out of the path of the stampede. Joe and Pony's horses had been swept along with the rushing herd, with many of the punchers' mounts.

Leaving Pony beside Joe, Ringold rode up the incline and onto the brink of the ridge. The Mexican shot by young McLowry lay spread-eagled in the morning sun, his big, gold-laced hat crumpled under him.

Ringold took one look at the corpse and then waved Pony up.

"Damn! That's nobody but Slim Jim Crane."

Pony squatted down and went through the pockets of the last of the Benson Stage robbers. "Well, that about takes care of th' bunch!"

"All but Doc."

"Yeah, but he'll get his comeuppance sooner or later." Deal turned back to continue rifling the dead bandit's pockets. "Here, look at this." He tossed a small notebook up to Ringold.

Ringold thumbed through the cheap, little, red-backed book. It was blank, except for two entries. One page had a scribbled pencil notation: *"Meet Lopez at Villa Verde on June 20. Bring off the raid on Old Man Clanton on the morning of June 23, if possible."*

Another page had a set of smudged figures, obviously in round dollars, running into the hundreds. There was also a group of names that appeared to be in some sort of code. The list included such odd handles as *Star, Stilts, Spade* and *Saguro!* Obviously aliases of the gang of bandits—all commencing with the letter *S*. But which was the *S* that topped the bunch? There was no way to tell. Then a prickle ran up his neck—*S!* That was the same cryptic letter that had been at the bottom of the secretive message taken from the body of Bill Leonard. Now let Thorne scoff, if he could, at the deadly conspiracy eating away at Wells Fargo's gold—and causing bloody destruction as it went along.

Placing the odd, little book in his vest pocket,

and motioning Pony to follow, he rode slowly back to the clustered cowhands.

The two wounded men were helping patch up each other, while the remainder of the hands were in the process of rounding up what horses they could find, preparatory to getting the cattle. The herd had slowed its rush and most of the animals were still milling about in the narrow confines of the canyon.

The Mexicans had never reappeared after the stampede and were, doubtless, back down over the border.

Ringold paid his first, and last, respects to Ike Clanton's father, where the old pioneer lay stretched out in his last sleep, with three of his punchers. Half an hour later, Ringold and Pony were heading back for Tombstone, with Hill's body draped over a spare horse.

"Poor old Joe," Pony mourned, staring back at the canvas-covered corpse, bobbing along in their wake. "Poor Joe. Well, that damned bunch lost their right-hand bower, and they'll sure pay even more for this day."

"Yes, especially when Ike Clanton and his brother get back," Ringold spurred the bay forward.

"Yeah, Ike's got plenty to collect for. Wonder what he'll do?" Pony rode up alongside.

Ringold, who had found himself wondering just where Cajeme had got to, after the beginning of the fight, and what the Yaqui had meant to discuss with him, was jarred from his reverie by the sight of Joe Hill's canvas-clad form jogging just behind Pony Deal. "I don't know, but whatever happens . . . it could just about split Tombstone right down the middle."

9 The Bisbee Stage

Two days after the fight in Guadaloupe Canyon, Joe Hill was buried out at his ranch, at the eastern base of the great outcropping of sandstone. There were only six mourners—Billy Breakenridge, young McLowry, Ike and Billy Clanton, Pony and Ringold.

Pony vowed to stay on and run the small horse spread, for the time being. "Joe'd like me to take keer of th' shebang."

Ringold, however, was willing to bet it wouldn't be long until Deal got an itchy foot, and was off on one of his many restless jaunts into the vastness of the Territory.

He wished Pony's abrupt departures wouldn't break out again until they had got a good tail-hold on the ones responsible for the stage robberies, attempted and otherwise. And he found himself realizing that he wanted to stay on in the Territory, until that happened. His many grumbles to himself at being stuck out in Arizona had, somehow, gone by the board. His current half-pay from the Texas Rangers, and the modest sum paid monthly by Wells Fargo—plus that $1500 reward money due to him from the deaths of Head and Leonard—none of that cut any ice. It was just the fact that he, now, felt dedicated to wind the clock on the Earps, Holliday, and the rest—and particularly on this *Mister S.*

At the burial of Joe Hill, Ike Clanton, contrary to his free-and-easy, blowhard manner, had been silent and almost grim when they lowered the coffin down into the sandy soil. Clanton remained tight-jawed after the preacher had been paid, and departed for Galeyville in his buckboard, and the six returned to the ranch house to kill a bottle of whisky in Joe's memory.

The younger Clanton was also thoughtful until McLowry joshed him over his horse-trading expedition to New Mexico in time to, luckily, miss all the shooting. Despite the death of Old Man Clanton, and the two recent funerals, the young fellows' animal spirits soon broke loose and within moments both were bear-hugging, and wrestling around the cabin and out the door.

"Damned fools," Ike glowered. "Pa 'tain't cold in his grave and them scamps has nigh forgot all about it."

"Easy, Ike." Ringold shoved the bottle across at Clanton. "Let the youngun's let off some steam. Your brother needs to kick up his heels a bit, and young Tom McLowry fought for your father and your cattle like a tiger. Don't forget he's the one that knocked the spots off of Jim Crane at that fight."

"Yeah, and one hell of a good shot." Pony

pushed the bottle back. "Joe was that kind of a shot, too. Poor Joe . . . if he could have got into action . . ." He broke off and wiped his nose on his sleeve. "Aw, hell!"

"And that damned Earp crowd is gonna find out there's other good shots around, too." Ike, coming out of his unnatural solemnity, winked and yanked the bottle back. "Yessir, lawman or not, Billy Breakenridge, I'll tell you right now there's gonna be a hell of a lot of fur flyin' in this county sooner or later."

Breakenridge reached in his vest pocket and brought out a handful of short-sixes, and passed them around the table, lighting up one of the evil-smelling little stogies. "Well, as I see it, Ike, you can surely make things mighty tough for Holliday. That is, if you stick to your story about seein' him ridin' cross-country th' night th' Sandy Bob Stage was jumped."

Ike stood up, swaying slightly, puffing at his cigar. "You can bet your bottom dollar, Billy Breakenridge, that I'll tell it in court. And I'm also gonna swear it was Doc and Wyatt that tried to gun me down not fifty yards from this here ranch house. And Ringo'll vouch fer that!"

Breakenridge, who was unfamiliar with that event, choked on his cigar, and stared at Ringold. "That so?"

"Yes, but it's water over the dam, now." Ringold didn't feel up to playing the hero, and glared at Ike—who grinned back, his sombre mood washed away by the liquor.

"Should have been reported to Sheriff Behan." Breakenridge raised his sandy eyebrows at Ringold. He appeared thoughtful, then shrugged. "Well, as you say that water's gone down th' crick." He pulled out the remains of his cigar, looked it over with growing distaste. "That Earp bunch! Whatever they do, never surprises me any. Guess Ike can smite 'em hip and thigh in court. It could put that bastard of a Doc away for a good spell."

"Yeah, but Doc's only a part of th' story . . . him and that Wyatt! There's more devilment hatchin' than you could shake a stick at! And when we find out who's back of . . ." Pony broke off as Ringold kicked him under the table.

"What sort of devilment?" Ike wanted to know. "You mean more of them damned Greaser raids?"

Breakenridge sat silent, puffing away at the remnants of his cigar.

"Pony's bottle-talking," Ringold laughed, and getting away from the table, motioned the little man outside. "Pony, come on. I want to see about a new mount. Mine's got a pulled tendon, I think."

"Yeah, and you got yourself a spring-halt leg, yourself," Pony joked, following Ringold outside. "Damn me, I'm sorry," he muttered. "Nigh come to spillin' th' beans, didn't I? Well, if Joe hadn't caught it . . . and all . . . I wouldn't have drank so much. No fear now . . . I'm gettin' sober."

Ringold shrugged it off, but he was bothered. Too much loose talk was bad, but nothing really had been said that tipped any hand. If Behan's deputy did size up something, he'd keep it to himself, if it might alert the Earps. Both Breakenridge and Behan were no friends of the Earps.

The next day, Pony rode up to Benson and returned immediately to report that Thorne had gone to San Francisco to talk to Detective Chief Hume.

Ringold wished to discuss the notebook taken from Crane's body, but now he'd have to await Thorne's return. Yes, Thorne would have to change his mind considerably when he inspected that notebook's list of names—all starting with *S*. Here was undeniable evidence of some sort of full-scale criminal conspiracy, similar, it appeared, to that of Henry Plummer's road agent gang up at Montana Territory's Virginia City over twenty years back.

That Mexican-staffed raid upon the Clanton stock was, doubtless, bound to be tied to the Tombstone gang's efforts—possibly for Ike's open defiance of Doc and Wyatt, and the phantom leader, whoever he was. Ringold's secret belief was that the fact of the McLowry cattle being involved in the raid was just happenstance. But happenstance or not, men had died because of that raid.

With Thorne away in San Francisco and a sizeable portion of Tombstone still in ruins, but already busily a'building to the noise of hammer and saw at all hours, and an empty ranch at Joe Hill's, with Pony in and out of town, Ringold cast about for something to do.

The weather had now reached its blazing peak, and no one set out on horseback jaunts, unless they had a definite purpose—except a few hardened rovers, like Pony. Ringold took meals at the Can Can, sleeping at the Cosmopolitan, and making the rounds of the gambling halls. Those, along with the Bird Cage Theater, were, fortunately, spared from the devouring flames that ravished the town from Fremont to Allen Streets.

Doc and Wyatt remained on public view each day. The lanky Earp served as bouncer at the Alhambra, while Doc kept his gaming table at the Crystal Palace.

Acting Marshal Virgil Earp continued his slow-paced rounds of town. With James, the silent brother, close at his heels, the pair spent a considerable portion of each day, perched on top of assorted piles of lumber, quietly superintending the erection of the various new buildings. Sometimes they were joined by the, equally, silent Fred Dodge.

Sheriff Behan was away days on end at Tucson on county business, so there was little friction to set the town on edge during the sweltering heat. Young Breakenridge, always ready with a grin, and a slap on the back, seemed friends with everyone—even the stray drunks that he had to lock up for the night.

For several weeks, Ringold stayed away from the Earp brothers and Doc, generally playing cards with Bones Brannon or Dick Clark at the Oriental, yet never let Wyatt or Doc too far out of his sight.

He even caught several performances at the Bird Cage Theater during the month, particularly when he noticed any of the Earps headed for the show.

Eddie Foy was now appearing at the theater with his company of comedians and singers the last week of August and the first week of September, and drawing full houses each night.

Ringold and Pony saw "Muldoon's Picnic" twice, partly to watch the trained donkey walk over Eddie Foy's plug hat without denting the topper. Pony was so certain of a misstep by that long-eared thespian that he lost twenty dollars to Ringold, who stood pat on a sure-footed per-formance.

• • •

The night of September 8, 1881, Pony and Ringold sauntered up to the Bird Cage to catch the last comedy to be performed by Foy and Company for the season, "Over the Garden Wall."

The entire Earp clan was in attendance, Wyatt having taken a night off from bouncing at the saloon. Doc was absent, and presumably with his case box, dealing his particular brand of Faro at the Crystal Palace.

At the end of the first act, while the packed audience was stamping its collective boots and bellowing with laughter, Pony poked Ringold. "There goes Earp." And the lanky Wyatt was edging through the crowd toward the rear of the theater.

"And there you go." Ringold leaned back in the creaking seat and thumbed Pony out into the aisle. "Drift along and see what he's up to."

"Probably out for a short beer," grumbled Pony, but edged his way out after Earp, returning just in time to catch the opening antics of Eddie Foy, playing an uproariously inebriated Julius Snitz.

"Well?"

"Like I said, he went down to th' Alhambra and wet his whistle. Had a couple shots and started back. I beat him, but here he comes now." The rest of Pony's remarks were drowned in fresh gusts of applause.

At the end of the next act, Ringold casually turned to see Wyatt in earnest conversation with his brothers. "Who'd he have those drinks with?"

"Nobody in p'ticklar. That lump of a Fred Dodge sorta passed th' time of day with him. And, oh yeah, Wyatt got hisself a light for his cigar off'n Pete Spence."

"Seen Indian Charlie lately?" As he spoke, Ringold found himself wondering about Fred Dodge, as much as Cajeme. Dodge? He was always close to the Earps and Holliday, ostensibly to keep his eye on them for Wells Fargo, but who really knew? It would bear some more thinking about, at that.

"You say Indian Charlie? Pete Spence's woodcutter? No, ain't seen him since that damned Greaser dry-gulch."

As Pony's features assumed such a down-in-the-mouth expression at the thought of that fatal ambush, Ringold turned back to the renewal of the stage high-jinks and dropped the conversation.

Next day he cursed himself for not having personally followed Wyatt to the Alhambra between acts when news broke out of the robbery of the Sandy Bob Stage, not twelve miles to the south of town.

"Hear the latest, I reckon?" Pony slid into a seat across from Ringold at the Can Can Restaurant.

"Yes," he answered shortly, feeling puzzled

and angry with himself. Obviously Earp had been involved in some way. He'd talked to both Spence, and Fred Dodge. Had the hefty Wells Fargo agent passed on the information of the coach's particular cargo? On the surface, at least, Dodge didn't seem to have enough gumption to turn a tricky dollar. But as for Wyatt and the other Earps, he was damned certain they were involved in this series of stage robberies. If not concerned with the execution of the latest strike, they must have been in on the planning. As for Doc, it was evident to Ringold that he was pure blackleg to the core. But who, in the name of heaven, was the unknown behind the whole set-up? That enigmatic *Mister S?* He stuck a thumb in his vest, touching Slim Jim Crane's notebook with its list—*Star, Spade, Saguro.* Who could it be?

"Whatcha thinkin' about? Wonderin' who turned th' trick and waltzed off with that twenty-five hundred? Well, I can tell you . . . now!"

"Now? What are you gabbing about?"

"I was over to th' Sheriff's office pumpin' that kid deputy about things in general . . . and th' word comes in on th' tely-graft and was fetched over. It's Pete Spence and Frank Stilwell, his pardner in th' Benson Livery Stable, wood cuttin' and all that. They's a warrant out for 'em at Benson. The Marshal down there was tipped off by th' passengers."

"Spence?"

"Yeah. Pete allus calls money . . . sugar. And th' damned fool up and asks th' passengers for all their sugar. They was masked, but that word, *sugar*, tipped their hands." Pony gulped down his coffee. "And, oh yeah, th' authorities, so-called, can't find th' big money, though they got Pete Spence and Frank Stilwell cold."

"Earp, or Dodge . . . or . . ."

"Yeah, I was thinkin' that some sorta message could'a exchanged hands last night at th' Alhambra. Hey! Look at that! There goes Billy Breakenridge and th' other deputy to pick up Pete and Frank and haul 'em back here."

Ringold finished his meal and went outside with Pony to catch the last glimpse of Billy Breakenridge and Dave Neagle dwindling in a cloud of dust down Allen Street toward Benson.

"Blazes! And look there!" And Pony indicated another knot of riders emerging from Fifth Street and turning onto Allen, in the wake of the lawmen. It was Marsh Williams, Wells Fargo agent for Tombstone, along with Fred Dodge, and Morgan and Wyatt Earp.

"Now what in Hades is that bunch up to?" Ringold wondered out loud, knowing that the only legally-concerned rider was Williams. Dodge, as a clerk in the Wells Fargo office and part-time driver, was acceptable, on the surface, as Marsh Williams's assistant—but Wyatt and Morgan were just tagging along, apparently, as

171

Wyatt would say: "for the glory." But it had to be more than that!

"It's hotter than th' devil's hoofs, but I think we oughta ride after 'em," said Pony. "We could look around fer someplace where Spence might'a stashed that loot."

"You're right as rain . . . for once! That's why they went down there."

"Who?"

"Those Earps! They've taken up with Williams . . . *and Dodge*. Their usual public-spirited move. Get our nags at the livery, and hustle."

Though they pressed their mounts as much as they dared in the shimmering heat, they hadn't caught up with either party by the time they reached the outskirts of Bisbee in late afternoon.

Meeting the up-stage coming back toward Tombstone, they were able to learn the exact site of the robbery without going on into town. The vehicle was driven by Sandy Bob Crouch, himself.

"That'd be th' spot, right thar!" Sandy Bob flicked his long, braided, rawhide whip at a cholla cactus, expertly taking off the top-most flower. "Well, gotta make time, huddup!" And with a parting crack of the looping whip, he and his stage were off down the road's slight slope, around a great mass of granite boulders and out of sight.

Pony and Ringold reined-up, surveying the sun-bleached, desolate locale. There was nothing unusual to view, just a typical southern Arizona desert landscape, sand, cactus, rocks and brooding stillness.

"By gobs!" Pony spat over the back of his paint pony, hitting a scuttling vinegarroon broadside. "What about them big rocks down there?"

"Figure that's where the money went?"

"Could be. There's just no other place to hide a big mail sack, stuffed with greenbacks. Th' ground hereabouts is as hard as Doc's heart . . . or Wyatt's head."

They rode on down the track and dismounted. The sun was now inclining toward the west, and shadows were stretching out from the gaunt, organ-barrel cactus in streaks of dull purple.

Before they could do more than begin a search of the table-sized boulders, keeping a watchful eye out for vinegarroons and rattlers, they caught the sound of hoofbeats coming toward them from the direction of Bisbee.

"That's bound to be Breakenridge or the Earps," Ringold clipped, grabbing Pony by the arm. "Here, get the horses back up the hill and into that Joshua thicket."

"Don't want'a see 'em?"

"No, you thick-skulled rounder! If it's Breakenridge, he might wonder why we're tagging after him. And if it's the others . . . it will be the Earps, by themselves, either coming back before or after Marsh and Fred Dodge. Get going!"

Within moments the animals were staked down on either side of the thick clump of Joshua trees, while Ringold and Pony squatted in their shadows, peering out through the thorny branches.

The road from Bisbee to Tombstone wound across rolling land, near the site of the robbery, and the approaching horsemen were heard long before they crested a rise and loped on past to disappear around the great, jackdaw nest of boulders.

"Well, Spence and Stilwell don't look very happy about things, do they?" Pony snickered as they watched the last of the six horsemen reappear only to vanish again into a hazy dust cloud beyond the boulders.

"Marsh Williams and Fred Dodge in front, with the jailbirds in the middle, and Billy Breakenridge and his side-kick deputy bringing up the rear," Ringold enumerated, rising from his crouching position and shading his eyes to gaze toward Bisbee.

"Makes you wonder where th' Earp boys could be."

"Maybe not far behind. Listen!" Ringold led the way out from the thicket. "More horses on the road."

"What do we do, if it is th' Earps?"

"We sit tight and watch what they're up to . . . if they stop and hunt."

"Bet you five to one they pull up and give them rocks a combing over."

"Don't bet on sure things. Here, get back, they're cresting that rise."

Two riders jogged up past the Joshua clump and halted. For a moment they sat nearly opposite Ringold and Pony, looking back toward Bisbee, and scanning the road ahead. Apparently satisfied they were alone and well behind Breakenridge, they rode on down the incline of the sandy road and reined-in near the upthrust heap of rocks.

"They're gonna start lookin' for th' loot," Pony whispered hoarsely in Ringold's ear. "Wyatt's gettin' down right now."

"Damn," Ringold muttered, "someone's coming from Bisbee, right on their heels."

Wyatt, who had started to dismount, hurriedly straightened in the saddle of his crowbait sorrel, with a gesture at his brother. The pair lashed their horses and galloped toward Tombstone, and were gone.

"Now what?" Pony ground out, staring fixedly toward Bisbee.

"Just a couple of damned ore wagons. And it looks like they're stopping on that rise for something."

Two lumbering ore wagons, wheels squealing perpetually amid protests, came up the Bisbee

slope and stopped about ten yards away from
Pony and Ringold. One of the vehicles appeared
to be in precarious condition, with a split axle
and on the verge of losing a wheel. The next hour
was occupied by the teamsters in a cursing match
as they made rude repairs. After several trips out
into the desert, they eventually returned with the
section of a log, which they chopped into the
proper length for a drag to fasten to the axle, thus
supporting the wagon.

By the time the pair had rested themselves from
their labors, taken several lusty pulls at a jug,
and lit a pair of lanterns to guide their progress
toward the Tombstone mines, the cherry-red
ball of the sun had burnt itself out in a thicket
of tattered clouds over behind the Whetstone
Mountains.

"Well, the balloon's done gone up," Pony commented. "Another ten minutes and it'll be as dark
as Wyatt's heart, providin' he's got such."

"Yes, and not enough moon out to see to scratch
your elbow," grumped Ringold. "If we had one
of those fool freighters' lanterns we could prowl
around and see for ourselves just what those two
were up to, providing it was the money."

"Oh, it was th' swag, devil a doubt. I'll bet you
th' bag's in them rocks right now."

On the chance that the Earps or someone else
might appear, they sat and waited. Wrapped
in a blanket of their own thoughts, they moved

only to light a cigarette or hobble the horses nearer to some scattered clumps of gamma grass. Overhead, the stars journeyed imperceptibly, dimmed to a pale silver from their usual blue-white brilliance by the continuing heat and drifting clouds. A wandering breeze edged itself through the Joshuas and keened softly across the open. Somewhere a pair of coyotes struck up a long-range duet, their quavering song blending with the lonesome whistle of the wind. A bobcat, somewhere nearby, punctuated the weird medley with its piercing cries as it hopefully trotted through the scrub on the track of an early breakfast.

"Let's go," Ringold broke the long silence. "It's got to be close to morning. If they come back, Earps or whomsoever, I'd be surprised. We'd best get an early start, and come back out when we can see straight."

They mounted up and rode back to Tombstone.

Ringold, who bedded down at the Prospector Hotel on Fremont, was up at sunrise. Getting Nugget from the livery while Pony still lay abed at the Cosmopolitan, he debated riding back down to the robbery site, without breakfast or companion.

As he jogged his mount past Behan's office, he was hailed by Billy Breakenridge, who sat on the front step whittling at a piece of lath. "Up early there," the grinning deputy called out.

"Thought I'd exercise this four-legged excuse for a horse, before it comes on another sizzler."

"I can tell you one thing, Ringo."

He reined-in and looked Breakenridge over. He might just pick up some information on the bandit pair, who were incarcerated in the small, log jail out back, without appearing too nosey. "What's that?"

"I can tell you that you surely ain't from Arizona or hereabouts. You'd not be callin' this kind of weather hot. Why man, it's just sort of pleasantly warm nowadays."

"Maybe yes and maybe no. But it's been more than warm for Wells Fargo!"

"You're sure right about that. Don't know how those two varmints pulled it, but that money seems gone for good."

"Spence and Stilwell tell you that?"

"Hell, no! Th' empty sack that a teamster fetched in last night after supper told me that!"

"Empty sack?"

"Yep! Him and his pard, one of 'em broke an axle and come nigh on losing a wheel, and so they ranged out in th' flats off th' road and got them a dried piece of timber for a drag. And that's where they found th' empty sack. Th' money, all twenty-five hundred in greenbacks to pay off th' boys at th' Tough Nut Mine." Breakenridge tossed away the whittled stick and put his knife up. "Yep, twenty-five hundred missing dollars!"

"Those teamsters found the money sack near where the coach was stopped?"

"Not a hundred yards from th' spot, and right close to that walloping, big pile of boulders at the turn of th' road."

Ringold tipped his sombrero over his eyes, nodded to Breakenridge, and turned his horse back toward the livery. Someone had plucked the robbery loot out of the rocks before the deputies, the Earps, or even he and Pony had got to Bisbee. But who? And where had the money gone?

Only the invisible *Mister S* knew. Ringold was sure of that—and damned little else!

10 Indian Charley

Two days after Stilwell and Spence had been brought back to Tombstone, they were arraigned on two separate charges in Judge Spicer's Court, that of theft, armed, of the Tough Nut payroll, and robbing the U.S. Mails.

While Pony rode up to Benson with their report, Ringold joined the crowd that sat in the fly-haunted, whitewashed courtroom on the second floor of the Tombstone City Hall at Fourth and Fremont. The Cochise County Court House, in process of erection at Tough Nut and Third, at the south-end of town, had been set to be completed in early 1882, but work had recently been suspended while all available roustabouts and mechanics labored from daybreak until dark to rebuild Tombstone's burned-out business district.

A few cases, in addition to the stage robbery, were heard on that warm September morning, but they were small potatoes—several drunk and disorderlies, with Virgil Earp as arresting officer, and one case of cattle theft. The latter defendant, a small rancher from the Huachuca area, was bound over until the next court date, and the *D-and-Ds* paid their fines and hustled out.

Then Spence and Stilwell came clanking up the outside stairway, followed by a puffing John

Behan and a grinning Breakenridge, both toting shotguns.

The courtroom crowd straightened up in their hard seats and settled back for an instructive morning, but they were abruptly doomed to disappointment.

Judge Spicer, a portly, old man, with mutton-chop whiskers and a flaming red nose, fanned himself languidly with a palm leaf fan while he entered the case as Number 56 on the docket. He then accepted the short, but burly Stilwell's plea of not guilty, as well as the cadaverous, round-shouldered Spence's duplicate plea of no guilt.

There were squeaking chairs, amidst a chorus of muffled coughs, and many shifting boots, at the speed Spicer accepted the pleas and set bond for the pair. Clearly the onlookers had supposed it was in for a regular, legalistic, time-killing morning.

Ringold was not surprised. As a Texas law officer he'd seen rogues and rascals back on the street almost as soon as they were fetched in. But what took him aback was the group, headed by Ike Clanton, that arose to make up Spence's and Stilwell's fifteen-thousand-dollar bond.

Ringold went out, with the rest of the dis-gruntled crowd, while Ike and two fellow ranchers, Ham Light and Bill Allen, lingered to sign the necessary papers, freeing the accused.

The first man he saw on the city hall sidewalk

was Wyatt. The elder Earp, pale with anger, was bitterly castigating Billy Breakenridge in an over-loud voice.

Ringold passed near enough to hear Wyatt cursing Breakenridge, Spicer and Behan. It brought instant reaction from the now unsmiling deputy.

"Earp, if I didn't think you'd been drinking, I'd run you in for disturbin' the peace. You-all can't call me or Johnny Behan such names! And I'm tellin' you right now your friend Judge Spicer is th' man who let your saddle-pards out . . . not us!"

"Saddle . . . !" Wyatt gagged on the word. "Billy Breakenridge, that kind of talk gets a man into a hell of a hole!"

Breakenridge, catching sight of Ringold amongst the growing group of spectators, turned on his heel, and walked away, still toting his double-barreled shotgun.

Earp, livid with rage, took two steps after the deputy, then with another curse, whirled so fast he nearly collided with Ringold. "Hell!" He dropped his hand from pistol butt, and with a muffled growl, shoved past Ringold into the suddenly quiet crowd.

"Ike's the real gent you should look to! He and a couple of friends just raised the bond," Ringold shouted after Wyatt. It was just something on the tip of his tongue. He'd told himself that Clanton had a big mouth—and here he was as bad as Ike. But it seemed that he was always looking for some way to crack the Earps and Doc wide open. It wasn't the way, perhaps, to break the bunch down, but he was positive that Wyatt and Doc, in particular, were into the robbery picture, head-over-heels. And not just that—murder! For though Wyatt and Doc, themselves, weren't in that bloody ambush at Clanton's, it was an action involving the gang—and so the whole bunch were guilty as sheep-killing dogs.

Wyatt, who must have heard Ringold, never turned, nor halted a step. Ringold knew he must be boiling inside, for this Earp wasn't the kind that forgot a thing—and he had plenty to remember. There was the time that Ringold had shot Doc and Wyatt off Ike Clanton's neck out at Joe Hill's. And there was the set-to he'd had with Wyatt at the Alhambra when he'd disarmed him at gunpoint. Yes, Wyatt Earp had no love for him, and that was just fine, because it could give him the edge against Wyatt if the time ever came for a no-holds, show-down. An angry man was most often a rattled man. He'd seen that borne out in more than one fight.

But as he strolled the other way from that taken by Earp, intending to go over for a card game at the Alhambra, he began to think about something. If Wyatt was part of that gang, as he was sure he was, *Star, Stirrup, Saguro*—or whoever, then

183

why was he so damned upset because Stilwell and Spence were out on the streets? They were a part of the robber bunch. They had to be! And hadn't he and Pony watched Wyatt's stealthy performance at the recent robbery site? Then— why in the devil was Earp raging around like a mossy-horned bull?

Ringold kept asking himself that question until he gave it up, and substituted another. What was Ike Clanton up to? He was certain that Ike was pretty honest, though certainly a big-mouthed, rattle-headed sort of a waddy. Then why had he shown up to bail out Stilwell and Spence? He'd never heard anything connecting Clanton to that pair.

Mulling over such riddles, he turned the corner of Fourth and Allen to behold the man who would shortly answer both questions.

The Yaqui, Cajeme, was unloading firewood on the east side of the Cochise Hardware and Trading Store, across from the Can Can. His glittering gaze fastened leisurely upon Ringold, and with a slight, almost imperceptible nod beckoned him over.

"My Sergeant, I have had much to say to you . . . but we cannot talk in this place." Cajeme shrugged a shoulder in the direction of the nearest corner.

Ringold, standing where he could still see down Allen, turned his head slowly to discover

Pete Spence and Frank Stilwell loitering in the doorway of King's Saloon, just beyond the O.K. Corral building.

"Stilwell and Spence are to be taken to Tucson the day after tomorrow for a hearing in Federal Court. That will give us time to talk."

"Where?" Ringold kept an eye on the pair at King's, while appearing to light up a cigar and blandly ignore the Yaqui, who had now gone back to the job of unloading his mules.

"Out at the wood camp," came the voice of the industrious woodcutter. "It is on the eastern slopes of the Dragoons. The other workers will be gone for some days, and I will be alone." He tossed a crumpled bit of paper near Ringold's boot. "I have marked the route for you. Come at sunset the evening after tomorrow. Then I can answer many questions."

Ringold, looking up at the pair in the doorway, nudged the paper ball toward himself with his toe, and then bent to retrieve it. Spence and Stilwell were in a heated discussion, paying no attention to anything beyond their noses. "Thanks, I guess I'd better amble. They're heading down this way."

The two suspects had, indeed, stepped out of their doorway and were walking in the direction of the Can Can.

"*Si*," Cajeme continued to deposit the small cottonwood logs on the ground. "Go before they

185

arrive. And when you come to the camp, there may be something for you beside talk."

Ringold continued on down to his hotel. He needed to get away and do some hard thinking about matters.

Pony was back the next day to stand with Ringold in front of the Can Can and watch Pete Spence, Frank Stilwell along with their escort of Behan and Breakenridge, taking the afternoon stage for Tucson and the court hearing.

"Damned fast work wasn't it, wranglin' a hearin' before a Federal Judge nigh as soon as they was out on bail?"

"Someone's pulling some strings, I'd say."

"That's so. I hear they never found hide-nor-hair of th' money."

"Yes, and it's just one of the puzzles of the case," Ringold replied, leaning against a hitching rail, watching the dust settling in wispy clouds of gold through the blazing September sunlight.

"There's others?"

"Come on across the street to the Corner Five and let's have a drink, and you can tell me what's doing with Thorne."

Seated over their dark, amber steins of beer in the cool interior of the saloon, Pony reviewed his meeting with the head of Wells Fargo for Arizona.

"Mister Thorne's certain mighty put-off about

this last holdup. He kinda thought we could'a got a line on it before it happened . . . us and that lump of a Fred Dodge." He downed his brew. "But I don't know how."

"I don't know how, either." Ringold moodily killed his brew and ordered another round. "Maybe he thinks we could have kept Wyatt in sight a little better. Did you tell him about his meeting with Spence that night?"

Pony grinned like a dog fox. "Ain't no use in rilin' him more than needs be. But I did tell him Injun Charley seemed to know a hell of a lot for a wood chopper . . . and him workin' fer Spence."

"You told him about what happened at the Mexican raid?" Ringold was secretly uneasy. He realized that Thorne would have heard from Pony concerning the book found on Jim Crane, but he wanted to discuss the affair in person. It was no secret that Joe Hill and Pony had been summoned to his aid by the Yaqui. But Florentino Cajeme was much more than he seemed, and as Kosterlitzky's agent on United States soil, he was a man with many irons in the fire.

"I said I just told Thorne that we'd picked up a funny sort of a little book from Crane and you'd be bringing it up." Pony wrinkled his brow at Ringold. "Hey, did you hear what I said?"

"Yes." Ringold came out of his brown study. "And when does he want to talk to me?"

"Oh, he's gonna be busy for a day or so.

Probably next time you're due to go up to Benson. Tuesday a week ain't it?"

"Yes, I guess it can wait." Ringold hoped Pony's loose jaw hadn't tipped Cajeme's hand, whatever it turned out to be—for Thorne was no fool, even if he'd scoffed at the actual existence of a secret gang. He decided not to tell Pony of his upcoming meeting with Cajeme. Pony was pretty straight, but his mouth was apt to open at the wrong time, like Ike's.

"Funny Doc don't want to go to Federal Court, ain't it . . . when Pete and Frank just honed to get there," mused Pony, downing the last of his brew.

"Doc must figure he can't beat the case. Ike swears he's got him dead to right." Ringold ordered one last round.

"Spence and Stilwell must think they can get off without a wiggle. And they probably can without any . . . what's it called, corpus delecty?"

"I'd say it's the lack of evidence, even if they do call cold cash . . . sugar, and obviously, someone else must think so."

"Someone else like . . . old *Mister S?*" chuckled Pony, putting away the beer.

"Questions. Questions! By hell it's getting so all we do is sit around and ask each other questions," cursed Ringold. "I'd damned well like to know why that fool Ike Clanton headed up the list of bondsmen for those bandits."

"Why not ask Ike, hisself, 'cause here comes

th' big sand stomper?" Pony nudged Ringold, pointing out Clanton as that worthy slipped into the saloon through the side entrance to belly-up at the bar.

About the same time, becoming accustomed to the dim interior, Ike spotted them and ambled over. But it was a sober-faced Ike Clanton. His splay-toothed grin was gone and he was possessed of an unusually thoughtful expression.

"Gawd! I sure need somethin' stronger than that there beer." He wiped his face and settled into one of the broad-bottomed saloon chairs, bawling for a bottle of whisky, unmindful of the curious stares of the other patrons. Tossing off a shot glass of the stuff, he wiped his face, again. "Ugh! Half a dozen more of them and I can begin to breathe easy."

"What's happened?" Pony positively vibrated with ill-suppressed curiosity. "Bet you had a run-in with Wyatt or Doc, eh?"

"Wrong! It was Virgil Earp. And how he gave me what for!"

"Virgil Earp! Why, he's in it just like his blamed beanpole brother. And that butter-won't-melt-in-his-mouth of a Morgan. He's in it, too. Hell's fire, they must all be in it," barked Pony, unmindful of the tilted ears of the surrounding drinkers. He subsided at Ringold's gesture for silence, and buried his sharp nose in his foaming glass, slyly peering around to see if he'd been overheard.

The only, apparently, interested person was Ike. "In what? Who's in what?"

"Oh, Pony's got an idea that the Earps had something to do with that fight out at your cattle drive." Ringold kicked Pony under the table. He found himself getting uneasy over Pony. Each day Deal seemed to get more and more on edge. He thought he'd speak to Thorne about the little horsethief, not that he wanted to get him sacked. But if Pony didn't settle down, he could let the lid off the whole affair. And if he, Ringold, were exposed as a law officer, the devil alone knew what could happen. A shot in the dark. Dry-gulching. Anything!

"What makes you think th' Earps had somethin' to do with them polecat Mexicans?" Ike demanded. "I know that renegade bastard Jim Crane was in on it, but that kind of scum'd do anythin' fer money."

"Just a damned fool idea," Ringold answered before Pony could open his mouth—again. "Pony here feels the Earps and that Doc are capable of just about any kind of devilment."

"Damned if I don't think so, too." Ike downed another shot. "Hell, you know Doc tried his best to call out my kid brother . . . which you stopped. And you saw 'em chase me all to hell and gone out at Joe Hill's, where you stopped 'em. Hell yes, they'll pull anythin'. And Virgil . . ."

"What *did* Virgil say to you? Give you hail

190

columbia fer bailin' out Stilwell and Spence?" Ringold seized an opportunity to turn the conversation away from Pony's blunder.

"Just what you'd guess. Told me I was a damned fool fer lettin' out such people. Told me a whale of a lot of folk had been talkin' about th' vigilance committee, including brother Wyatt, of course. Told me that some dark night I might find myself dancin' from some cottonwood, along with Stilwell and Spence. Whew!" Ike downed another jolt of whisky and rubbed at his red neck.

"Mighty odd talk for a law officer, ain't it?" Pony absently fingered his own throat.

"Yes, mighty funny," Ringold answered, turning back to Ike. "Just why did you post bond for that pair?"

Ike glanced around cautiously, then leaned forward. It was a movement that brought an answering attitude from Ringold and Pony. "Well, I just know things are goin' to get worse before they get any mite better. And I need all th' friends I can git."

"What kind of friends?" Pony wanted to know.

"Friends with guns. Friends that ain't afraid of some fireworks!"

"You know Pony and I will back you against Doc and Wyatt, and the rest . . . providing it's legal," Ringold replied, suspecting what Ike was getting at.

"Hell yes!" Pony echoed Ringold.

"Knew I could count on you both, but you already done too much, Ringo. You pulled my chestnuts out'a th' fire at least twice. I don't like askin' you to risk your hide for me over and over. And you both also pitched in to fight them polecat Greasers."

"But why are you tryin' to build up a gun-slingin' outfit fer? Don't you know Spence and Stilwell could get th' whole book heaved at 'em over to Tucson?" Pony looked thoughtfully at Ike's whisky.

"Here, take a snort." Ike pushed the half-empty bottle at Deal. "I'm gamblin' that they won't, that's all. And Doc's bound to come up with a stretch whenever he comes to trial."

"If he ever does," interjected Ringold.

"Yes, if he ever does. But he may, and there'll be hell to pay . . . fer me as both my kid brother and me are witnesses against Doc, like I told you before. And you know I've blown around some about puttin' Doc behind bars, and it's gonna cause me trouble . . . so I need that fire-power sooner or later."

"Talk gets folks in a lot of trouble, sometimes," Pony solemnly offered.

Ringold left Pony and Ike with the bottle and went back to the Alhambra to play cards with Bones Brannon, until time to ride out to see Cajeme. All he could do was hope Pony would remember that last kick he'd given him under the table.

He rode into Spence's wood camp an hour before sunset. Located on the slopes of the Dragoons, it gave a clear view of Tombstone, miles away across the mesquite flats, glinting white in the late evening light.

When he swung down from the outlaw bay, Cajeme greeted him at the edge of a magnificent stand of pines. "*Señor*, you are in time for a simple meal, and some talk."

"You said you'd have something for me, besides talk," grinned Ringold, downing his second cup of coffee, for there had, actually, been little of that, as yet. Cajeme had immediately served him with a savory plate of frijoles and cornbread, but had done little more than remark upon the beauty of the fading twilight, and busy himself at the campfire.

"*Si*, you are right, my Sergeant." Cajeme walked to Ringold's horse, where it was picketed by a pile of logs. "I will take the bay to good grazing beyond those pines. Any questions you have, I will try to answer when I return."

The Yaqui led the horse into the gloom of the trees, while Ringold, seated on a log near the fire, loosened the Colt in its holster. He sipped at his coffee, keeping an ear cocked at the small, nearly imperceptible sound of the gathering night along the mountain slope. Crickets chirped their brittle music in the peaceful dusk, and the flick and rustle of bedding birds stitched an audial tracery through the hushing whisper of the ever-present breeze.

Off to the south, across the rolling expanse of olive-toned mesas, a scattering of lights, mere quiescent sparks of gold, studded an insignificant lavender patch that was Tombstone. Beyond the town, the ragged blue silhouettes of the Mule Mountains rimmed the darkening horizon.

As night edged out of the pines, the firelight at Ringold's feet intensified into a definite, outflowing circle, pressing back the gloom as far as the low, log cabin that housed Spence's woodcutters.

As quietly as he had departed, Cajeme returned leading a black horse around the cabin. It was Blackbird.

Ringold scrambled up from the log, spilling his coffee. "Blackbird! How the devil did you get him?"

Smiling, Cajeme led the horse over to Ringold. "I have had your fine mount here for near a week. I rode him back from a recent trip."

"Agua Prieta?"

"*Si.*" Cajeme handed the reins to Ringold. "And now we will talk."

With Blackbird tied to a tree, Ringold rested on the log, talking to the Yaqui. It was a mighty interesting conversation that continued while the great bowl of stars overhead arched into a silvery splendor that dimmed the distant lights of Tombstone and rivaled the firelight. The moon was not up, but the brilliance of the heavens made that orb unnecessary.

"You say the names of the stagecoach gang are known to Kosterlitzky and the Federales?"

"*Si.*" And the Yaqui enumerated them, as Ringold listened with intense interest. "*Storm* is Stilwell, Spence is *Sunset,* Wyatt Earp is *Stilts,* his brother Virgil is *Shrike,* brother Morgan is *Stride,* Holliday is *Sidewinder,* Leonard was *Star,* and Crane was *Stirrup.*"

"*Sidewinder* is a perfect name for Doc," Ringold marveled. "You said Spence is *Sunset* and Stilwell is *Storm?*" Ringold repeated the two names as he kicked a smoldering log back into the heart of the fire.

"*Si.*"

"Why do you still work for Spence, if he's a gang member?"

"The best way to keep an eye on such rascals." Cajeme emptied the last of the coffee into Ringold's cup and set the pot aside.

"But you still don't know who this *Saguro* is?"

"No, however, we do know he was to blame, as much as any, for the raid on our *ranchos* south of the border."

"He, whoever he is, he's worked hand-in-glove with those murdering raiders?"

"That is true. The Colonel, as well as our police in Mexico, are aware that one or more of the Earp party has been below the border recently to set up the raids . . . while they were on, what they called, their *hunting trips*. But this *Saguro* . . . this fox with the cactus name, must have planned the stealing of cattle. We think the Earps have not enough cleverness to direct such things . . . what the Colonel would call 'tactical skill.'"

"When do you think we'll have enough on the Earps, and that damned Doc, to haul them all into court and make the arrests stick?"

"Soon, if all goes well. But it will have to be your case. I must not be known to have anything to do with such matters, or my usefulness would be at an end."

Ringold sat thinking about the entire, revealing conversation and the complete unselfishness of the man. What a risk he ran! If the Earps knew that the poor, ragged woodcutter they called Indian Charley was aware of their devilment—he wouldn't last a day. And if any of that bunch were finally tossed into the pen, and they held Cajeme to be responsible, there was nothing that could save the Yaqui from a savage vengeance.

"You are silent, my Sergeant." Cajeme bent to add another log to the ebbing fire. "I have instructions from the Colonel to fully cooperate with you. So, what might your orders be?"

Before Ringold could answer, a gunshot split the night. The empty coffee pot flew into the air to rattle across the ground.

Ringold was on his feet instantly, six-shooter in hand, peering across the crimson blur of the campfire.

Cajeme had vanished, in that split-second, melting into the shadows.

"Hey! Put up that weapon. I just wanted to make myself known," a swaggering voice called from near the cabin. "Guess I got a right to say hello any damned way I wanter . . . seein' it's my own layout." Pete Spence, drunk as a lord, but still cat-like on his feet, eased around the building into the firelight.

Cajeme, also, materialized from the outer darkness, with an inscrutable look in his black eyes. He made a gesture of warning to Ringold, and held out his hand, palm up, at the approaching Spence. "You have returned soon, *Señor.* The troubles in Tucson is finish?"

"Hell yes, they're finished," Spence snorted. "Couldn't make a damn thing stick. Thought they'd caught a couple of suckers, but no such thing. We come off scott-free. I bought me a horse and rid back early. Stilwell, he took himself a deetoor by Clanton's." He looked Ringold over curiously.

"I was out on a little jaunt and stopped off for a cup of Arbuckle before riding on down to Tombstone." Ringold thought he'd beat Spence to the draw in any conversation.

"Eh? I know you, don't I? You're John Ringo, ain't yer? Th' rooster that backed down Earp and Holliday." While he killed the last of a pint bottle, Spence's legs gave out and he sank heavily onto the log. "Here . . . you Charley, rustle up some coffee fer me, too. Got enough of a load in Tucson to last till next week. I need to thin it down somehow."

Without a word, Cajeme picked up the coffee pot, and plugging it with the cork from Spence's empty bottle, filled the pot with water from the canteen hanging on a corner of the cabin.

Spence sat and stared, yellow-eyed, into the fire, rubbing hands on his knees. "And, yeah, Charley, I left that horse back in th' pines. Go git him and turn him inter th' corral." His gaze took in the sleek shape of Blackbird on the edge of the firelight. "Hell of a horse there! Your'n?"

"Yes, and I suppose I'd better get on board and ride to town." Ringold stood and untied the black's reins from the pine branch, keeping an eye on Spence. This fellow needed watching—*Sunset* in the gang's lingo. That bullet holing the coffee pot could just as well have gone through his back, or the Yaqui's. Spence was as unpredictable as a cougar, and his pardner Stilwell was just as dangerous. And yet Ike Clanton had backed them both.

"You ride on, *Señor*?" Cajeme returned with the coffee pot, settling it on the bed of coals at the fire's edge.

"Yes. And thanks for your hospitality . . . Charley, wasn't it?"

"*Si.*" The Yaqui looked stolidly at Ringold as he mounted Blackbird.

As he rode down the slopes along the winding road, under the blazing canopy of stars, he cursed to himself. Spence's unexpected arrival had cut short his meeting. He'd have to see Cajeme later. Perhaps they could get together in Tombstone, or elsewhere, but wherever, he knew the Indian would discover a way.

With Spence and Stilwell on the loose, who knew what could turn up next? He knew, now, that there was a definite, organized gang at work in the Tombstone-Benson-Bisbee area. That much he would tell Thorne, but not where his information came from—aside from presenting Thorne with Jim Crane's—the defunct *Stirrup's*—notebook. Well, Crane came out of his stirrup when young McLowry pulled the trigger on him at Guadalupe Canyon.

No, he'd not reveal his source of information—yet. He mulled over Spence's statement concerning his pardner's detour to see Ike Clanton, and just as soon as Stilwell had shook the dust of Tucson.

"Bandits and bravos!" He slapped the reins on Blackbird's neck and the great horse leaped on through the starlight, obviously happy at carrying Ringold upon its broad back again. "Bandits and bravos!"

There was bound to be some hell popping—and soon. As sure as Pony was a horsethief!

11 O.K. Corral

While Pony remained out at the ranch, attempting to sell off Hill's excess saddle horses, Ringold rode up to Benson on October 23 to have his regular bi-monthly meeting with Thorne.

Seated in the seclusion of the Wells Fargo's back office, Thorne accepted Ringold's expose of the gang, which he now characterized as the *Crooked S Bunch*. But Thorne failed to appear as disturbed by their evident existence as Ringold would have supposed.

"Let's sum up the matter." Thorne cocked a gaitered foot up on the corner of his desk and polished away at his glasses. "We know there have been three robberies since you arrived in Tombstone. The first seems to have been laid at the door of Doc Holliday, and this Crane, Head and Leonard. I understand that a certain Lute King was picked up by Sheriff Behan as a horse-holder during that robbery, but someone left the door open and he's gone out of the country. That's small potatoes, though. The second robbery is a bit of a mystery, the one at Charleston. No money was taken and so it's of rather small consequences. But the Bisbee Stage is another matter. Twenty-five hundred dollars in greenbacks and no one in jail for that, unfortunately."

Thorne squinted through his spectacles, and put them on again. "You say that you suspect Wyatt Earp, even saw him talking to Spence just before the robbery on that evening. You further state that you were witness to Earp's rather odd activities near the site of the robbery later on . . . yet Spence and Stilwell were found to be not guilty, and we just don't know where Earp fits into the affair."

"He fits right in the middle. That code name of his . . . *Stilts,* puts him there, just as Spence's *Sunset,* and Holliday's *Sidewinder* place the whole bunch in one pack." He looked closely at Thorne. "If I recall, you were pretty certain that it was all a bit of play-acting."

"Yes, that's true." Thorne wagged his head, then extracted two cigars from his desk and handed one to Ringold. "That's shrewd work, ferreting out all of those names, but I won't ask how. It's your business."

"What does Chief Detective Hume think of our . . . of my failure to stop this gang in its tracks?"

"I had a telegram from Hume just this morning. He said he'd be traveling here to take a closer look at things around the first of November. I think he feels that you, and I, and this office are doing just about all we can . . . under the circumstances."

"It would help a lot if we could bring Doc Holliday's case up, instead of letting it drift along month after month."

"He's got a good lawyer, and won't come to trial for some time."

"That's just bound to cause trouble sooner or later."

"What kind of trouble?" Thorne flicked the ash from his cigar and stared speculatively at its glowing head.

"Ike Clanton."

"Clanton?"

"Yes, Ike Clanton. He's chief witness against Doc. You know there's been several attempts upon Ike's life. And I don't think his young brother is safe either. He's also apt to be called as a back-up witness."

"I see what you mean." Thorne ground out the remains of his cigar on the floor with his heel. "But do you feel the gang will keep to such dangerous maneuvers without giving themselves away?"

"Yes, I do. I feel the raid on that Clanton herd could have been a way of getting back at Ike . . . only someone slipped up, and Ike was over in New Mexico when it came off."

Thorne polished his glasses, again. "What do you propose?"

"Not much. I can only hope that Ike stays out of Tombstone for the next month or so."

. . .

Two days later on October 25, 1881, Ringold discovered that Ike was not about to stay out of Tombstone.

On that morning he was lounging in a chair in front of the Alhambra with several Tombstone gamblers and sports, including Bones Brannon, and Speck Owens of the Palace, when Ike Clanton came driving a light spring wagon up the street toward the Cochise Trading Store. Young Tom McLowry rode beside Clanton on the seat. Both waved as they rattled past in a small cloud of dust.

"Clanton's got as much sand as that road-bed," Brannon chuckled, tossing a half-smoked cheroot after the spring wagon.

"Hope th' blamed idiot stays away from my joint," Speck muttered. "If he tangles with Doc in there, or th' Earps, they'll probably wipe up the place with him."

"Wonder where his man Stilwell is?" Bones inquired of no one in particular, lighting up another stogie.

Ringold cocked an eyebrow at that. "What's Stilwell got to do with Ike Clanton?" He knew everyone was aware of the bond Ike had raised, but had someone talked, revealing Ike's actual reasons?

"Oh, I don't know where I heard it, but word is out that Ike thinks Stilwell and, maybe, Spence will back him if th' Earp bunch try to push him around."

"Ike's more of a fool than usual, then," grunted Speck. "Stilwell's made himself scarce for th' past weeks, since gettin' off scot-free at Tucson. He's probably holed-up at Spence's wood camp or sticking close to that two-bit livery barn in Bisbee. But one thing's sure, he ain't around Tombstone!"

Ringold nodded. Speck was right. Stilwell had not been around town since that appearance of Spence out at the wood camp when he and the Yaqui, Cajeme, had been interrupted in their meeting. At that time Spence had volunteered the information that Stilwell had ridden on to Clanton's. What had gone on there he could only guess. And, in fact, this was the first time he'd seen Clanton, since they'd talked in Hafford's Corner Five Saloon after Ike had posted bond for Stilwell and Spence.

Ringold and the Alhambra crowd were not the only ones taking note of Ike's arrival. About ten minutes later, Doc Holliday and Morgan Earp walked slowly up the street to be met by Wyatt, who came around the corner of Fourth with Virgil. They all stood in front of the Can Can, in close confab, looking across Allen from time to time to where Ike's spring wagon was hitched in front of the Cochise.

When several ponderous ore transports had

rumbled by, Doc, hitching up his belt under his long, black coat, walked over and confronted Ike as he was emerging from the store, arms full of groceries.

Though it was a good half-block from where Ringold and the others sat, they could hear the shouts, while the three Earps stood across the street watching.

"You son-of-a-bitch of a cowboy, get your gun out and get to work!" Doc stepped back two steps and, flinging the flaps of his coat open, held his hands, claw-like, over the butts of his two, ivory-handled Colts.

"Go on and draw, you cowardly bastard!" came Wyatt's shrill tones from the opposite side of the street. Morgan and Virgil stood staring, making no comments.

Ike shook his head silently, and turned first to the right and then to the left, showing Doc and the rest that he was unarmed.

"Sons of bitches!" Ringold sprang up from his chair, turning it over with a clatter.

"Hey, where you goin'?" Bones Brannon's long, slim fingers grasped Ringold's sleeve. "Those jaspers are out to do some killin', and Ike ain't even heeled!"

"Well, I am!" Ringold shook off the gambler's hand, and hurried down the board sidewalk toward Ike and Holliday, unmindful of the trio of Earps on the corner.

But it was all over by the time he got to the store. Ike, white-faced and shaking with rage, had called Tom McLowry out of the building, untied the horse, mounted the spring wagon and lashed the horse toward the far end of town.

Holliday, with a sour look at Ringold, recrossed the street to the waiting cluster of Earps. All immediately walked back up Fourth in the direction of the City Hall, where Virgil, alone, had any legitimate reason for entering.

Ringold stood and watched them go, then went back to Bones and the Alhambra bunch for a game of stud that stretched itself into the long evening hours.

About nine o'clock Pony Deal came in, ordered a drink, and pulled up a chair to watch the battle of the pasteboards. Ringold was ahead of the game by one-hundred-and-fifty dollars, having cleaned up on Bones, Johnny Behan, and of all people—Ike Clanton, Tom McLowry and Virgil Earp.

Pony, noticing the tense, abstracted air of the group, particularly Ike, McLowry and Earp, maintained his silence as long as he was physically able, and blurted, "Well, I see cards is still th' great leveler! Here's Ike and Virgil a'playin' as if there's no tomorrer. And I been told that, not five hours ago, Doc Holliday was tryin' to light a fire under pore old Ike, here!"

It was obvious that Pony had been hitting the

bottle. Ringold scowled at the little man and tried to kick him under the table, but only fetched up against Sheriff Behan's shins.

"Oh! Damn it there! Keep your boots under your own chair," Behan grunted at the players, in general. "Let's try to be easy here. Ike don't want any trouble. I don't want any . . . and . . . ," Behan's Irish flaring up, he raised his voice and slapped his cards face down. "And, by gravy, there ain't goin' to be no trouble! And that goes for th' hull damned crowd here, and elsewhere." He glared at the gamesters.

"Why don't you go out to the ranch and sleep it off, Pony?" Ringold suggested to his, erstwhile, undercover partner, wishing he could plant a healthy kick on his hinder parts.

"Yeah, I got enough on my mind now, without any wiseacres a'tryin' to rattle me," muttered Ike, a weak smile flitting over his broad, sweat-streaked face. He darted a furtively-puzzled glance at the stolid Virgil Earp, where he sat across the green baize-top table, studying his cards.

Behan picked up his hand, discarding, and asked for three from Ringold, the dealer. "Don't bother yourself, Clanton. There won't be any trouble tonight or tomorrow. But when might you be goin' back to your ranch?"

"Goin' back sometime tomorrow after we get th' rest of our buyin' done," spoke up Tom

McLowry, youthful features thoughtful, grey eyes flickering across the table at Virgil.

Ringold watched the group, while his fingers riffled the deck, shuffling and dealing out the required number of cards to the five contestants. Just how the game had come to include such a divergent group, even he couldn't say. He'd been playing with Bones Brannon when Behan had wandered in. Bones had asked the Sheriff to sit in, and Ringold agreed, hoping to get in a few words with the portly, little lawman, regarding the apparent tensions building between Ike and the Earps. But before any such talk could get going, Ike Clanton and Tom McLowry had entered and asked to sit in. Ringold was almost certain that Ike and his young friend, neither packing a gun, were looking for a haven of safety for the evening.

After half an hour or so, Virgil turned up and stood watching the fall of the cards until Behan urged him to join them. And so the game had progressed, with Ringold getting the deal, and piling up the chips—until the last member— Pony—had showed up.

The play continued until three in the morning. By then the regular saloon rounders had all staggered off to bed, the bar was closed and only the radiance of one oil lamp, overhead, enclosed the odd group within its yellow circle.

At last, Behan, yawning prodigiously, had

dropped out, followed by Bones, and a luckless Pony. Ike folded and left Ringold butting heads with McLowry and Virgil Earp. Three more hands broke Virgil, and he arose ponderously, shifting his pistol belt, and with a surly nod to all, shoved out through the batwings and was gone.

"All or nothin' on th' last hand, what say there, Ringo? They say you're a dead-game sport." The young McLowry winked at Ike, who stood waiting for him and casting a leery eye at the door. Fortunately for Clanton, Behan and Bones both lingered, waiting along with the fat, negro swamper with his broom at the ready.

"Why not?" Ringold pushed his pile, nearly two-hundred dollars, out to match the young cowboy's winnings. He shuffled thoroughly, turned and "burnt" the top card and dealt the hole cards. Looking at his, he saw a black ace. He dealt three cards to McLowry, who stood pat. He took a ten face up and stopped.

"Show 'em, Ringo," McLowry chortled, looking again at his hole card, with nineteen showing. The youngster vibrated with excitement, grinning around at the waiting spectators.

"No use!" Ringold, with twenty-one, scooped the cards in. "Take the damned pot. I busted!"

"How's that for luck!" McLowry grabbed up the money, and reaching across, slapped Ringold on the shoulder. "Better luck next time!"

"Why'd you do that?" Pony wondered, as he and Ringold walked down the empty, echoing boardwalk toward the hotel. "You had that squirt. Damned if you didn't. I bet you did!"

"I don't know," Ringold answered slowly. He didn't know, himself. "Guess I figured a kid with as much grit as he's got, deserved to win. Remember how he pitched into those Mexicans at the ambush, when his pards showed yellow?"

"Yeah. And I remember how you and me and poor Joe did th' same thing . . . and nobody's antyin' up a pot for us. Fact is that blamed fool Ike Clanton is still gonna wind up gettin' us into his fight. Did you see Virgil eyein' Ike and McLowry like a tabby cat at a mouse hole?"

They arrived at Ringold's hotel, and stood outside in the quiet street watching the big October moon glossing the distant mountains into waves of pure silver.

Pony, who'd sobered up somewhat, cleared his throat. "Oh yeah, I forgot to tell you. Indian Charley come across me in them Dragoons over there where I was huntin' some strayed stock. Said he'd like it right much to see you about tomorrow noon out at the wood camp. Spence and Stilwell are still in Bisbee, I guess." He cleared his throat, again, seeming to await some comment from Ringold. "Well, I got to go on and get my plug. Left him down at th' O.K. Fact is, Ike and young Tom's down there, campin' out under Ike's spring wagon. Think they'll get out of town in th' mornin' without any more ruckus?"

"I don't know. But I'll see them on their way, if I have time," replied Ringold. He stood, smoking a final cigarette as he listened to the jingle of Deal's spurs ringing their way toward the peacefulness of the O.K. Corral.

He arose late in the morning with a foggy head and an empty wallet. Shaving at the cracked, yellow washbowl on the rickety wash-stand, found him reflecting that it was a good thing Wells Fargo's payday came in less than another week. He'd been a bit of a fool to let young McLowry rake in that pot after those long hours of play. But it was just water over the old dam. More where that came from, and he was sure the kid could use some extra cash.

Breakfasting in the Can Can, amid a crowd of miners, freighters and cowmen, he heard excited shouts outside. Downing his scalding coffee, he paid his bill and exited along with half of the restaurant.

"Earp just pistol-whipped Ike Clanton," a bar-keep from the Crystal Palace told the gawking crowd.

"Which Earp?" Ringold inquired.

"Virgil Earp. Him and Morgan come up behind Ike over on Fremont. Found him carryin' a

Winchester and packin' two Colts. They disarmed him, and hit him a hell of a lick and took him across th' street to th' Court."

"Clanton in th' pokey?" A cowman wanted to know.

"Naw. Ike claimed he was packin' all that iron fer pertection . . . feared th' Earps was about to do him some harm. But th' old judge, he fined Ike twenty-five dollars, and tossed him back out on th' street."

"Clanton's on the street without firearms?" Ringold looked up and down Fourth and Allen, but saw nothing of Clanton or any of the Earps.

"Yep. And if Ike don't pull freight pretty soon, well . . ." The bartender shrugged as the buzzing crowd drifted away.

Half an hour later, at eleven-thirty, Ringold noticed Billy Clanton and Tom McLowry's brother, Frank, leading horses toward the O.K. Corral. Young Tom, head wrapped in a blood-stained bandage, walked along with them.

"Hey there." In spite of his obvious injury, Tom McLowry gave Ringold a sunny smile. "Guess I ain't quite as lucky as I been thinkin'. What'd you think of my present from that egg-suckin' saloon bouncer of a Wyatt Earp?"

Ringold, who'd been boarding Blackbird at the O.K. since he'd got the horse back, joined the trio. "Wyatt Earp? Earp buffaloed you too . . . like Ike got it from Virgil?"

"Sure pop! Seems like th' Earp bunch is really on th' warpath today."

"How'd this happen?"

"I was up town tryin' to find Ike," Tom answered, gingerly fingering the top of his head. "And darned if Wyatt didn't come around the' corner and pull a six-shooter on me. He wanted to know if I was 'heeled or not.' And when I said I wasn't, he whalloped me full-length into th' gutter for no good reason, and then walked off."

"Then he showed up in front of that store on Fourth, right after we rode into town," spoke up the grinning Billy Clanton. "When Frank and I come out, darned if he wasn't out front jerkin' our horses around, and claimin' they'd been tied on th' sidewalk, which they wasn't. But Frank here scared him off by offerin' to punch him one. When we run into young Tom, here, and got his wooden head patched up, we come down to put up th' horses in th' corral while we got our grub."

"We're all goin' on a cattle buyin' trip east to get us more stock for both ranches," the irrepressible Tom McLowry volunteered, slyly thrusting out a foot and half-tripping the chuckling Billy Clanton.

"When are you going back out to the ranches?" Ringold was getting an uneasy feeling, for some reason he couldn't define.

"Early as we can, I'd say," Frank McLowry answered. A thin, serious-faced young man, with a long, dark mustache, he seemed more a farmer than a rancher, with his checked pants stuffed into cowhide boots. "It's got so every time we come into town, one or th' other of those Earps seem to get all fired-up at us."

"Yeah," Billy grinned. "But that's generally because you're seen in Clanton company."

"I still say it ain't fair to larrup a fellow, because of th' bad crowd he runs with." Tom McLowry winked at Ringold as they walked the horses through the pole gate into the enclosure.

The proprietor, Abe Stark, followed by a stable-hand, came up and took the animals. "Stayin' long, boys?"

"Just long enough to get some stuff up at th' stores," said Billy. "Did Ike get back yet?"

"Yep, he was here a while ago with a big knot on his head. Guess he run into th' same door-knob as you, eh Tom? But he's gone off again. Said th' hull lot of you'd be pullin' out about one o'clock or so."

Ringold pulled out his watch. It was now almost halfpast noon, and he was a good thirty minutes late already for his meeting with the Yaqui. He was still edgy about possible trouble, but hated to miss Cajeme. It must have been important or the Indian would have come into town and looked him up at his leisure. The man must have felt the need for a hasty conference.

His mounting anxiety over the bull-headed

215

hustling of Ike and his people was relieved, somewhat, by the appearance of John Behan at the corral gate. "Ike Clanton got picked up by Virgil Earp and fined twenty-five dollars for carrying arms in town. Now, you boys . . ." Behan halted, staring at Tom McLowry's head. "You had trouble with th' Earps?"

"Yep," Billy spoke up. "Frank and I got bullied by that damned beanpole of a Wyatt! He said our horses was on th' sidewalk over on Fourth. Yanked 'em around and darned near started a fight right there." He jerked his head at Tom. "And Wyatt hit McLowry there for no good reason. Tom wasn't even armed."

"Well, there ain't goin' to be any more of this today. I already spoke to Wyatt and Virge," Behan barked. "Wyatt ain't got no more authority than my pet owl, and him tryin' to enforce ordinances!"

"I'll tell you, Sheriff, we don't want any trouble either, and we're goin' back home as soon as we visit a couple more stores. Hell, we don't get to town once in two months, 'cept for Ike, and we ain't goin' to let them four-flushin' Earps and their side-kick, Doc, shove us out before we're ready," Frank McLowry offered stoutly.

"That's all right, as far as it goes." Ringold motioned for the stable-hand to bring out Blackbird. "But you all know that Doc, and Wyatt, in particular, are going to keep after you

216

fellows, Clantons especially, because they don't want you around to testify against Doc. I really think they'd take up a collection if you packed up and left the Territory for good."

"And I'd do th' same for them," Behan laughed shortly. "Well, go on up town if you have to, but remember don't take any arms, pistols or whatever with you. There's an ordinance on th' books against totin' firearms." He looked pointedly at Ringold's pistol on his hip, as Ringold swung up into Blackbird's saddle.

Ringold ignored him. He knew that ordinance was only enforced when Behan felt like leaning on someone. And Virgil had never looked even cross-eyed at Ringold's weapons, or Pony's, or a good dozen others that he could think of. No, Virgil wasn't about to bull-doze a real man! Poor Ike was a natural-born sucker. But if Behan really sat down hard on both factions, everything would simmer down, and Ike and his bunch would soon be back out of Tombstone again for a spell.

"Where's Breakenridge?" Ringold asked, guiding Blackbird from the corral.

"He's due back right now from servin' a paper out east of town." Behan hauled out his big, gold watch. "One o'clock! He's back by now at th' office, I'd say."

"Don't hang around here wet-nursin' us Clantons," Billy laughed, slapping Blackbird's shining flank. The horse broke out through the gate and Ringold, looking back over his shoulder at the little knot of men, gave a wave and then let his mount have its head, loping down Allen toward East Street and the Dragoons. He was a good hour late already, but it couldn't be helped. He hadn't wanted to leave Tombstone until he was satisfied that Behan would be able to control a potentially dangerous situation.

Even as he rode up the mountain trail toward the Yaqui, who was seated, reins in hand, in the shade of the towering timber, he couldn't rid himself of a nagging feeling, whether from the impending meeting with Kosterlitzky's agent— or from thoughts of Ike and his people back there in a troubled Tombstone.

"You have the black look, my Sergeant." Cajeme urged his mount up to Ringold. "The Earps have caused this?"

"How'd you know that? But it's the Clantons and McLowrys, too! They're all back there, bristling-up like a pack of cats ready to leap on a bunch of feisty dogs."

"Then our meeting needs be most brief. I wished to tell you, myself, that Spence and Stilwell are filled with fury at the Earps and that unknown *Señor*, called *Saguro*. I have heard much talk at camp, when they thought me asleep, or at work in another part of the forest. They got themselves no money from that last robbery. Betrayed, they say, so they plan to stop the Benson Stage at Walnut Gulch, outside of Tombstone when it carries the bullion from the mines. This will be on the night of December 14th!" Cajeme gentled his fractious roan. "They will keep the money, this time."

"Does Pete Spence suspect you, or that you have given me information?"

"I do not think so." The Yaqui permitted himself a slight, unexpected smile. "Poor old Injun Charley is good only to load up the donkey and peddle the woods."

"Thanks, Cajeme." Ringold reached out, seized his hand and shook it.

"One more thing, my Sergeant. This *Saguro,* somehow, sent an unknown messenger down to Bisbee right after the robbery and had that mail sack stripped of its twenty-five hundred dollars . . . thus looting his own gang right in their teeth. He is most sly . . . this old wolf of a *Saguro!* But we will den him at last!"

"Right! And in the meantime, I'll see if we can't put Spence and Stilwell out of the stagecoach business for good."

He rode toward Tombstone with all the speed he could get out of Blackbird. The desert's vast stretch of yellow sage, in the glory of its autumnal bloom, flew past. The sun blazed, but it already slanted toward the tawny-green and sandy gold of the distant Whetstones.

Within thirty minutes he was pounding over Goose Flats. And there rode Pony. They met at the corner of Eighth and Bruce on the outskirts.

"*All over!* Y'might as well pull in that horse, and not kill him. Hurry won't do a damned bit of good anymore."

"*What?*" But Ringold knew what Pony was about to recount—even before he re-opened his mouth. He sat on Blackbird, stunned and silent, without interrupting the overwrought Deal. "I come back to town about two o'clock from th' ranch. Everyone, barflies, gamblers, punchers, miners and, even th', so-called, respectable folks was all out on th' streets talkin' about th' Earps.

"Virgil was standin', big as life, acrost th' block with a shotgun, and makin' all sorts of big talk about runnin' Ike and his bunch twenty miles. Wyatt and Doc was with him, flourishin' six-shooters and hollerin' for Morgan to come and join th' committee. Vigilanty, I guess they thought they was.

"Anyway, I went right over to look for Breakenridge. Wasn't any of my business, I guess, but I looked. Billy was still out of town. Then I tried to dig up Behan. John was gettin' shaved at th' barber's on Allen. I told him th' Earps and Holliday was loaded for bear and th' talk was that this time they meant to clean th' Clantons' clocks for good.

"Damned if when we got out on th' street,

again, there come th' whole Earp gang, and of course that pasty-faced devil of a Doc, in his long, black undertaker coat.

"They looked right through Behan as if he wasn't there. 'Hey you, hold on! Where do you think you're goin'?' says Behan. But on they went. Doc and Virgil totin' those killer scatter-guns, and Wyatt and Morgan with their six-shooters on their hips . . . all ready.

"Damn it, Behan, that's a lynch mob, I says. He admits it, and tells me he'd got th' Clantons and th' McLowrys, who come in with 'em, to put away their weapons. Now, he could see they was just a bunch of sittin' ducks, if he couldn't stop them crazy Earps.

"We run down as far as Baur's Butcher Shop tryin' to head 'em off, but they cut ahead, cross-lots, and come right at th' Corral. I'll give Behan credit. He hauled out his pistol and hollered for 'em to hold on. But th' Earps were pure blood-crazy by that time.

"I pulled on Johnny Behan's arm. Told him he'd get us killed, too. I felt like a yellow dog, but I had a feelin' we was too late to do anythin' but get killed. And I thought of poor Joe Hill. He's dead and what good did it do? Maybe if we'd had you . . . or Breakenridge, we could have stopped it.

"It wasn't more'n half a minute and it was over. Pure damned murder! No other name for it. There was two horses by th' entrance. Frank McLowry's and Billy Clanton's. Ike was back there by then with his kid brother and th' two McLowrys and young Billy Claiborne, who rides for Ike sometimes.

"I heard Virgil bawl out, 'Hold up your hands!' Billy Clanton held up his hands and yelled, 'Don't shoot. We don't want to fight.' Frank McLowry threw up his hands too. Billy Clanton had a pistol on, but didn't go to use it. Most of their guns was in Clanton's spring wagon, where Ike had put 'em after comin' back from leavin' his pistol and Winchester at th' Judge's office. Th' only ones armed was Billy and Tom.

"Billy Claiborne up and ran for it about th' time Wyatt poked a pistol smack inter Ike's belly and tried to fire it. Ike wrestled with Wyatt, and th' pistol discharged, missin' Ike, who run off hard as he could out th' end of the Corral and by Fly's Photo Gallery. About that time all th' Earps and Doc started firin' when Virgil yelled . . . 'They're gettin' away, let 'em have it!'

"Billy Clanton was hit bad, and staggered over to th' side of Fly's shop. He sat down and pulled out his Colt and begun to fire back. Lead was flyin' like hail stones while Behan and I scootched down, peerin' under th' railin'.

"Next to get it was young Tom McLowry, who still had his hands up. Doc pumped both barrels inter his chest! Frank McLowry had a

Winchester on his horse, but no pistol. His horse kept swervin' and dancin' around, and Frank took a couple of slugs in th' chest and back as he went round and round with that damned fool horse, holdin' th' reins, tryin' to get a'holt of his saddle-gun. But he didn't make it, and fell dead out past us at Fremont and Third.

"Sounds like a long time, and it sure seemed like it! But it was all over in less'n a minute, like I said. Th' Earps was wounded. Virgil and Morgan only, worse luck. Just flesh wounds.

"Billy Clanton was th' last one. He died screamin' fer his maw, not half an hour back as I was ridin' out to look fer you.

"John Behan, he tried to arrest those murderin' bastards, but they backed him off and lugged Virge and Morg away to patch 'em up. I let 'em."

Ringold sat staring westward where the golden October sun continued to slide toward the deep-shadowed mountains. His eyes were wet.

"Well, what do you say?"

Ringold straightened in his saddle and turned Blackbird toward Tombstone. Life kept on. Two ore wagons were rumbling toward him, and the air vibrated to the clank and chuff of the mine engines. He looked at Pony. "I say we drive every one of those scurvy bandits into the pen . . . all of them, or out of the Territory for good. If we don't kill them first!"

12 Pony's Bet

The days following the killings at the O.K. Corral sped by as swiftly as Blackbird at full gallop, or so it seemed to a deeply-troubled Ringold. Immediately after the shootings, a storm of rage, sorrow, threats and counter-threats broke over Tombstone.

The bodies of the McLowrys, as well as Billy Clanton, were dressed in decent, black broadcloth, placed in rosewood coffins, and displayed in the Fremont Street windows of Ritter and Ryan, the undertakers, with a sign "murdered in the streets of Tombstone."

The funeral was attended by half the town and a goodly portion of the outlying area. Leathery-faced ranchers sat side-by-side with sallow clerks, pallid gamblers and horny-handed miners at the October 29th service, then thronged back to the saloons for a long round of drinks to the departed. There were mighty few toasts to the Earps, and those, almost to a man, were scurrilously uncomplimentary.

Ringold and Pony had attended the garish affair, along with a grim-faced Behan and Breakenridge. Ike Clanton, Pete Spence, who had been out of town during the shooting, and others of the Clanton and McLowry faction sat in the front row of the funeral parlor. But none of the Earps, including Virgil, were in evidence. The word was out that both Morgan and Virgil were still laid up, Morgan with a bullet wound in the leg, and Virgil with a creased shoulder.

The Earps were only seen in a body when they made their appearance in Wells Spicer's court. Doc and Wyatt came in along with their fellow defendants to meet the charges of "Murder, involving the deaths of Thomas and Frank McLowry and William Clanton." As Case Number 94, the Territory of Arizona Versus Morgan, Virgil, Wyatt Earp and J.H. Holliday, to be heard in Justice Court, Township No. 1, Cochise County, A.T.—the examination was started on October 31.

Ringold and Pony, along with as many spectators as could be packed into the second-story, whitewashed courtroom, watched the proceedings day after day. The hearings went on, through most of November, with the poker-faced Doc and a frozen-featured Wyatt, along with his stolid brothers, sitting it out while their lawyer, a high-powered attorney from California, named Fitch, handled their case.

Ringold saw Thorne attend several of the early sessions, but thought little of it, on reflection. Folks came from all over half of the Territory to attend the hearings. He avoided getting close to Thorne during the intermissions, but saw the

Wells Fargo head talking to Pony, the lawyer Fitch, and once with Holliday.

"Oh, Thorne knows Doc all right," Pony remarked at Ringold's question. "He likes his game of cards and him and Doc used to play lots of hands at Benson when Doc first lit, and worked a couple of places up there."

Day after day, first one witness and then another testified, consuming twenty-two full days of testimony. The deponents for Clanton presented an interesting cross-section of Tombstone. Saloon-keeper Andy Mehan testified that Tom McLowry had left a pistol with him between one and two o'clock on the day of the fight, remarking that he still had the weapon.

According to James Kehoe, a butcher, "Frank McLowry was not armed when at my shop just before the fight."

Another saloon man, J.H. Allman, testified that the pistols and rifles belonging to Ike Clanton were behind his bar before and after the shooting, and that the first two shots were fired by Holliday and Morgan Earp.

Young Billy Claiborne, the only one to escape the killings beside Ike Clanton, swore that he resided at the neighboring village of Hereford, and was twenty-one. He testified: "Frank and Billy were the only two on that side that did any shooting. I saw Tom McLowry during the shooting. He threw open his coat and said, 'I am not armed.' I helped put him on the wagon and he had no weapon on him at all. After Billy Clanton was shot he said, 'Don't shoot me, I don't want any fight.' I saw him draw his pistol only after he was shot down. Doc Holliday shot first, Morgan second, almost together."

Wes Fuller, one of the Crystal Palace gamblers, told the court that: "Frank McLowry, just at the time the shooting began, was standing, holding his horse. I saw his hands, and he had nothing in them. Billy Clanton throwed up his hands and said, 'Don't shoot me, I don't want any fight.' The Earp party fired the first shots; two shots, almost together."

Johnny Behan took the stand, about in the middle of the sessions, to the accompaniment of a volley of murderous looks from Wyatt and his bunch. Dressed for the occasion in a new black, broadcloth suit and wearing a gold watch-chain across his expansive chest, Behan looked as much a banker as a lawman. But the little Irishman, staring coldly at the Earps and Holliday, set his jaw, thrust out his chin-whiskers, and let fly: "Billy Clanton said, 'Don't shoot me, I don't want to fight.' Tom McLowry, at the same time threw his coat open and said, 'I've got nothing.' Billy and Frank were the only ones armed. They had their horses ready, leading them, and were leaving town. Their rifles were on their saddles. They had their hands up when the Earp crowd fired on them. Doc Holliday shot Tom McLowry with a shotgun. And Morgan Earp shot Billy Clanton while their hands were up!"

The last major witness for the Clanton-McLowry side, before the Earps took the stand, was Ike Clanton. All during the trial he had been rarely seen in Tombstone, coming from the ranch and generally putting up at a local hotel—but never habituating the saloons. It was as if the deaths of his father and the recent end of his younger brother had sapped something out of the blustering Ike—if only for the time being.

He was sworn in, late in the month, before an overflow crowd. He testified that he had not been armed and that Frank McLowry's and Billy Clanton's hands were up, and that Tom McLowry was throwing open his coat when he was shot down. According to Ike, the first two shots were fired by Doc Holliday and Morgan Earp. Unarmed, and not about to stand around waiting to be shot down, like the rest, Ike had run for the safety of a nearby store—with three shots sent after him by Wyatt, who was well aware that his target was weaponless.

When Ike stepped down from the stand, at the end of the day, he ignored the Earp-Holliday clan, as they sat across the courtroom, staring fixedly at him. He nodded shortly at several friends, including Ringold and Pony, as he made his way out of the building—not waiting to hear the Earp rebuttal.

Ringold, who'd sat through the long, hot days of droning testimony and recesses, watched Pete Spence and Frank Stilwell follow Ike out. He felt like a trapper at the edge of a wild animal den, knowing the team of Stilwell and Spence would soon be making a try at Wells Fargo—in defiance of the Earps, Holliday and their shadowy leader.

"Here comes the king of liars now," grunted Pony as Wyatt stepped up and announced that he would not put his trust in a faulty memory as some witnesses had, but would read from a carefully prepared "statement." Virgil and the rest had clearly chosen Wyatt to attempt to sway the court with his glib tongue.

The attorneys for Clanton objected to this maneuver, but Justice Spicer ruled against them. The paper, read in Wyatt's nasal, droning voice, was long. It stated, in part:

"My name is Wyatt S. Earp. Thirty-two years old the 19th of last March. Reside in Tombstone, and have resided here since December 1st, 1879. Am at present employed in a saloon. Also have been deputy sheriff and detective."

It continued: . . . "I went as deputy marshal . . . as a part of my duty and under the direction of my brother Virgil."

The audience sat up and listened closely to Wyatt when he wound up his rambling discourse with: "The first two shots were fired by Billy Clanton and myself . . . I never drew out my pistol or made a motion to shoot until after Billy Clanton and Frank McLowry drew their pistols . . . believe Tom McLowry was armed and fired two shots at our party before Holliday, who had a shotgun, fired at and killed him . . ."

There was more, but Ringold, and the more observant members of the audience, found it apparent that Justice of the Peace Wells Spicer had already made up his mind to rule for the Earp party. On the day following Wyatt's testimony, December 1, Spicer rendered his decision. He absolved the defendants of all blame and discharged them.

It was a most unpopular decision. There were rumblings and muttered threats, not only against the Earps and Holliday, but also the Justice, himself. "Hell, this is one case of plain no justice at all," Pony complained to Ringold as they sat in the Palace barroom, watching a smug Doc Holliday warming long, pale fingers at the pot-bellied stove in the saloon's corner, prior to riffling the pasteboards through another night's work.

"You've plenty of support for such feelings," Ringold bit down on his cigar. "Listen to what the editor of the Nugget has to say: 'The examination of Earp and Holliday, on charges of the murder of Frank and Tom McLowry and William

Clanton, on the twenty-sixth of last month, was concluded yesterday by the discharge of the prisoners by Wells Spicer, the magistrate before whom the examination was conducted. This was not much of a surprise to anyone, inasmuch as Spicer's ruling and action for some days previous to the close of the case had given sufficient indication of what the final result would be!'"

Ringold tossed the paper onto the table. "And that's that! The dirty pack is running free. But for the time being we've got something else to think about."

"Yeah, Spence and Stilwell." Pony looked around the crowded room, then leaned over casually. "You still want to play this one close to th' vest . . . tellin' Thorne nothin' yet?"

"This time, yet. He might want to call in some law to help set up an ambush . . . and if he tipped off the drivers or guards, they could get buck fever and shoot too soon. And I want those two!"

"Odd the way they went out with Ike before Earp got up to blow."

"Not so odd. I think Ike's going to try to use them on the Earps. But if he is, he'd better use them before we get them," said Ringold.

"You think Ike's dead set gettin' his dues from th' Earps? You know Ike and his usual hell-roarin' ways . . . and he ain't even raised his voice, while most of Tombstone has had their say about th' hearin'."

"That's just why I think Ike is laying plans. He's been too quiet, and out of sight too long since he left court."

Ringold rode up to Benson on the morning of December 13th to collect his mail at the Benson P.O. and see Thorne at the Wells Fargo office. After thinking things through, he'd decided that the proper procedure, according to his Ranger training, would be to inform Thorne of the imminent raid on the Benson Stage. If Cajeme's information was correct, and there'd been no change of plans, it would take place the following night.

Riding back out of Benson, an hour later, without seeing Thorne, who'd gone over to Phoenix, he fell to cursing the chill winds, wailing down from the snowcapped Whetstones to the west. He, also, consigned Pony to perdition for not being around to keep him company. The little horse-sharper was off on another of his clandestine trading expeditions and would not be back before morning.

So, without any mail, no pay—and a long, chilling jaunt back to Tombstone ahead of him, he stopped at the hamlet of Contention and paid a visit to that burg's one saloon. There he had several drinks to fortify himself for the rest of the journey. Never a heavy drinker, he took on board more than he needed, and, forgetful of eating, was in an odd mood the rest of the ten miles to Tombstone.

The pressure of the many months away from his native state of Texas was commencing to tell upon Ringold, despite an unusually even-tempered nature. Putting Blackbird up at the Pioneer Livery off Tough Nut Street, he'd never been able to enter the grounds of the O.K. Corral since that fatal day, he drifted toward the Palace.

The oil lamps of the place were aglow, their yellow brilliance sweeping across the smoke-thickened room, to hold back another long, winter evening at the threshold.

Going up to the long, mahogany bar, he ordered a double shot of rye and gratefully sipped its amber fire. Acquaintances spoke or waved a hand from various sections of the room, but he greeted them without his usual courtesy. He merely grunted at Wes Fuller, when the gambler clapped him on the back, offering to buy another round.

Fuller, a good games-of-chance-man, and a sight reader of human nature, merely shrugged and moved on to more congenial companions.

Ringold downed one more shot, and, turning to the barkeep, Frank Leslie, tossed down a ten-dollar gold piece, ordering drinks for Fuller and the others along the bar. He briefly acknowledged their thanks and was making his way out of the place when he was halted at the icy sound of Doc Holliday's voice.

He hadn't noticed Doc before, due to his moody preoccupation and the dimness of the corner tables. But now he spun around as he caught a portion of Holliday's unmistakable conversation: "Damned whelps! I'd pull triggers on such again, and don't anyone forget it! I ain't th' gent to back down from blowhards like th' Clantons or anybody else." He ceased abruptly as one of his fellow gamblers called his attention to the oncoming Ringold.

In Ringold's present mood, the sight of any of the Earp crew would have made his hackles rise. But when his ears were ringing with this consumptive killer's brags, it was more than he could stand.

He was determined, then and there, despite the consequences, to force Holliday to slap leather, or back down in public—like a yellow cur dog. "Holliday, how's it seem to have a straight deck to draw to? How's it seem to face up to a man, and not a bunch of unarmed kids?" He kept his mackinaw open and his right hand close to his holster.

"By God, you can't talk to me like that!" Doc's pale fingers began to twitch and move—then his arms were pinned, as Billy Breakenridge materialized from the shadowy side of the room to hold the struggling, cursing gambler in a bear hug.

"You, Ringo!" Breakenridge shouted. "Get

your hands away from that pistol! You're both under arrest!" An audible sigh went up from the tense crowd of gamblers, miners and hangers-on.

Ringold marched beside Breakenridge and a murderously silent Holliday back through the windy night to Behan's office, where both were fined twenty-five dollars apiece—"for disturbing the peace."

Behan, himself, took the fines, smiling sardonically but said nothing to either Holliday or Ringold, except to thank them for their "contribution." Breakenridge handed them back their six-shooters, minus cartridges.

Ringold, as angry at himself as at Behan and his deputy, turned his back on all concerned and stalked off to his hotel, where, to his surprise, he found a tense Pony Deal.

"Where you been? Heard you got inter another tussle with Doc. But that don't cut no ice. Spence and Stilwell are goin' to hit th' up-stage fer Benson jest as your Injun Charley told you they would!"

"How do you know, for sure?"

"I come back sooner than I thought, over th' mountain, and pulled around by Spence's wood camp. I see a fire goin' in th' cabin, so I staked out my buckskin and snuck up to listen. T'warn't no risk. Both was drunker lords. You could'a hear 'em a mile. They was rantin' around because Injun Charley was off huntin' and they had to rustle up their own grub. Grub? Not much! They took it out of bottles, for sure. So, whilst I scooched by th' door, they went over the whole scheme. They're gonna hit the stage at Walnut Gulch, when she come through about eight o'clock, with that mid-December bullion run!"

Ringold sank back on the brass-bound bedstead and tugged off his boots with a battered boot-jack. His ankle pained him a bit, but with a good night's sleep, he'd be ready to tackle those rascals. And Cajeme had been right, as usual, even to the exact date. "All I can say is that you are gettin' to be a proper gumshoe." He told a grinning Pony Deal.

Pony twirled his hat in his hand, and opened the door. "Well, I'm gettin' a lot of experience from a damned good teacher." He shrugged, but Ringold could see he was pleased. He went on out the door and shut it behind him. Then it reopened and he stuck his head back in. "I'll bet you one thing. If th' Earps get wise to this stickup, it'll blow th' rest of Tombstone apart before Christmas!"

13 Guns in the Dark

The evening of December 14 came on blustering, with fitful winds and the barest suggestion of snow in the chilly air. Ringold and Pony ate supper at the San Jose House on Fremont and then went their separate ways, about five-thirty, to get their horses. Each carried his Winchester carbine, wrapped in a blanket, with extra cartridges stuffed in the deep pockets of his mackinaw.

Blackbird emerged from the warm depths of the livery barn, shaking his head, obviously resenting the interruption of his night's repose, but when Ringold mounted the big black and gave him the reins, the sturdy horse loped down the frozen length of Tough Nut, rapidly bearing his rider out into a night, luminous with great stars that flamed like the points of a million diamonds.

Later the stage would be pulling into Tombstone, around six-thirty, and taking on passengers, plus a box of bullion from the local mines, for the run up to Benson.

He gave Blackbird a touch of spur and they flew through the whistling, frigid air toward his rendezvous with Pony Deal at Walnut Gulch. They had to be there and in position before the two road agents arrived and took their own places for the attempt. He had no way of knowing just when Stilwell and Spence would show up, but judged that it would be within the hour. That made for a cold and troublesome wait, but it couldn't be helped.

He covered the four chilly miles, in less than half an hour, to where the El Paso & South Western tracks crossed the Benson road, just beyond Walnut Gulch. It was a lonesome place, with scattered thickets of saguro stretching gaunt arms into the windy night—and for a moment he thought Pony was late. But as he halted Blackbird to stare into the cold, starlit gloom, Deal came riding up out of the shallow gulch.

"Hold on there. Hold your fire, stranger!" It was Pony all right, and about half-cocked. "Colder than Doc's gizzard." Deal hauled out a flask and poked it at Ringold. "Take yourself a belt, it'll warm you up fer your work."

"Heard anything?"

"Quiet as a tombstone. Ha! That's kind of a joke, eh? Tombstone'll be poppin' hell again, if th' Earps and Doc ketch on to what's up, eh?"

"Probably." Ringold took the bottle and downed a warming jolt, then corked it and stuck it into his own mackinaw pocket. "I'll hold the firewater." He swung down from Blackbird and motioned for Deal to dismount. "I don't know how long this will take, but let's get set."

They discussed the best way to get the drop

on the bandits, settling for a strategy that placed Pony down in the gulch, and Ringold out behind a saguro thicket about ten paces down the road.

"But what if they land on our places?" Pony debated out loud as he led his buckskin down into the shadowy depression of the gulch.

"We just take our chances, but if they come down from the direction or the wood camp, they'll probably take cover off on the other side of the tracks." He paused, but the only sounds were night noises of an open land. A pair of coyotes were holding a long-range duet, their quavering yelps drifting up toward the brilliant, indifferent stars. For a moment, the fitful night wind, keening through the dry grasses and mesquite paused, and in the breathless hush, the minute rattle of vagrant snowflakes mingled with the bridle jingle and muffled stamping of the mounts.

"Hark!" Ringold lifted a hand. "Someone's coming." Nothing was to be seen in the vague starlight, but the sound grew—the thudding of hooves on the frozen roadway, coming from the west.

"Could be them." Pony led his horse further down the draw, staking him by an outcropping of rock, and returned, carbine in hand.

"When I pull trigger twice, fast, throw down on them from your side, and I'll do the same,"

Ringold ordered. "Give 'em a chance, though, to cave in," he added, thinking of that shooting back in Texas, seemingly years ago. He hustled across the road, leading Blackbird into the saguro.

He was surprised to find Stilwell and Spence so much ahead of time, for it was almost an hour before the stage was due. But there was nothing for it, but to lie low, and hope the pair didn't tumble. As he stood between the giant saguros, holding a gloved hand over Blackbird's nose, gentling the great horse, he saw dim silhouettes—riders approaching.

They dismounted and Ringold glimpsed the sheen of starlight on their weapons. Each led a horse off on opposite sides of the road, about twenty yards from Pony's position and thirty from his.

Minute followed dragging minute. The wind, rising again, moaned and whistled as its phantom fingers tugged and plucked at his sombrero. The cold grew. Stilwell and Spence remained in their own positions.

Losing track of the hour, he was taking a second belt of Pony's rye when the unmistakable rattle and creak of a horse-drawn vehicle came from the direction of Tombstone. The coach!

Spence and Stilwell were calling hoarsely to each other, and he heard the metallic click of their rifles, as they jacked shells into the weapons' chambers.

Then, with a clatter and clash, the Benson Coach was rocking past.

Everything broke loose at once. There came the crack of the robbers' guns, jumbled with the curses and shouted commands of Spence and Stilwell, along with the voice of Pony, who reared up out of his hollow, shrilling for the bandits' surrender. Even the stage driver, Joe Snell, a hard-shelled old reprobate, fearing neither man nor devil, added his roared defiance at the sudden order to "hold up!"

With the fat in the fire, Ringold ran out into the road and sent a shot at the dim outlines of the milling bandits.

Pony emptied his carbine in Spence and Stilwell's direction, increasing the danger to the swaying, jouncing vehicle, which kept up its headlong flight down the Benson road. Someone aboard fired back at the robbers, and then the speeding coach was out of sight.

"Hold it! Hold it!" Ringold shouted at Pony, and ran back to Blackbird, for the outlaws, horses at hand, had forked their mounts and were gone in the darkness.

Mounted first, Ringold rode down to Pony as he came puffing up out of the gulch, tugging along his buckskin. "Come on!" Ringold rode full tilt down the frosty road for half a mile, seeing nothing. He could hear the rattle and pound of the coach in the distance, but no more gunshots.

Clearly the bandits had been frightened off and had taken to the open country.

It would be impossible to track the pair in the dark. They'd not head back to the wood camp, and could have scattered in any direction. Ringold had been on too many wild goose chases to attempt to trail at night. He waited for Pony to come up.

"If this is all we get for our trouble, I guess we pack it in and go back to bed." Pony pulled off his sombrero and poked a finger through a hole in the crown.

Ringold silently agreed, and they headed toward Tombstone with the wind at their backs. It had been a wasted night.

For some time all the talk around town seemed concerned with the latest robbery attempt. Spence was back in Tombstone the day after, bold as brass, making the rounds of the saloons. However, Ringold noticed that Spence seemed to keep clear of the Earps and Holliday, though he didn't hesitate to frequent their haunts. Stilwell, apparently, had left the country.

Pony rode up to Benson on December 16, and returned to report that Thorne was certainly "on th' prod" over the Walnut Gulch affair. "He wanted to know why we wasn't on top of th' thing. I tole him we was certain it was just a couple of down-at-heels miners tryin' to make a raise fer Christmas."

"That's probably the best way to handle it. No use in getting Thorne any more excited than he seems to be." Ringold was watching Pete Spence, who had just come into the Palace on the heels of Pony, and was standing at the bar, staring at Virgil Earp, where the acting police chief was involved in a billiard game in the saloon's corner. Spence went back to his drink and made small talk with a pair of miners whenever Earp glanced around.

"Guess Pete didn't recognize my voice th' other night, and I'm right glad of that," Deal observed, seating himself at Ringold's table and ordering himself a beer. "And I want to thank you fer cleaning out my bottle of corn then too!" Pony gave a wave of his hand at the unsuccessful bandit when Spence glanced over. "Wonder what Pete and Frank would say if they knew it was us that busted up their little game?"

"I wonder what Virgil Earp would say?" Ringold paid for Pony's drink.

"I'll go you one better. Where does this *Saguro,* this *Mister S,* whoever he is, fit into all this?"

"I haven't any idea, but I imagine that he is madder than the devil at Stilwell and Spence, for I don't think they are part of the gang, anymore."

"I'll see you and raise you! Wonder what Ike Clanton is up to, and why he's been so scarce lately?" Pony flagged a waiter for another beer.

"We might find out before Christmas rolls around," answered Ringold.

"Clanton'll play Santa Claus, you think?"

"He'll play hell . . . I think!"

Ringold loafed around the various saloons and gambling halls, day after day, sometimes with Pony and sometimes by himself. With the advent of winter, Pony was restricting his horse trading expeditions and sticking close to Tombstone. He'd closed down the horse ranch, and was looking for a buyer, but so far there'd been no takers.

Ringold could feel the little man's restlessness. He was restless, himself, but there was nothing to do but to stay under orders and continue to work for Wells Fargo for the time being. According to Thorne, they needed to keep a closer watch on possible holdup men, and, of course, Thorne was correct, but an officer, ofttimes, was only as good as his informants. Pony seemed unable to turn up anything—and Cajeme, the Yaqui, had been absent for so long that Ringold was sure he'd gone back to Mexico.

Ringold cultivated Fred Dodge, somewhat, for he had begun to have a theory that the holdup men, whoever they were, and whoever this *Saguro* was, were gaining information on gold shipments and payrolls from someone within the organization. But any conversations with

Dodge over a drink or a game of cards seemed to produce nothing but boredom. As Pony put it, "Dodge is just too cussed thick between th' ears to be a crook." But Ringold, somehow, felt that Fred Dodge, the undercover man for Wells Fargo at Tombstone, could be much more clever than he appeared to be.

Despite Ringold's apprehensions, Christmas came and went. Celebrated by Tombstone in high, old style, with loads of mountain turkeys, shot by vagrant hunters, and served at all the hotels and restaurants, along with bear meat, venison and imported oysters, and washed down with keg upon keg of beer, the miners, mine-owners, cowpunchers and townsfolk, including the dead-sport gamesters and their ladies, frolicked, danced and gambled, topping off their saturnalia with avid attendance to the latest offerings at the Bird Cage Theater.

During the holiday season, a California repertoire company presented "The Ticket of Leave Man" at the Bird Cage. Ringold and Pony attended the rousing melodrama several times just to kill the monotony of the long winter evenings.

On the night of December 28, along with several hundred other theater-goers, they left the Bird Cage discussing the drama and the slick way in which Harpshaw the Detective had saved an innocent man from the brink of prison and sunk the hooks into the hardcases who actually deserved it—when three or four heavy reports thudded out in the night, for all the world like the sound of shotguns.

Pulling their six-shooters from under their coats, Ringold and Pony ran across Allen and onto Fifth, where the racket and ensuing shouting had come from.

Pistol shots cracked out over on Tough Nut and then came the humming sound of quiet that rings through the air after the cessation of gunfire. But the shouts and cries of an agitated mob continued to grow.

"They got Earp! They got Virgil Earp!"

"Ike!" gasped Pony, pointing as they approached a milling knot of people in front of the Eagle Brewery Saloon. And it *was* Clanton! Ike stood gawking in at the place as Johnny Behan and Billy Breakenridge came out the door into the street.

"Clear out of here, folks," Breakenridge spoke up pleasantly, while Behan opened his coat to display his pie-plate badge. "You, Ike, you'd better get along now." Behan motioned at the open door. "Wyatt and Morgan's in there. They might try to start something, again."

Ike, who had not spotted Ringold or Pony, as yet, bristled up at this. "Hell's fire, you know I ain't a'scared of them slumgullions! Tough for

Virgil, but I guess most folks would say it was bound to happen."

"That's not good talk this time of night, and here in particular," snapped Behan. "Now all of you folks go along home and let us see about this." He paused as he noticed Ringold and Pony. "And you gents there . . . we sure don't need you around here no more'n Ike."

"Just wanted to give you a hand, Johnny, if you'd be needin' one," Pony grinned, dropping his gun back into its holster and buttoning up his coat.

"Who shot Earp and where did they go? Shotguns, wasn't it?" Ringold inquired, sheathing his own six-shooter.

"Hey there, Ringo and Pony!" Ike grinned at them in much the same manner of the old, carefree Clanton—despite the deadly attack on Virgil Earp.

"Come on, Ike," Ringold beckoned to him. "We haven't seen you since . . . the trouble. Come on over to the Palace and have a nightcap with us."

"Yeah, go along, everybody." Behan breathed noticeably easier. "That's right, folks, nothing you can do for Earp."

"We know somethin' we'd like to do to all th' damned Earps," a voice cried out from the dispersing crowd.

"And Holliday too," another called.

"Let's go warm up somewheres." Ike shrugged,

pulling his sheepskin collar up around his ample ears. "Just got to town. Been up to Benson on business, and it's a damned cold jaunt."

"Should'a took th' coach," grinned Pony, giving Ringold a dig in the ribs. " 'Course it's still risky to ride th' old Concords."

"I heered about that up to Benson. They tried fer th' coach agin t'other night, but somebody or other run th' scoundrels right off," laughed Ike.

"That's so," Ringold replied, but was interrupted as the door behind them banged open and a group of men, including Wyatt, Morgan and Doc emerged, carrying a groaning Virgil Earp between them. Virgil's shattered arm dangled down and he was obviously in great pain.

"Hell! Look at that," muttered Ike. "Th' whole damned clan, and in one bunch."

"You should have waited a bit, Ike," Ringold said, watching Clanton closely in the dim light of the flickering street lamps.

"Hell, what makes you think I had anythin' to do with that there?" Ike scowled at the silent party moving past. Doc was the only one who noticed them watching from the shadows—but he merely glanced coldly at the trio and stalked on behind.

"Old Doc thinks you showed up at th' wrong time, but doesn't want to try anythin' tonight . . . for fear he might get himself on th' business end of a scatter-gun fer a change," chuckled

Pony while they walked toward the Palace.

Breakenridge and Behan stood in a close conference and then one moved off toward the center of town, while the other walked down toward the darkened Chinese quarter.

"Looks like them shotgun men took it on th' run fer Hop Town," said Clanton, staring after Breakenridge. "But Billy and John might as well save shoe-leather. They won't find anyone in this town to pin that ambush on, I'll bet."

"Sounds like you know more about this than you wanter say," Pony said.

"Listen, Deal . . . and you too, Ringo. When I get those Earps, I'll do it legal-wise. I ain't done with 'em by a jug full! And when I turn loose on 'em, it's gonna be with a lawyer. You'll see." Ike was clearly angry, voice tight with emotion. "You really think those varmints can kill us Clantons . . . because I know they was somehow to blame for killin' my pap, as well as my kid brother . . . you think they can up and kill us and walk around free as birds?"

"All right, Ike," Pony took Clanton by the arm, accompanying him down the wooden sidewalk to the front of the Palace, followed by Ringold. "It's all right. We know you better than to think you'd stoop to back-shootin'." His voice was soothing, as if he reasoned with a sulky child. "But you sure ain't gonna leave many of that gang in one piece . . . if Virge is any example."

249

He ducked away, laughing, as Clanton lunged bear-like at him.

"Oh hell, try to talk straight sense to you!" Ike, joshed out of his dark mood, gave Pony a shove and slapped Ringold on the back ahead of him into the saloon.

Once inside, and bellied up to the bar, Ringold bought the first round. While he paid Buckskin Frank Leslie, the bartender, muttered sotto voce, "Gent down at th' end would like to make some talk with you . . . but only you, he says."

And Ringold, glancing down the level stretch of mahogany and brass, beheld Emilio Kosterlitzky, dressed in a plain, brown sack suit, raising a glass in salute.

"Here, go on over to that table and I'll come in a minute," he told Pony and Ike. "I have to talk to that fellow over there. Knew him from some other place."

Leaving the pair to their drinks, he approached the end of the bar—and the saturnine Ruales Chieftain.

"You seem a bit nonplussed to see me," Kosterlitzky smiled slightly.

"Well . . . you are right, and especially on a night like this."

"You are referring to the shooting this evening?"

"Yeah, and the fact that one of the Earps got it . . . from unknown gunmen."

Kosterlitzky laughed easily. "You are pleased with your big, black horse? Cajeme returned him to you promptly?" He seemed unaware that he had changed the conversation.

"Yes, and I want to thank you for that." Ringold lowered his voice. "But you haven't answered my question. What brings you up here in such foul weather?"

"Rest assured, it was necessary. That much I can tell you . . . now."

"Now?"

"*Si*, as my adopted countrymen would say." He glanced around the room casually, seeming to blandly ignore everyone in the room. "That little, ferret-faced man with the brown mustache, who came in with you and that big, blond fellow . . . that would be Charles Ray, alias Pony Deal?"

"Yes, that's Pony. What's he got to do with all this?"

"Actually nothing. But this is the nearest I have ever been to one of the most clever horsethieves in the States or Mexico, for that matter. You choose your friends most carefully, I see." And Kosterlitzky smiled carefully. "Well, I did not ride all the way to Tombstone to hold such trivial talk. Can you come to my room at the American Hotel on Fremont in the morning?"

"What about tonight?"

"It will keep overnight. I suggest you rejoin your friends before they become too curious.

251

This matter needs most careful consideration, and I believe we both need a good night's repose . . . at least I do."

Ringold nodded and went back to Ike and Pony where they sat deep in conversation. Pony glanced up when Ringold sat down. "Well, what did old Emilio want?"

"You know him?" Ringold was a bit staggered.

"You bet! I made too many trips through his bailiwick not to know that bird. What did he have to say about th' shootin'?"

"Shrugged it off, and didn't seem surprised that it had happened."

"Hell, it was bound to have," Ike grunted, lighting up a cigar. "Don't know who that feller is . . . but he's got good sense." He puffed deeply on the weed. "Only thing is, though, they should have shot closer. I guess next time, maybe they might."

14 The Deadliest Game

Ringold was knocking on Kosterlitzky's door at the American Hotel next morning, while the town still buzzed with gossip of the night attack upon Virgil Earp.

Pony had ridden out from Tombstone, after breakfast, accompanying Ike back to the Clanton Ranch—"just in case." Deal, while they had eaten breakfast, expressed his mystification at the upcoming meeting with the Ruales Chief—but didn't pursue the matter when Ringold changed the subject as they split up to go their different ways.

At the second knock upon the oaken panel of Number 22, the door cracked open to reveal the alert features of Kosterlitzky. He nodded, and opened the door wide enough to disclose a second person, Wells Fargo's Chief of Detectives—Jim Hume.

"Come in, Sergeant," Hume spoke up, waving an expensive cigar in invitation. Kosterlitzky closed the door quietly behind Ringold, after scanning the empty hallway.

"And now you see why I did not wish to get involved in any discussions in that noisy saloon." Kosterlitzky waved Ringold to a chair and sat down upon the bed, with head cocked on one shoulder. "But instead of holding down the floor, shall we not allow Chief Hume to have his say? After all this is his case . . . and country."

"You may be a bit surprised to see me here in Tombstone, unannounced." Hume paced over to the window and looked out at the watery sunshine. "And I don't blame you . . . but things seem to be coming to a head down here, as indicated by that shooting of last night. And there seems to be a fairly well organized gang at work on our coaches, headed by some sort of robber chieftan . . . *Saguro,* if I recall the alias. So, it appeared time to come out and see for myself, just what we can do about this *Saguro* and his forty thieves."

"I passed on the information to Chief Hume that was contained in the letter taken from the dead bandit at Agua Prieta," Kosterlitzky smiled. "I presume you did the same with your immediate superior, Thorne?"

"I did just that, and Thorne, at last, has seemed to come around to my way of thinking about the organized gang."

Hume lit up his cigar, a Gold Coast Twister, and looked at Kosterlitzky. "There's got to be something to it. Thorne's one of the best, but we all have our blind spots."

"Sergeant," the Ruales Colonel cleared his throat. "You have been supplied with helpful information from Cajeme?"

"Sure. We tried to nail Spence and Stilwell in the act when they tried for that Benson Coach at Walnut Gulch . . . but it fell apart." He watched Kosterlitzky.

"And you are wondering why the head of a police unit of a foreign country should be here in Tombstone . . . and cooperating with Wells Fargo, are you not?"

Ringold nodded, but remained silent.

"If we are correct, Chief Hume and I, considering what information Cajeme has furnished to us, there will be more attempts upon the coaches, and by the same men who are wanted in Mexico for various matters, as well as here."

"The Earps and Holliday?"

"Possibly." Kosterlitzky smiled cautiously. "You may as well know there are warrants out for two of the Earps, including Holliday . . . all issued by the Governor of Sonora Province in Mexico."

Hume, puffing hard on his cigar, broke in. "And that is where you, particularly, come in on the scene. There's no kind of law organization in Arizona Territory, comparable with your Texas Rangers, capable of enforcing a foreign warrant. Someday, soon, there may be some sort of ranger company for A.T., but not yet. There's just one U.S. Marshal for hundreds of square miles, and some local sheriffs . . . such as John Behan."

"And so, Sergeant, we want you, and your

255

friend Deal, if he will, to help spring the trap . . . and it seems that you had best do it soon, or whoever has declared open war on the Earps will, how do you say it, gum up the works," Kosterlitzky took up the commentary.

"I'll be glad to help, if you'll tell me just how we go about it."

"Sergeant, this is most confidential," Hume spoke up. "These people, and the unknown leader, are fanatics, devoted to taking just what they want and killing when they have to . . . without compunction. So, we, and you, in particular, must stop them, by any means we deem necessary."

"Well," Ringold drew upon the cigar handed to him by Hume, and held it up to the light to inspect the fine head of ash. "I'd say that to pick up the Earps and Doc should just about solve the problem. The rest are pretty small potatoes . . . just sweepings of a frontier. And as for our mystery man, he'd have to look around for another set of varmints."

"This is just what we wish to do," Kosterlitzky responded. "Pick them up with our warrants, the next time you get anything on them. And when that happens, they'll be spirited out of town and across the border to stern Mexican justice!"

"So, what happens now?" Ringold inquired.

"According to our good friend from below the line here, his Cajeme has informed him that the gang won't give up, despite the shooting of Virgil and is getting ready to really lambaste Wells Fargo in the coming months toward spring," said Hume.

"Does Cajeme think this would include Spence and Stilwell, or just the Earp bunch, now the rest seemed killed off," Ringold inquired, accepting another of Hume's fine stogies.

"From all he has overheard at the camp, and in certain reliable quarters of Tombstone, while Spence and Stilwell are part of the outer circle of the gang, Holliday, and Wyatt, in particular, are the pair most apt to be involved in more robberies," Kosterlitzky replied.

Ringold arose and stalked to the window, and stood puffing on his weed, staring up and down Fremont. "I know that I'll have my eyes peeled, and so will Pony, if he is still o.k. with you, Mister Hume."

Hume joined Ringold at the window. "Oh, Deal is all right, as far as that goes." He poked Ringold in the ribs with a thumb. "But it's up to you just how far you want to trust an, ah . . . horse trader." He drew deeply on his Gold Coast Twister, sending up a billow of blue smoke at the dingy panes. "But, one thing, Sergeant, there is to be no mention of this meeting to Deal, or anyone else."

"Anyone?"

"Right! And that includes even Thorne, for the moment. I'll inform him at the proper time. And most particularly there must be no loose talk about our visitor from Mexico here. We must be careful of international difficulties over those warrants, until things happen."

"That's all right. Pony doesn't pry. He's got his own business secrets, and I don't push him to level with me about them."

"Very well. In due time, I'll fill Thorne in on all aspects of this matter, as I have said. And now for the present, try to keep from any head-on collisions with Holliday or the Earps. I imagine they're about as jumpy as rattlers by now . . . though I can't imagine who the assailants were at the moment."

"I've an idea on that score," Kosterlitzky said, joining them at the window. He faced Ringold. "One never knows when the paths of friends will cross, and this has been such an event." He held out his hand to Ringold, who shook it firmly. "In the event that you are able to bring any of the bunch to justice, Cajeme has the warrants hidden in a safe spot . . . and you will have my deep gratitude, as well as that of Mexico, if you would help him serve them upon the proper culprits."

"And you have my permission, as special deputy of Wells Fargo, to not only do that, but aid in the transportation of Cajeme's prisoners right down to the border, and over, if you are needed," Hume added, also shaking hands with Ringold.

"I trust your leg has come along and that you are not troubled with it," the Ruales Chief walked to the door with Ringold. "And one final item. I have my own methods of information, as you may be aware. Anyway, here is one thing your Adjutant General King in Texas might not have told you as yet, perhaps as it just occurred. One of those men sent to the Texas Penitentiary at about the time you left the state to come to Arizona, a James Rush, I believe, has escaped confinement and vanished. You know who that might be?"

Jim Rush! It was odd that his folks, or King, hadn't written about that. But as Kosterlitzky said, it was too soon for them to get a line to him. "Yes, the leg seems to be mending o.k." He opened the hotel door and waved a farewell to both men. "By the way, that'd be an old acquaintance who's flown the coop. Well, let him fly. I sometimes think that jail isn't always the right answer."

"No," said Kosterlitzky closing the door. "It more often should be *ley del fuga*."

All through the remainder of the fairly mild month of December, and on into January of 1882, Ringold and Pony kept close to Tombstone, Pony making the rounds of the lower-class grog-shops, and Ringold playing cards around the better gambling places.

They learned nothing—with the exception that Virgil Earp was slowly recovering from the ambush, but with a permanently damaged arm.

Wyatt and Doc, making veiled threats against their "foes," from time to time, hung around their usual places of business—the gambling dens.

Morgan took on the job of guard at a string of business houses still rebuilding through the winter on Fourth, between Fremont and Allen. If any of the bunch meditated further raids on the coaches, Ringold and Pony couldn't turn up any evidence pointing that way.

The Yaqui, Florentino Cajeme, was in and out of town with wood for the restaurants and saloons. Several times, Ringold saw him unloading his cargo from the patient burro, but Kosterlitzky's agent made no effort to signal to him—so he kept on his way.

Spence and Stilwell came and went from Tombstone, seeming to keep to themselves pretty much. Yet Ringold could feel a tension slowly building with the dragging passage of each dull winter day. It seemed to him that old blind Fate had come into the arena to play its own hand in a game that bade to grow deadlier as time elapsed.

Ike Clanton stayed out of town—visited once by Pony, who reported him as still gleeful over Virgil's downfall, but vigorously disclaiming anything to do with midnight ambuscades.

Both Ringold and Pony made trips to Benson to report the complete lack of activity to a rather phlegmatic Thorne. "If he's not worried about someone crackin' his damned coaches, don't know why we should be," said Pony, very closely echoing Ringold's own feelings.

And yet he, *Ringo,* John Ringold, would never be contented nor willing to leave Arizona until Holliday and the rest were paid back, in spades, for the O.K. affair, if nothing else!

Then in the middle of February, making another attempt to jail the Earp bunch, Ike Clanton came back to Tombstone and swore out warrants for the arrest of Morgan and Wyatt Earp, and Doc Holliday, charging them with "the willful murder of his brother William Clanton, as well as the ensuing deaths of Thomas and Frank McLowry." The papers were served on the trio by Johnny Behan, and they were lodged in the city jail. This made the third time that Doc had been in the Tombstone jail, within a year.

The arrests made quite a noise for a day or so, and then with the release, on bond, of all three by Judge Spicer, Ike left town in a high state of disgust. Some saloon hangers-on, familiar with both parties, surmised that Clanton didn't feel up to facing the enraged Earps.

"He said he wouldn't give up. It was die dog or eat hatchet this time as far as he was concerned," Pony related to Ringold. "Wonder if he really had anything to do with that shooting of Virgil?"

"A straight flush to a bob-tail pair, someone around Tombstone knows more than he has ever let on," Ringold replied, thinking of Emilio Kosterlitzky's cryptic remark.

Despite the fact that Wyatt and Doc, in particular, moved around town breathing fire against Clanton and their midnight assailant, it was evident to Ringold that they were clearly spooked, and getting desperate. At last, the luck that had buoyed up the Earps and Holliday was beginning to desert them. They might have more devilment up their sleeves, but the deadly game they'd played across half of the west, from Kansas to New Mexico to Arizona was beginning to turn into a losing game.

On Friday evening, March 17, as a mild southern breeze out of Mexico was sweeping an early spring into Tombstone, Morgan Earp was shot and killed in Hatch's Saloon on Allen Street.

Ringold happened to be standing out on the boardwalk talking to Fred Dodge and Billy Breakenridge, and waiting for Pony, who'd ridden out to Clanton's Ranch to check on Ike, who'd laid low since losing his latest bid to imprison the Earps, when a series of shots blasted the night apart.

"B'gum that'd be from inside there!" Breakenridge stiffened at the sudden outcrash, and whirled to dart back through the swinging doors, now open to the mild weather. "Come on, lend a hand here, Ringo!"

As they dashed into the smoky interior of the place, all was uproar. Glass shards, blown out of the alley window, powdered the rear tables and two men were down on the sawdust-covered floor. One was a small-time gambler named George Berry, and the other—Morgan Earp!

Both died in the space of an hour. Berry succumbed to an old, reopened wound. Morgan, laid face down on one of the pool tables with a shattered spine, died surrounded by a frozen-faced Holliday, a wild-eyed Wyatt and Virgil, and a group of fellow gamblers that included Turkey Creek Johnson and Sherm McMasters.

"I'd say that just about puts th' cap-sheaf on th' hull gang, don't it?" Pony wanted to know as he and Ringold rode toward Benson to a mid-monthly meeting with Thorne, on Saturday following the Friday night shooting. Around them the desert was slowly coming to life as the blazing Arizona sun gleamed through brassy clouds that swept down from the surrounding mountains. Some hedgehog cactus were already touched with pink blossoms and here and there the yellow, wheel-shaped blooms of the desert marigolds brought a new vivid glow to the dull sandy mesas. Roadrunners were out after the vagrant, darting green streaks that were the early lizards, and overhead the curve of wings against a brightening sky bespoke the passage of many birds, from the great golden eagle to the numerous red-tailed hawks.

"I say, somebody's sure certain to help in whittlin' down th' Earps, without us firin' as much as a shot, eh?" Pony repeated his inquiry, aware of his companion's sombre mood, but determined to get the conversation moving. "Tell me, again, just what you saw, and how you figured out th' hull deal?"

"As I said, Breakenridge yelled at me to come on . . . him being the only lawman on duty, and we hustled into the saloon not half a minute after those three shots . . . all pistol shots. And by that time one of the Hatch's employees, Tipton, the dice man, had ran out into the alley, but saw no one."

"Or so he said."

"Or so he said, but whoever fired those shots must have known exactly where Morgan Earp was standing . . . because he got him dead center, in spite of the lower glass being painted white."

"Talk is that Spence, Stilwell and that Injun Charley, who you call Cajeme, was all in town that night. All left town mighty soon after th' killin's," said Pony.

"You're saying that one of those three pulled the trigger on Earp?"

Pony spat downwind from his buckskin and pushed his dingy sombrero back on his head. "Well, if it ain't Ike, and I left him at th' ranch talkin' cheerful to a bottle when I came back to town, then it just might be Spence or Stilwell or th' Injun. I can't see that Clanton would try anythin' quite so low-down. Ike claims he'll get them legal in th' courts."

"He hasn't had much luck, so far," Ringold replied, thinking to himself that Pony might be right about those three, and wondering just what Kosterlitzky had been hinting at. Well, whatever, he had an idea that time was running out for them all.

15 Doc's Prescription

The meeting with Thorne brought a number of revelations to Ringold and Pony.

The Wells Fargo man appeared to have made a complete turn-around from his former stand that there was nothing to the idea that an organized band of cutthroats was hard at work robbing Wells Fargo. His first words, uttered in the confines of his closed office, dispelled all that.

"From what Hume said, when he was here on a flying-trip recently, he, apparently, has gained access to certain information that we have not been aware of, and that information seems to bear out the fact of a highly-professional gang at work. Do either of you two have any idea who the leader, *Saguro,* could be?" Thorne polished away at his specs, a sure sign that he was thinking.

Pony and Ringold glanced at each other, and shrugged. "Could be anybody from Tombstone or Benson for that matter, or Gawd knows where," Pony muttered.

Ringold noticed that Thorne had seemed unaware of his meeting with Hume and Kosterlitzky at Tombstone and wondered what Thorne would say if he knew the Wells Fargo Chief had expressly forbade mention of the matter. "I have an idea that it wouldn't be Wyatt, as he's too apt to fly off the handle. I have reservations about Doc Holliday, though. For that rascal is cold clear through, though he rather fell down on the job back when he was definitely identified for his part in the robbery of the Benson Stage last March. So, it has to be some man used to using his head, which Holliday can do, when he's a mind to."

"There has to be something in your view, but it is pretty hard to believe that any of our business-men would be hand in glove with such people as Leonard, Head, Stilwell and Spence, and that half-breed that hangs out with him," replied Thorne, holding his glasses up to the brassy light coming in from the alley window. "But one possibility that has come to me recently is the fact that someone in the Tombstone office of Wells Fargo has been doing the master-minding, or at least tipping off the outlaws." He paused, and then adjusted his specs back upon his nose. "You know who I am referring to?"

"Couldn't be Marsh Williams and . . . , or could it?" Pony stared open-mouthed at Thorne.

"Fred Dodge? It is just a thought, but who else down there has access to secret informa-tion regarding the bullion shipments?" Thorne reached into his drawer and extracted a folded sheet of paper. "No, though Dodge is operating as our undercover man at Tombstone, and I grant you does not appear to have too massive an intellect, it would be a thought worth pursuing a bit more vigorously."

"I've got to thinking that myself over the past few weeks," Ringold sat up in his chair and rubbed his chin.

Thorne lapsed into silence for a moment, drumming his fingers upon his desk. "Yes, I'm inclined to agree, but it is a matter that had best be pursued very quickly if we are to get anywhere." He took up the sheet of paper and regarded it with obvious distaste. "I just don't know how to break this to you, but let me read the message. *'Main Office, Wells Fargo, San Francisco, California. This is to inform you we must dispense with the services of John Ringold of the Texas Rangers, now on detached service. As of the first of the month, Sergeant Ringold is relieved of any duties connected with the protection of monies and bullion transported in our strong-boxes, as well as in the pursuit and apprehension of any criminals responsible for robberies of Wells Fargo shipments. You are hereby ordered to pay him up to the first of the month. Signed Hume.'"*

Pony sat, jaw ajar, staring at Ringold, having taken in the unmistakable fact of his partner's true identity and rank in the Texas Rangers.

Ringold was too surprised by the contents of the letter to do more than give Pony a short grin.

After a long pause, Thorne cleared his throat

and spoke. "Really this is too bad. But typical home office procedure. I'm not exactly sure that Jim Hume initiated the idea. Probably came from one of our vice-presidents, after looking over the expense sheets."

"Does that mean me too?" Pony wanted to know, still looking at Ringold.

"No, not for the moment." Thorne stood up behind his desk. "Well, I really didn't know how to break it to you. But I'll be issuing you a pay voucher the first of the month, including the reward monies due for the slaying of Head and Crane. So, until then you are still on the payroll. Any idea what you'll do after?"

Ringold had no ready answer. "I don't know. Stay around for a while, I suppose . . . until I get straightened out with the Rangers. Then back to Texas, I reckon." He looked at Pony who was scratching his head and staring out the window. No need to mention it, but he wasn't about to pack and ride for Texas—yet. There were too many loose ends dangling. Damned if he wouldn't still try to nail the Earps and Doc— and help Cajeme serve those Mexican warrants. It was odd that Thorne lumped the Yaqui with Stilwell and Spence. He'd not thought much about it, but Kosterlitzky had hinted that there was someone gunning on the sly for the Earps. And maybe Cajeme was that one?

With little more than a handshake they parted

from Thorne and, getting their horses from the livery, rode back through the pleasant March day and were in Tombstone before nightfall. After the initial jolting disclosure as to Ringold's identity, Pony, apparently, shrugged it off and continued to call him *Ringo.* It was obvious that, as *Pony Deal,* he had ample experience with aliases on his own.

Both were still puzzled by the meeting with Thorne. Ringold could not figure out why Hume would let himself be pressured by pen-pushers in the home office—but had to admit that his record as thief-taker was pretty poor. Possibly Hume had to go along with his superiors.

When they turned in their mounts at the Pioneer Livery on Tough Nut, Pony put it into words. "Something damned funny about all this, but the best thing to do is wait and see what turns up. Wyatt and Doc are bound to be up to something pretty soon. I hear Virge's doctor bills and Morg's funeral expenses just about ate up their rolls. So, I guess we wait and see."

"Yes, and keep a closer watch on Fred Dodge," Ringold replied as they parted to go to their respective hotels, Ringold still at the Residential and Pony at the Occidental.

Pulling off his boots in his room that night, Ringold had a long soul-searching session with himself. Unable to disclose to Pony, Hume's recent clandestine appearance and, still baffled by the turn of events, he felt himself puzzled and frustrated. But he was still determined to see the Earp-Holliday gang behind bars, whether in the Territorial Prison at Yuma or in a Mexican jail, it didn't matter.

He debated sending a wire to Uncle Bill at Ranger Headquarters in Austin, but held off. It would seem like a calf bawling for its mother, he told himself.

Another puzzlement was the actions of the Yaqui, Cajeme. While killing time around town he'd noticed the woodcutter delivering fuel from his mule wagon at various restaurants and saloons, and was sure Cajeme had spotted him, but the Indian still made no moves to contact him. So, how in the devil would he get a line on the next stickup if he didn't have advance information from the Yaqui? It all added to the growing frustration building within himself, and to cap the whole affair came the suspicion, suggested by both Kosterlitzky and Thorne, that Cajeme could be the nighttime assassin.

"You seem to have dried up on th' talk overnight," Pony observed as they met for breakfast at the Can Can on Sunday morning. "I could get more speech out of Ike Clanton than you, and I ain't seed him in a couple'a weeks."

"Nothing to talk about," Ringold replied, wondering if Pony was fishing to get some

271

information concerning his background in the Rangers.

"Well, here's somethin' to chaw over with those flap-jacks." Pony leaned across the coffee cups. "Take a gander at that!" And he shoved a folded sheet across the table.

It was an unaddressed note, written in pencil in a crabbed backhand, upon good, lined paper. *"Make final plans to stop the bullion box on the night of March 20th. Take T.P., plus two more and stake out at the spot agreed upon last month. Hit it hard and we'll shake Arizona's dust forever."* It was signed, *Saguro.*

"Great Nelly! Where'd you get that?" Ringold was jolted out of his depressed mood.

"Right out of th' pocket of Mister Wyatt Earp." Pony smiled like a sheep-killing dog. "I got as many hidden talents as you, I guess."

"But how?"

"Wyatt got himself a snootful last night at th' Palace, where I was playin' cards after we got back from Benson. I up and volunteered to help him home, along with Turkey Creek Johnson, who ain't too bright. So, we led him off—with me feelin' mighty sorrowful over all th' dirty skunks who been makin' a shootin' gallery outa th' Earps. And while Turkey Creek was shuckin' Wyatt out'a his boots, I hung up his coat and stuff. And I just, natcherly, went through his stuff."

"The night of March 20th . . . that's tomorrow night! And where'd they stop the coach? We don't know the spot they're talking about. And who in blazes is this T.P.?"

"I'm more awake than you, even if I'm jest a simple saddle tramp and no Texas Ranger." Pony grinned slyly and tugged his scraggly mustache. "But I had all night to think that one over. Who's there left for pore old Wyatt to ride with? Only Doc Holliday ain't it. And *T.P.* ought to mean *Th' Physician,* right?"

"You may be right, but that still leaves the other two and the site of the holdup." Ringold looked over the note. There was an obvious attempt to disguise the handwriting, and yet it had a familiar look. Then he recognized it as being very close to the crudely printed letter taken from the dead bandit, Leonard, in Mexico. Here there was no use of the usual code names. Doubtless *Saguro,* the mystery man was under too much stress to go into such niceties.

"One day! What say, we take a ride about noon down to see Ike and check over the possible robbery sites while we're gone. Make the rounds of the bars before then. Let it out we've decided to go visiting." Then he was struck with a thought. "What will Earp do when he finds the note gone? Will it cause them to call off the raid?"

"Oh, it's a chance we got to take, I'd say, but

273

from th' looks of things, I don't think they've got much time to make any changes. Earp'll think he lost it along th' way and go about his business. He wouldn't get th' word to old man *Saguro* that he made a blamed fool of himself, and lost it. You bet he won't!"

"I know you and your bets. Get along and drop the word we're riding down to see Ike, for we don't want anyone following and reading our trail. This has got to be the time we nail Earp and Doc to the barn wall. Remember I'm gone for Texas after the first of the month—off the payroll for good."

The chance had come at the last minute to clean up the bunch, and while he was still in the employ of Wells Fargo, and he meant to grab it with both hands.

The ride down to the Clanton Ranch was completely unproductive. Ike was not at home. A ranch hand said Clanton had been gone for two days.

Ringold and Pony rode back to hit the Bisbee-Tombstone Road, arriving there in the late afternoon. Storm clouds were lowering over the Dragoons, blanketing the serrated blue tops with grey shreds, reminiscent of shrouds. The light of the late March evening seemed subdued and wan, and even the sun, when it fought itself out of the gloomy heavens, was pallid looking.

Riding first toward Bisbee, with the high-shouldered bulk of Potter Mountain on their left, they neared the rocky defile where the Bisbee Stage had been waylayed by bandits, and where Pony and he had waited and watched the Earps rein-in to search out the vanishing loot. Pausing, they soon rode on, Ringold wrapped in thoughts of that night, and filled with all the gloomy possibilities of another unsuccessful attempt to foil another robbery. But, he told himself, he had to pull this one off. There wouldn't be another chance!

Their course took them back toward Tombstone, with several stops to check out other possible ambush spots.

Pulling up on the top of a rise that looked toward the spindling mine shafts and smoking smelter stacks, they paused to breathe their mounts in the grey dusk.

"We've wandered at a good dozen places where them blacklegs could throw down on a coach, and damned if there ain't two dozen more all th' way to Benson, including that spot up at Walnut Gulch," Pony gloomily remarked. "Just where in blazes are we goin' to squat tomorrow night?"

"Yes, it's like trying to catch raindrops in a sieve," returned Ringold, looking off toward the purpling slopes of the Dragoons, where lay the wood camp of Pete Spence. He kept thinking of the Yaqui. Was Cajeme suspected by that brutal pair, Spence and Stilwell? And how could he get to him to see those Mexican warrants were served?

"If that Injun Charley could slip us th' information as to where th' raid was comin' off, it'd sure help," said Pony, kicking his buckskin into motion to keep abreast of Ringo's great black.

"If there's two rival gangs, and one of 'em is Spence and Stilwell, I don't think the Yaqui will be much help. It looks like this one will be all Holliday and Earp, and I don't believe they'll call in Pete Spence and Frank Stilwell." Ringold spurred on toward Tombstone and supper.

"Guess you're right. Anyway, maybe we can turn up somethin' or other, for we got till tomorrow night," Pony shouted, lashing his piebald mount after Ringold. "We might get lucky and grab th' hull damned bunch. Damned if I don't feel lucky fer some reason. Yeah, Mister Wyatt Earp and cold-fish gunman Holliday . . . this is th' time we git you. And I bet on that!"

Before midnight of the same evening, Pony had lost another bet. The Benson Stage was successfully held up five miles out of Bisbee, exactly on the same spot of the former robbery, attributed to Spence and Stilwell.

Killing two birds with one stone, Ringold and Pony had been playing a four-hand game of red dog with Marsh Williams and Fred Dodge in the back room of the Wells Fargo office—taking their money and keeping an eye on both employees, when the coach pulled in at 11:30 with an agitated cargo of voluble passengers, and cursing crewmen.

The last passenger to disembark was none other than Jim Hume. He spotted them immediately and beckoned them over. "Well, here's hell in a hand-basket!"

"Got th' jump on us agin. Pulled 'er off a day before, just on th' chance somebody got at that damned message," Pony whispered out of the side of his mouth as they waved to Hume and approached the irate lawman.

"Mister Hume," Ringold acknowledged the burly Wells Fargo Chief. "Did they get much?"

"Get much?" Hume pulled back his checked frock coat to display a pair of empty pistol holsters. "Got my six-shooters, and all the cash I had on me . . . plus cleaning out the passengers!"

"But . . . did they get the bullion?"

Hume narrowed his eyes in the raw glare of the lanterns being swung here and there, as Johnny Behan, Marsh Williams and Fred Dodge inspected the bullet holes in the coach. "No, that bullion from the Bisbee smelter was due to come through tomorrow night, then it was changed back to tonight. I found out about that and, just on a crazy hunch, I had it slated back to tomorrow night. They missed that."

"Spooked into pulling this one too soon," said Pony.

"But outsmarted," Ringold told Pony.

"Too soon? Outsmarted? Just what in hell are you two talking about?"

In a few words, Ringold informed him of the note plucked from Earp, and its contents. As he figured, he was overheard by Johnny Behan, who came over and introduced himself to Hume.

"Know you by reputation, Mister Hume. This is a damned bad thing to happen, but no one was hurt, so the driver tells me." Behan glanced shrewdly at Ringold and then Pony.

"What do you propose to do about this latest outrage, Sheriff?" Hume tackled Behan. "This robbery was as close to Tombstone as to Bisbee, or nearly, and I figure you could raise up a posse here faster."

"Well now," Behan rocked back slightly and sat his lantern down. "Did you identify the perpetrators? I find from talking to the driver and the passengers that no one got a good look at the robbers' faces."

"No, we didn't get to see the blackguards' faces, but I can bet a Chinese dollar to a plugged peso that it was those Earps and Holliday. Here, show him that note." Hume took the folded piece of paper from Ringold and thrust it at the Sheriff.

Behan took the paper and held it up to his

lantern, squinting at the writing. "Humm. Well, that don't say who it was, as I can see."

"No, but it came out of the pocket of one Wyatt Earp of your town!" Hume took the note back and replaced it in his own pocket. "Where is Earp and Holliday? Do you know?"

Behan didn't and admitted it. "I just got back from Tucson this evening from taking a prisoner over, and my deputy, Breakenridge has gone off to San Francisco on a trip. So I guess we'll have to start to make inquiries." He looked at Ringold in the lantern light. "If it's any of my business, how'd you get that note away from Earp?"

"Pony, here, saw him drop it the other night."

"Why didn't you turn it over to a proper lawman, Deal?"

"You been out of town, remember?" Pony grinned at a puzzled Behan.

"Here! Here! Let's stop this," Hume bristled, obviously still under great strain. "What about that posse?"

"Maybe we can get one up in the early morning." Behan held his low-crowned sombrero in one hand and ran the fingers of his other hand through thinning hair. "Y'know this is really pretty odd at that!"

"Odd? What's odd?" Hume scowled.

"I know that Ringo, here, will see it . . . being from Tombstone." Behan moved closer after looking around at the milling crowd. "I'm going to serve papers on Wyatt and Doc, and when I find 'em, tonight or tomorrow, they get papers served on 'em!"

Ringold felt a hot thrill run through him. This could be it at last! And if they could pin this stickup on Wyatt and Doc—*that'd be it!* "Who swore out your warrants?"

"Ike Clanton had them made out in Tucson two days ago, and I picked them up when I delivered my prisoner over there."

Ringold and Pony looked at Behan. "Well, Ike don't give up easy, does he?" remarked Pony.

"Need help with those warrants?" Ringold asked Behan.

"Got to find them first. Don't know as if any of 'em are in town at the moment," replied Behan, looking thoughtfully at the bullet holes in the Concord.

"I'd give a good hefty bet that they're nearby, but out of sight," said Pony, adjusting his pistol belt.

"Well, gentlemen, if there's a chance that the Sheriff can get after the culprits . . . Earps or whoever, let's leave it until early morning." Hume picked up his telescope bag and raised an eyebrow at Ringold, who nodded.

"I'll go on up town and show Mister Hume where to bed down," Ringold said, pointedly ignoring Pony and looking at Behan. "If you need help with that posse, bright and early, I'm your man."

As he set off with Hume, he managed a word with Pony. "Keep an eye on Fred Dodge, he didn't look as flabbergasted as I'd have thought he would."

Pony nodded and slouched back into the Wells Fargo office after Dodge and Marsh Williams, while the coach made ready to go on toward Benson with such passengers as felt up to the continuing trip. Several had hastened up town to the nearest saloon with their baggage.

Hume thanked Ringold after he'd signed the register of the American Hotel. "No need to come up, Sergeant. I've got to get away by myself and think this thing over. The robbery and that business you told me about, as we walked up here . . . that message purporting to come from me at the home office, cutting you out at the first of the month. Danged funny that!" He held out his hand. "Good night. See you in the morning when your rather reluctant Sheriff finds himself a posse, providing he doesn't serve his warrants tonight."

"Oh, Johnny Behan is straight enough, but I don't think he'll do anything before tomorrow." Ringold went back across to his own quarters. He didn't feel like prowling the streets for the Earps or Holliday, who he knew would be back in town by now with cast-iron alibis. He wanted a good night's sleep, for he had a feeling Monday, March 20, 1882 would be a red-letter day on Tombstone's calendar—and the Earps'!

The disinterested night clerk at the Cosmopolitan yawned as he handed over a sealed note. "That Injun Charley stopped by earlier and left this for you. Probably a wood bill."

Ringold paused in the hallway and hurriedly scanned the message in the flickering yellow lamplight: *"The birds of prey will fly tomorrow. I have my government's warrants with me and will serve them. You could be of great help, if you would meet me at the Tucson railway station at six in the evening, before their train leaves. In the meanwhile, I will stick as close to them as the cockle burr."*

The unsigned, but well-written note was an eloquent indication of the Earp gang's finale in Arizona Territory.

So, they were running for it, and tomorrow. As he sat on the edge of his bed, his mind whirled with possibilities. Two sets of warrants! Wyatt, Doc and Company were finally boxed in tight. That damned bullion was really set to go up for certain!

Came a knock at the door and Pony sidled in. "Fred Dodge went to th' Palace and had himself two drinks, but only talked to th' bartender . . .

far as I could see. Then he left before Doc and that crippled-up Virgil come in."

"They were at the Palace already? Doc must have made good time."

"That's what I was thinkin'. Anyway, right after Dodge left, Johnny Behan come in too. But he didn't seem to want to nail 'em. Guess it was because Wyatt wasn't with th' pair."

Ringold rubbed his game leg, which had been acting up with the changeable weather, while he filled Pony in on the big news.

"Hunh! They're really lightin' a shuck at last. Well, it figgers."

"What figures?"

"After Dodge left and Johnny Behan stood around blinkin' at Doc and Virge like a barn owl, I sidled up th' bar close enough to listen to 'em. I heard just part of their lingo, before they noticed me and moved over to a corner table. Doc was sayin', that when th' hull damned deal goes up, his prescription fer th' boys was to *take one horse each . . . and ride to hell out fer good!*"

16 Murder in the Mountains

Ringold and Pony met in the early morning and made their way over to the Sheriff's office, without waiting for Hume to show up. This was one game in which Ringold wanted to handle the cards, himself.

He'd not been too surprised to hear from Pony Deal that Wyatt had got back into Tombstone very late on a fagged-out horse, and refused to accept Behan's warrant. According to what Pony heard, Wyatt had threatened to fight Johnny off if he tried to use force to serve the papers.

Upon reaching Behan's office, they discovered that the entire Earp party, including Virgil and Doc, had set out for Benson at daybreak.

"Didn't think they'd pull right out, lock, stock and barrel, but they did, and now we got to haul 'em back on suspicion of that Bisbee job, as well as Ike Clanton's complaint," stuttered a badly shaken John Behan, as he waved a sheaf of warrants for Wyatt and Virgil Earp, as well as Doc Holliday, and Turkey Creek Johnson—all signed by Judge Fitzgerald of Pima County.

"If I could ride with you two, I'd be proud as Punch," Behan continued as he swore them in as special deputies in his lamp-lit office. But Johnny wasn't going along. "I'm just too short-handed to ride out and leave this town wide-open, what with that kid of a Breakenridge off in San Francisco!"

Ringold had taken the warrants and stuffed them in his inside coat pocket. He ignored Behan's real reason—the threats made against the Sheriff by Earp and Holliday, the night before. No, John Behan was too wise an old prairie owl to risk his neck in an ambush by that pair.

And so Ringold and Pony loped off, with the March sun heating their backs, heading for Benson, where, according to Sim Blake, the livery man, who'd heard their talk, that the Earps had definitely intended to catch the afternoon train for Tucson and points beyond.

"They all went a'poundin' through here," the fat storekeeper at Drew's Station, reported. "Knew it was Holliday and th' rest of them Earps, bekase they drew rein, right in front of th' Emporium, and was jined up by that Injun wood-cutter of Pete Spence's, who rid in at about th' same time."

Ringold wasn't too surprised, for Cajeme's message had informed him that the Yaqui would stick as close to the Earps as he could. But riding with them? He had a cold premonition that the mounting sun couldn't warm away.

Arriving at Benson shortly past noon, they checked in at the Wells Fargo Office on Grant and found, to their puzzlement, that Thorne had been gone since Doc Holliday came striding in at nine in the morning.

"Don't rightly know when Mister Thorne actually left," the head clerk reported. "When I knocked on the door about eleven, the place was empty. Of course, I wouldn't have thought much about that, for Mister Thorne often comes and goes out the back way. But when I found that the office safe was rifled and papers all over, I ran up the street to inform Marshal Jackson."

Pony and Ringold exchanged glances.

"Know if Thorne's been seen since?" asked Ringold.

"Not in the past several hours. But there must be a logical reason for his absence, if I could think it through."

"Well, keep thinking." And Ringold and Pony went out the front door, without a look at the empty back office.

"You hightail up to that Marshal, and see what he's doing about this, but don't mention the warrants . . . it's not his business," Ringold ordered Pony. "I'll check the depot and see if those sidewinders showed up to buy tickets for Tucson, though I don't think they did."

"Why not?" Pony stopped in his tracks and stared at Ringold with an odd light in his eyes.

"A couple of things. If they've got Thorne, they won't take him onto the train here. I think they'll hit through the mountains over to Tucson."

"Think they got him for a hostage?"

"Right now I'm not thinking. I'm too riled up about Florentino Cajeme. I'm bothered they might see through him and pull triggers."

"Hell, a damned Injun like that!"

"Shake it up," Ringold told Pony. "We've not only got to find Cajeme, but Thorne! Because if Doc and the Earps have them, I don't think either one will live to get over to Tucson." He'd ignored Pony's comment on Cajeme, for Deal had not been aware of the Yaqui's undercover work—beyond the fact that the Indian had spied on Spence and Stilwell for Ringold.

When he rode Blackbird across to the brick and stone station, he found there was no reliable information to be had. The station master had not seen Holliday, or the Earps, or Thorne. No one answering their description had shown up to buy a ticket anywhere. And, according to the station master, the next train for Tucson wasn't due until supper time. No, the Earp Gang was sticking to its horses, with its guests—willing or otherwise.

He found Pony in front of the Marshal's small adobe jail house. "That old lawdog in there is about one cut below Johnny Behan. Says Thorne has probably gone off with Doc. He just ain't worked up about it at all. He's a real trouble-dodger, if you'd ask me." Pony closed up and moved down the wooden sidewalk as a paunchy, red-faced man, with a silver badge pinned to his checkered vest, ambled out and stood rocking on his heels, chewing at a toothpick.

"As I said there, *Mister* Pony Deal. I think Mister Thorne can take keer of'm self. We'll wait a day and see what turns up . . . and I'll bet you aces to queens it'll be Ben Thorne. He's took a day or so off before for a sociable game."

"Thorne gamble much?" Ringold asked the pudgy officer.

"Well Mister, if'n it's any of your business . . . yes. Ben Thorne likes poker about as well as th' next man. Hell, him and Holliday, he's supposed to be off with, has been buttin' heads and hands ever since that damned Doc lit in th' Territory two years and more back."

"Where to now?" Pony asked, fiddling with his stirrup before untying his buckskin from the hitching rack.

"Well, if Holliday, and the rest aren't in any of the local gambling spots, and we'll chance it they're not, I'd say they're on the trail for Tucson. They've got five hours to catch that evening train over there. And if we don't get there before that, somebody had better watch out." He still hadn't mentioned Cajeme's role with the Mexican warrants and the part he and Pony would have to play in serving those papers.

Pony took one look at Ringold and kicked his mount into a gallop that took him westward out of Benson. Ringold followed hard on his heels with a spurred-up Blackbird.

By three o'clock they had forded a branch of the San Pedro and were edging up into the foothills. The upper mesas were now covered with the tall spikes of the early-blooming penstemons, with their gaudy, bell-like blossoms ranging from pale violet to blazing scarlet. These gradually gave way to the vivid red of the star-studded skyrocket gilias, interspersed among the bushy junipers. Mantled chipmunks and rockchucks darted from their path as the horses lunged and jolted up the constantly increasing incline, while mountain jays circled in screaming annoyance.

By the time they reached the great stands of timber, wreathing the Rincons, they rode along, dwarfed by the huge, sentinel-like ponderosa pines and giant white firs. Daylight, flattening out with the declining sun, became so diffused it seemed near evening although a good three hours of daylight remained until nightfall.

"This is the best way over to Tucson?" Ringold inquired when they paused on the summit of Rincon Mountain to let their horses blow. It was the first words he'd spoken since they'd left Benson. And Pony brightened at the words.

"Sure pop! See that big, split pine? A pretty easy track leads on down from there to th' bottom of th' mountain, and on inter town."

They took the trail down through thickets of

western box elder that eventually opened into stands of silver fir and black locust to give way to an open grassy area. Riding out into the still sunny clearing, a huddled bundle at the base of a great fir caught their eye.

"Say! Ain't that th' Injun? They must have popped him and dumped him here," Pony shouted.

They were off their mounts and both approaching Cajeme on the run.

Ringold stood silently looking down upon the unmoving Yaqui while his mind churned slowly. He tried to speak, but seemed unable to voice his bitter anger as he clenched his fists helplessly.

Pony, however, never completely lost his voice. "Hell, if they give it to him . . . they must'a got Mister Thorne too! That *Saguro*'s been cleanin' house, whoever th' black hearted devil is."

They spread out after another look at Cajeme's corpse, where it lay with a good half-dozen bullet holes in its body—two in the head and four in the back. It was a simple case of cold-blooded, brutal murder. No other way.

They scouted around over the clearing where nothing moved but the wind sighing through the trees and a bird or two that seemed songless. There was no indication of why the Yaqui had been killed there, except for the beginnings of a small fire, now only a few charred pieces of log that had been kicked around by the great fir tree's base.

"Looks like they was goin' to have some coffee or somethin' and then changed their mind," Pony offered, poking a charred stick with his toe.

Ringold carefully searched the dead man's pockets. They yielded little beyond a tobacco pouch, a small mirror, and a scattered handful of Mexican and American coins. There was no sign of the Mexican warrants.

He backed off from Cajeme, and mounting up, signaled Pony to ride. The rest of their route down the narrow mountain trail, winding among the thinning stands of timber, was filled with ominous silence.

Pony, jolted into a silence of his own, had little to say, except to indicate his bewilderment by a shrug now and then, with sidelong glances at Ringold.

Ringold, himself, maintained a poker-faced calm that he didn't feel. As he rode, he racked his brain over and over—as to who *Saguro* could be. Perhaps *he'd* meet up with the gang at Tucson, and leave with them. Anyway he and Pony were narrowing the distance between *Saguro* and his band—and the day of reckoning was nigh at hand, as the old-time preachers would put it.

At last they were out of the timber, had traversed the open stretches of the lower slopes and were nearing the sandy barrens surrounding Tucson. In the distance toward the north there was evidence of some buildings and closer at hand a narrow stage road, which they presently took in the direction of town.

Riding down the empty road, they found it swinging close to the railway. Within the hour, the road brought them to the outskirts of Tucson. The slanting sun was lowering behind a bank of red-streaked thunderheads. The sky above was darkening, as much from the nearing storm as from the time of day. A low rumble was followed by another, and another.

"Gonna rain like Billy-Be-Blowed," observed Pony, finding his voice again after the silent journey.

"How far up to the depot?"

"Oh, she sits about two blocks from here up in th' yards. Tucson is th' make up point for trains runnin' as far off as Californy and up to Colorady." As he spoke, the first drops of the storm came pelting down into the roadway, like small bullets kicking up the dust.

They rode past the brewery on 16th and crossed Simpson, unnoticed by the hurrying groups of Tucson citizenry, interested only in getting out of the storm. Dismounting, they tied up at the iron-pipe railing in front of one of the Southern Pacific storage sheds, just as the California bound Immigrant Special came chuffing through the yards, trailing a long, smoky banner of steam behind its coaches.

"Made it!" Pony yelled above the hissing clank of the passenger's slowing progress. "We'll still get th' dirty devils!" He shook his pistol as the Special pounded past them, filling the damp air with the acrid odors of burnt grease and coal, to eventually grind down to a halt by the brick-red depot.

"Yes, if we see them," Ringold shouted, loosening his six-shooter in its worn leather holster. He was suddenly gripped with the fear that they might not catch sight of the Earp party, and *Saguro,* in time. Perhaps the gang had ridden up on the line to get the train at some upper station. "How long will she lay over here," he queried Pony.

"Five to ten minutes," Pony bellowed and then dropped his voice. "Want me to get out th' Winchester and open up from here?" The steady falling rain, coupled with the clouds of billowing steam from the several panting engines in the yard, was obscuring their vision badly.

"No, you damned fool! You could hit any number of innocent folks!" While he spoke, the rain began to peter off somewhat, but the thunder clapped and roared right over their heads. The light of evening was still ominously red, as the near direct rays of the sun, setting behind the Tucson Mountains to the west, threw dozens of scarlet beams onto the depot and adjacent railway buildings, bathing all in a crimson glow. Pony's features were transmuted to the color of a red Indian.

"On your way up there," said Ringold. "If they're not aboard yet, they soon will be." He indicated a knot of people drifting out onto the wet station platform. "If the Earps are there, they probably won't be expecting to see you . . . but they'll sure be looking for me after what they did to Florentino Cajeme. Move!"

Pony dog-trotted up toward the depot to mingle with the crowd of drummers, miners and cattlemen along the platform. He was back in less than two minutes. "You'll never guess who's up there . . . not half a block from th' Depot. Ike!"

"That damned fool of an Ike Clanton in town?" Ringold squinted through the scarlet sunset and the red-tinted rainfall. "What about Earps?"

"Didn't see hide-nor-hair of 'em. But they still got five minutes or so. Might be in th' saloon across th' street, waitin' fer the last moment."

Ringold was caught off guard by the news of Ike's appearance. Then as he wiped the rain from his face and stared up at the depot, Pony let the rest of his bombshell loose.

"Ike's got hisself company. Frank Stilwell's up there with him, standin' there bold as brass."

"Stilwell and not Spence?" Ringold felt things

had begun to move, and move fast, yet found himself strangely motionless. He pulled his pistol, spun the cylinder, and rolled a stone over with the toe of his boot as he debated his course of action. "Why Stilwell, and not Spence?"

"Y'hear me? I said Stilwell, for he's always got th' most sand of that pair. Spence talks hard, but he's too much like Ike . . . all bluff. Stilwell's a little lion. Never says much, but'll fight from hell to breakfast. *And I think Ike's gonna set him on th' Earps!*"

While Ringold still hesitated, trying to make up his mind which way to move, with Johnny Behan's warrants, a long freight, which had partially obstructed their view of the station, began to chuff its way out of the yards on a southbound track.

At that instant, a group of men emerged from the depot and made their way through the loungers. One shuffled along, being supported by a companion, who carried a rifle. Several others in the party packed along weapons.

"That's Virge, still all crippled up. Must be goin' north with 'em to Colorady. And look!" Pony pointed at a short figure that came around the station and slipped into the shadows. "That's Frank Stilwell. Crazy Ike's let him loose! Hell's sure to pop now!" As if in answer, thunder cracked and banged across the darkening heavens.

By this time, the entire group of armed men had approached the first coach of the Special and were mounting the car's steps. Virgil was boosted aboard and vanished inside with the majority of the onloading passengers. The engine gave several shrill screams but remained motionless, its bell mournfully tolling through the murky evening was muffled by the diminishing downpour.

"Where's Thorne? They must have him penned in between them somewheres in that crowd." Pony was trembling with excitement as the tense moments stretched out. "What're you gonna do now?"

"There's Ike," Ringold said. "Where'd Stilwell get to?" He felt they should be getting up to the coaches, but something, some instinct, held him back—though the cars would be moving any minute now.

The bulky figure of Ike Clanton, broad-brimmed hat pulled down over his nose, was slowly following the trigger man, but staying clear of the passengers. Stilwell was now running down the tracks between the Special and a standing freight. They caught glimpses of him until he reached the end of the coaches.

"There's Doc!" Pony barked, pointing out another group emerging from the depot. "And that'd be Wyatt." He hesitated. "And that third one? Who'd that be?"

"Not sure," Ringold replied, cocking his Colt. "Could be Turkey Creek . . . or . . ."

"Nope! Turkey's taller'n that. Besides I think he got on right after Virge. Probably he's on board already with a gun stuck into Mister Thorne's ribs . . . though we must'a missed him too . . . and his guard!"

"Let's go pronto! We'll damn soon see who's who! Ease up to the head of the coaches and I'll get onto the rear car. Don't try to be a blamed hero. Tell them to pile out . . . and I'll flash Behan's warrants. But if they go for any trouble . . . give 'em what they gave the boys at the O.K!"

But before Pony and Ringold could get started toward the coaches, Doc and Wyatt suddenly began to run down toward the end of the train, where Stilwell had emerged from the other side of the cars to stand like a feisty little bulldog, feet apart, gun in hand—waiting!

Clanton had vanished from view, completely.

"Look out!" Ringold grabbed Pony's arm. "Get over there by this tool shed and let's see what they're up to." The train gave another mournful series of wails.

With the last shuddering whoop of the whistle, the rain, which had nearly ceased, began to fall heavily, while the last beams of the dying sun flamed around the Earps, until Ringold seemed to be viewing a procession of devils gallivanting after a lost soul.

There came the crack of a pistol—and then the rapid shots of a pair of repeating rifles.

"They've opened th' ball fer sure," gritted Pony as he and Ringold ran around the shed and across the wet cinders with drawn six-shooters.

"Yes," clipped Ringold, "and we'll close it for them!"

More shots echoed in the rainy dusk. It was Stilwell's reply to the Winchesters of Wyatt and the unknown man. Holliday, bereft of his scatter-gun, was throwing shots at the little fighter with a long-barreled Colt. The stabbing flashes of the explosions were vivid in the gloom.

Ringold and Pony came to a halt, near a line of cattle cars on a siding, twenty yards from the Special and the battling gunfighters. "Doc's using Wyatt's Buntline," panted Pony. "Wouldn't you know it!"

"Hell, why not? He couldn't hit the broadside of a bull's hinder, anyhow," answered Ringold, straining to see through the gathering darkness, looking for Ike, and tensely waiting to make his own move against the trigger-happy Earp bunch.

There was a sudden pause as the group at the rear of the train scattered or crouched. Three more shots barked out, and Stilwell crumpled to fall face-first into the cinders.

"Hold up there! Hold up, Earp! Over here! Put those guns on somebody more your size," Ringold shouted, leveling his six-shooter on the shadowy figures. Pony waited tensely with cocked pistol.

The gangling figure of Wyatt, and his companions scrambled up from the downed Clanton gunman. "It's Ringo! Let 'em have it!" howled Earp, as he and the others pumped Winchester and Colt's slugs at Ringold and Pony. The steel-jacketed bullets blasted clouds of splinters around their ears from the cattle car. They broke in opposite directions, Ringold going down on one knee for a better aim, while Pony dashed to the end of the car, as they exchanged shot for shot with the bunch—the guns' explosions ripping through the rainy night with stabs of sudden orange.

"Hell!" Doc gave a shriek while Wyatt's notorious six-gun spun out of his shattered fist. "That does me! Them bastards got me square in th' gun hand! Think every bone's broken!" And Holliday lurched around the passenger coach and out of sight.

Two more shots exploded. One from Wyatt's rifle and the other from a battle-wild Pony. Earp gave a muffled curse and hurled his Winchester toward Deal, where it slammed against the side of the cattle car to fall onto the rails with a clatter. "Jammed or empty," Wyatt bawled, darting up the other side of the train, like a departing bat, his long, deacon coat-tails flapping in the half-light.

The third man was down flat, beside Stilwell,

hit by either Ringold's or Pony's last shots. Suddenly the night was empty—except for the steady rainfall and the hoarse, shuddering high-ball whistle from the engine. The Immigrant Special jerked and creaked, the coaches banging into each other. Up ahead, red and green signal lanterns swung in the rain, while the train crept forward with purposeful panting.

"Come on!" Pony called. "We got to get on board there! Doc won't be no trouble anyhow. Sure as hell, they'll take Thorne along with 'em . . . if we don't stop 'em!"

"No, they won't," Ringold replied, pausing to look down upon the two prostrate forms in the wet cinders. "Thorne's not going anywhere!"

Scratching a match on his boot heel, he held the small flame over the face of the "third man." Its tiny, blue flare illuminated the features of Ben Thorne for a flickering instant before a raindrop blotted it into hissing oblivion.

"Mister Thorne!" Pony jammed his pistol back into its holster, and dropped on his knees in the wet cinders. "Those dirty devils! Is he still alive?"

"Still breathing. Get his boots and I'll take him by the shoulders, and we'll carry him over here by the freight shed." The Special was now half-way out of the yards. If the Earps and Doc were aboard, there was nothing he could do now. The crowd at the station milled about on the platform and gawked down toward them. A lantern or two began to bob in the direction of the tool shed.

"Here comes someone to check on the gunfire. And they can look at Stilwell for starters." Ringold nodded at the huddled form of Ike's gunman.

They deposited the barely-breathing Thorne in the shelter of an overhung section of shed roof. Scratching more matches, they stared at the wounded man while they cursed the vanishing train.

Thorne, glasses gone, blinked up at them. "Oh, Ringold . . . and Deal." His voice was halting and his words seemed hard to articulate.

"Mister Thorne, how'd you get away from those Earps? Did they plug you?" Pony hovered on one side of the wounded Wells Fargo Chief, while Ringold bent closer to study the man's face in the flickering light of the matches.

"Too late. Too late, now," Thorne murmured, the rain running down his pallid features. The thunder still cracked and banged overhead.

"Yes, *it is too late*," Ringold replied in a clipped, unemotional voice. "It's too late for everything . . . except to own up . . . *Mister Saguro*, alias Thorne!" He glanced over at Pony's incredulous expression. "What other jobs were you and the Earp crowd up to . . . before you all spooked and ran for it? Were you on the way with them, or were you running off to another hole?"

Pony stared, open-jawed, a sputtering match in his hand. With an abrupt grunt, he shook burnt fingers. The light went out.

"I was hoping . . . to leave . . ." Thorne's voice trailed off again, breath becoming labored.

"Damned unpeaceably, I'd say," Ringold answered. Through the thinning rain, he could see the conductor's lantern waving in farewell from the rear platform of the Special, as that train finally vanished into the night, bearing away Doc Holliday and his shattered hand—a hand that would never again manipulate the pasteboards, or handle a firearm to murder unarmed cowpokes. That same train, its whistle eerily echoing back from a distant crossing, was also bearing away the Earps—what was left of them—all leaving Arizona for good and into whatever remorseless oblivion reserved for that sort of border trash.

"He's in real pain." Pony was chafing Thorne's hands. "Think I ought'a go for a doctor?"

"I'll . . . be all right . . . Deal," Thorne spoke haltingly, reaching up a trembling hand to wipe at the rain on his face and seeming to feel for his vanished glasses. "Lost my specs somewhere, but that's all right."

"You've lost more than your glasses," Ringold answered. "How did you get yourself into such a fix, and who killed Cajeme?"

Thorne's answer was barely audible. "Might

302

I . . . ask you, a question, in turn? How you tumbled to me?"

"Yeah," Pony interjected. "How?"

"I'd been thinking for some time that you were the only one around with enough information . . . and enough brains . . . crooked or not . . . to run such a show."

Pony let out his breath, but, for once, said nothing.

"But," Ringold continued, "you haven't answered my own questions, how you got into this business."

"Holliday," Thorne replied, voice growing stronger. "When I first came into the Territory, Doc was already here . . . got me into some games . . . regular tiger-killing games in the back room of a Benson saloon. That was before he went down to Tombstone and teamed back up with Wyatt." Thorne coughed until Pony lifted him up by the shoulders. That appeared to ease him, for he went on. "Took me for so much I was forced to go along on some scheme. Told me one strike at the gold shipments would be all . . . then went back on his word . . . the devil!"

"But you were *Saguro,* the man that called the tunes?"

"Called the tunes? Maybe. But Doc and Wyatt collected for the dance." Thorne pushed himself up to a sitting position. "You asked who killed the Indian. Wyatt and Holliday riddled the poor devil as he began to cook us breakfast back in that mountain clearing. They said they'd suspicioned him spying on a couple of their own jobs down below the border . . . and so they sent word to him through Pete Spence that they'd pay him to go along on the trip to Tucson to cook or whatever they needed him for." Thorne began to slump down against the boards of the shed. "They said . . . they thought he was in on the shooting of Morgan Earp . . . and . . ." He slid back into the wet. "Sorry," he mumbled. "Sorry about the chicanery, Sergeant Ringold."

"Thorne! Thorne!" He shook the man, and nodded to Pony for a light. It was obvious that Thorne was going fast. His voice was now just the ghost of a whisper. Ringold bent down with his ear to the dying man's lips. "May have let something slip . . . when drinking . . . to Holliday. He found out, somehow, about you and Texas. He'd worked the gambling dens over there. Sent a letter to someone. It could make . . ." Thorne stopped talking—and breathing.

"Dead?" Pony whispered.

"And a lot better off," Ringold gritted, looking up to see the bulky form of Ike Clanton in the knot of people, who were inspecting the sprawled body of Stilwell, by the light of several lanterns.

Noting Ringold and Pony, Ike came over to the shed. "That you, Ringo . . . and ain't that Pony?" Ike stopped short at the sight of Thorne. "Gawd!

304

Who played hell here? Them Earp skunks?" He gestured across the tracks at the group surrounding Stilwell. "They settled his hash a'fore jumpin' that damned train and runnin' for it." Ike cursed and slammed his fist into his palm.

"Thorne there, he was in cahoots with th' Earps . . . same as you with Stilwell over there. And it don't matter now who was right and who was wrong. Both dead as door-nails. Funny ain't it?" But Pony didn't smile.

Before the crowd around Stilwell could fan out over the yard, Ringold and Pony bade Ike a curt farewell, and eased through the lines of freight cars. After doubling back to pick up their horses, they rode several blocks west through the poorer district and put up at a seedy, but quiet hotel— the Tucson House on Samniego Street.

Ringold knew the law would be called in when they discovered Thorne on the railroad property, but was pretty certain that if Clanton were spotted, Ike would have enough sense to keep his mouth shut about the shootings.

Ringold and a very subdued Pony turned in early, both agreeing to ride back to Tombstone the next day.

With six-shooter under his pillow and both Winchesters stacked in the room's corner, Ringold drifted off to sleep, mentally composing a telegram to the Texas Adjutant General, concerned with the smashing and scattering of the stagecoach gang. He couldn't get the words to Uncle Billy just right, but it didn't matter—he'd sort them out in the morning, and send the wire before leaving Tucson.

His last coherent thoughts were concerned with the fact that his time in Arizona Territory could be nearing the end—then, exhausted and wrung out by the events, he slept dreamlessly in the rickety, double-bed, despite Pony's rasping snores.

17 A Rider for Texas

Next morning Ringold walked three blocks over to the telegraph office on Stone and sent a telegram to the Adjutant General at Austin, Texas.

The operator shifted his green eye-shade slightly, but gave no other indication he was not handling a run-of-the-mill dispatch dealing with the price of silver bullion or a current quotation on beef cattle.

The phraseology eluding Ringold the night before, came to him clearly and concisely on the walk past the miners' shacks on Ochoa and the string of saloons along Meyer:

"Adjutant General William King, Austin, Texas. Gang involved in Wells Fargo robberies during past year broken up. Thorne of Wells Fargo killed. He was head man. Others including Earps and Holliday driven from Territory. Kosterlitzky agent killed by Earps. Awaiting orders. Signed, John Ringold, Sergeant Rangers."

It was a long message but he wanted Uncle Billy to have the full particulars. Paying the agent, he went back to the hotel and an early lunch with Pony at a nearby beanery.

While they ate, he kept on the watch for trouble. Someone might have recognized him from the shooting at the station.

"I say we get as soon as we can," Pony volunteered for the third time as they finished up their coffee and pie. "Expect an answer from your wire?"

"Yes, and I want to get it before we leave town," said Ringold. "I might as well tell you . . ." he hesitated. "If I get the right answer, I'll probably leave Tombstone within the week."

"Figured as much." Pony nodded at a group of cattlemen who were loudly rehashing the previous night's events at the railroad yards. "Y'hear? They say th' City Marshal's askin' a lot of questions from any strangers, tryin' to get a line on who plugged Thorne. And they say he figures Earp and Company cut th' string on Stilwell before th' train pulled out."

"I can hear."

"But what you don't hear is any mention of Ike Clanton."

"Why should anyone mention Ike?" asked Ringold as he paid the gaunt proprietor of the Elite Cafe for their meal.

"Because everyone over here knows Ike on sight, and would be puttin' two and two together . . . seein' his pal Stilwell got it. In other words, Ike's holed up good and tight, or he's left for Tombstone already."

"You're right. And we'll make tracks ourselves as soon as that wire comes in," said Ringold, walking outside, hitching at his gun belt. "No use getting into any bind with local law. Could take a hell of a lot of time with affidavits, statements and all the rest of such rigamarole, not counting court hearings."

"Want to get back to ridin' old Rio with your Ranger pards?" Pony flashed Ringold a crooked smile. "That's all jake with me. I got my own plans, now Mister Thorne's got no more use for my services, such as they happened to be."

"Here, sit down for a spell on this bench and level with me just why in hell you pulled that green slicker dodge on me back at Owl City, and Agua Prieta . . . if you feel like killing a little time."

The little horsethief gave Ringold the briefest of side-glances and grinned as they stood on the saloon's shady porch. "Fess up time, eh?" He plunked down on a bench and tilted his boots up on the wooden railing. "Might as well tell you. I was certain you'd got onto me, what with my extry trips and horse deals. Thought you could'a been sent over to nail me, and was just waitin' th' right chance. Y'know I had you figgered as bein' out'a Texas when we first met, but didn't guess you for a blamed Ranger at that. Anyway, I thought my old green slicker would get you a'foul of them Greasers." Pony took his boots down and shuffled them on the planking. "Never wanted you to get shot at, y'know . . . just, maybe, heaved inter jail for a spell until I had time to figger out if I should fly th' coop or stick around." The little man paused and cleared his throat.

"And then?" Ringold growled, secretly amused to see Pony squirm.

"Then on top of that, Thorne got me doin' somethin' else that made me feel sorta hangdog like. Had me fetchin' your mail outa th' Benson P.O. and takin' it back after he'd steamed th' stuff open. Th' postmaster was wise to what was goin' on, but Thorne paid him off. Thorne pulled a lot of things, but I never had him pegged for head lobo, damn me, if I did!"

"Thorne probably tipped Doc about my Ranger connections, and Doc wrote back to someone in Texas, whoever that was, according to Thorne." Ringold stared out at the lumbering mine wagons and a rattling stage. "If that's the Benson Coach, it must be getting on toward noon." A look at his watch verified his words. He got up and telling Pony to fetch their gear from the hotel and their horses from the livery, follow him down to the telegraph office.

As he suspected there was an answer waiting:

"Sergeant John Ringold, Tucson, A.T. General King absent from state. Return to Texas immediately to resume duties on full pay status. Fugitive horsethief Charles Diehl alias Charles Ray alias Pony Deal reported in Tombstone area. Apprehend if possible and turn over to nearest U.S. Marshal. Signed, Brown, Captain."

He stood staring at the yellow flimsy. So, they wanted him to grab Pony and heave him into some bug-ridden Arizona jail. It would have delighted him to do that to Earps and Holliday, but Pony? *No way.* A friend was a friend! He took out a match, scratched it on the wall of the telegraph office and then seeing the red-headed operator squinting up at him from under his cracked, green eyeshade, blew it out. He put the order back into his vest pocket and went outside to see Pony riding up with the horses.

"Got your wire and all ready to shove off?"

Ringold nodded and took Blackbird's reins from Pony.

"Y'ain't sore at me are you?" The little man went on hurriedly as if fearful of some explosion from Ringold. "Thought I might get some word about Ike. But that ain't our worry. Ready?"

Ringold swung into the saddle and guided Blackbird beside Deal's buckskin down Stone toward the stage road.

• • •

For the next few hours they back-trailed over the same country they'd ridden the previous afternoon. The downpour of the past night still was apparent in the small pockets of moisture among the rocks and boulders of the sandy plain south of town. Traversing the scrub and brush of the foothills and on into the first stands of timber, they began to feel the increasing heat of the first day of spring.

Here they caught glimpses of shy whitetail deer, moving out of their path in the comparative coolness of the oak and pine shade. Their passage did not go completely unchallenged, as more than one scuttling, skipping ground-squirrel stopped long enough to chatter its disturbed feelings at the two riders, while a golden-eyed bobcat glared fearlessly at them from the limb of an oak before vanishing around the trunk.

Cresting the mountains eventually, they skirted the site of Cajeme's murder and rode on down the eastern slope, coming out near the Benson Road. They had already agreed to report the Yaqui's demise to Behan and let John come over and handle the inquest and subsequent burial.

Five miles on, Pony pulled in his buckskin a rifle-shot away from a small cross road, commanded by a rundown road ranch, owned by a boozy character named Marsh. He tugged off his sombrero and wiped the sweat from his eyes.

"What say we ride over and have a few beers, before we get into Benson?"

Ringold, still tense and on edge following the fire-fight of the previous night, and at loose ends with himself, recognized the need to unwind a bit and agreed.

They tied their mounts in front of the place and entered the semi-darkness of the interior, ready for a relaxing half-hour before resuming their journey. But Pony, once he'd buried his nose in the first beer's amber foam, insisted in not only treating Ringold, but a half-dozen cowpokes and loafers of the dive.

Ringold had begun to feel strangely uneasy, although he was unable to determine the exact cause. They'd got away from Tucson without any undue commotion. He had his Ranger's badge and the current wire from the Adjutant General's office at Austin for his credentials, if they had been challenged by Tucson authorities—yet he'd only feel right when he'd got back to Tombstone, packed his war bag, and was on his way out of the Territory.

As he moodily sipped at his drink, he also felt a growing sense of depression. Everything was over. And the Earps, though not captured or all shot dead would never be back. Holliday, in particular, would be a long time, if ever, regaining control of his gun hand. Doc would never, again, be able to deal off the bottom of the deck with such technical virtuosity. Yes, Doc was on the downhill slide—and to hell with him!

After an hour or so, he bought Pony a bottle of whisky, and one for the saddle bag and the long jaunt back to Texas. "Now here's where we part company . . . if you keep on this way," he told the drink-happy, little horsethief. "I want to get on to Tombstone and back out tonight, if I can. I've had a year and a half of this damned Arizona, and that's enough for a long spell."

"No need to rile up, I'm ready." Pony was following Ringold out the door when Ike Clanton, tired and dusty, came in, slapping dust from his clothing. Seeing them, he broke into a hilarious roar. "Hey there! Now then, Pony, old hoss . . . and Ringold. Thought them's your plugs out there. I sure owe you plenty of drinks and I mean to pay up." He dropped his voice a notch. "You fellers sure put th' kibosh for good and all on them Earps. Saved me plenty of lawyer fees. And damn me if I ain't grateful." Clanton settled himself down at the table just vacated by Pony and Ringold.

"Thanks, Ike. Buy my share for Pony. I've got to get on over to Tombstone." Ringold wondered where Ike had come from, but Clanton was as unpredictable as ever. He'd get Ike's story from Pony when Deal got back to town. He'd noticed that Ike had said nothing about his own part in that melee in the Tucson railroad yards, and of the death of Stilwell.

Mounting up out front, Blackbird suddenly shied at a bit of wind-blown paper, and Ringold felt his game ankle give as he fought the suddenly skittish horse.

When he had the great black gentled, he rode off north-eastward, deciding to bypass Benson and head directly for Tombstone. His head had begun to throb with the extra drinks and the unusual heat of the late March day, and he wanted to get the ride over as soon as he could, then rest before starting his long return journey to Texas.

When he was nearly to Sulphur Spring Valley, in the Dragoon foothills, his ankle was paining more and more. He reined in and took a nip from the bottle in the saddle bag. Though never a hefty drinker, he'd sure needed that extra snort. Now he'd ride on a mile to West Turkey Creek Canyon, near the Coyote Smith Ranch. There was a fine stand of live oak along the creek. Just the spot to let Blackbird rest in the shade, and a place where he could shed his boot and cool off that damned trick leg in the water, before riding on down to Tombstone.

At three o'clock he reached the clump of oak along the creek and dismounted, tying Blackbird to a sapling near the steep bank of the curving stream, where the horse could crop the sparse grass.

From where he stood, he could just see the top of the Smith ranch house. A slight wind, hot as the sky, shifted and turned the oak leaves. For some reason, he couldn't place, there came the passing thought of someone or something close by, though there were no sounds other than the rustle of the foliage, the stamp of his horse and the sibilant chuckle of the creek, washing over the snags and rocks of its gravelly bottom.

Shrugging away the feeling, he limped down the bank to the water's edge. Seated on a boulder, he slowly tugged off his boot. Peeling his thick sock, he eased his aching foot into the water and lay back against the cool bank, letting the current slowly wash away the pain.

After a while, he pulled on the sock and, boot in one hand, sombrero in the other, its crown filled with water, he gingerly hobbled up the bank.

He placed the hat, still filled with creek water, in front of Blackbird, and sat down in the fork of a double-trunked live oak, near the creek bank, to tug off the remaining boot.

Sinking back into the natural seat, provided by the forked trunk of the tree, he breathed a sigh of relief. There was nothing for it, but he'd have to ride on to Tombstone with a boot off, until the swelling subsided.

He wondered about Pony. They'd not discussed the route back to Tombstone, but supposed Deal would catch up after he and Ike finished their celebrating. Pony could cut any trail without trouble.

Again came that odd tingling in his spine. Apaches? He'd not thought of them lately, though the papers had carried several stories of isolated raids south of Tombstone and Tucson. But there'd been no word of any renegade Indians this far north.

Apaches were not the only renegades still loose in the Territory, for even with the Earp bunch and Thorne gone, there were still a few second-stringers left.

Then came the thought he'd held at arm's-length for months. *Jim Rush!* But even as he thought of Rush, he dismissed the idea. There just wasn't any way Jim could track him all the way to Tombstone—unless, and again that frosty finger traced a path down his backbone for an instant—unless that was Doc Holliday's last ace.

His ankle continued to throb. He debated going back down the bank to soak his foot, but as he stood up, gingerly favoring his game leg, a slight sound came to him—softly amongst the wind-flutter of the oak leaves.

He listened intently, but again there was nothing except the faint racket of an axe biting into a log at the ranch house over the hill, and the ever-purling ripple of the dun-colored water of the creek. Just that—leaf murmur, and the occasional jingle of Blackbird's trappings as he

317

shifted his cropping of the scrub green grasses.

It would be just like Pony, tanked up on Ike's beer, to try to play some fool trick, or it could be someone else following along. Whoever it was, he wasn't about to be suckered—not this late—with his job done for good in A.T.

He pulled his Colt, and thumbing back the hammer, got up and painfully eased around the massive oak in his stockinged feet.

From where he now stood, he could see that his boots, placed side-by-side, gave the appearance, or illusion, of someone resting in the crotch of the great tree.

Sharp as a carbine shot, a twig cracked in that hushed moment. There was someone near. Nearer than he'd thought! He stepped sideways around the tree—blinded in that instant as the unknown's pistol crashed out to be instantly re-echoed by his own six-gun!

Frozen by the twin explosions, again seeing in his mind's eye the figure of Jim Rush half-crouched not ten feet from the west side of the great oak—pistol raised—and then the double roar of the weapons!

All was humming silence. The wind still muttered amongst the leaves, the creek rippled onward. His horse stamped and shifted while another mount moved among distant trees.

He went forward slowly and knelt beside the motionless figure.

Somehow, Jim Rush had followed him after all—after all those months and that breakout at the Texas Pen. He'd followed on a demented, one-man vengeance committee for that worthless Rufe Higgins. And now he was as dead as Higgins.

Averting his eyes from the white, blood-spattered face, he went through Jim's pockets. There was some money, which he threw on the ground, a pocket knife, a box of matches, tobacco—and a letter.

Rising, he saw the top of Rush's head was blown off by the big .44 slug. He limped back to the bole of the oak, and sank down sweating yet deathly cold.

Where in hell was Pony? There'd been no sound from the ranch house, up beyond the trees, except for that axe that kept up its interminable chopping. If the ranch folks heard the shots, they must have figured it for someone hunting deer along the creek, or shooting at some varmint.

He unfolded the letter. It was four months old, and directed to Rush at the Texas Pen—and written by that foxy skunk of a Doc Holliday!

Somehow he'd expected that.

"Tombstone, A.T.
December 12, 1881
Dear Friend,
Though you may not know me, I am

319

dropping a line to say that an acquaintance of yours is here in Tombstone, big as life and twice as natural. When you are able, you might come over and look him up. I understand he owes you a little matter from a year back.

Yours, Doctor John Holliday."

Just that note, and Rush had broken out of the pen to trail him into the Territory. It was plain that Jim must have been in touch with Doc, but Doc had hauled freight before he could give Rush any assistance at dry-gulching.

Holliday had played his hole card, with Thorne rigging the game, but Jim came up with the losing hand.

The sharp rattle of hooves, coming down the river road, woke Ringold to further danger. He stuffed the note in his pocket and was behind the tree, pistol in hand when two riders dismounted near the dead man.

"By hell, they got Ringo!" The voice of Ike Clanton came to him, pitched high in surprise.

"Aw fer Gawd's sake . . ." Pony's strident tones broke with excitement. "Hi, that's not Ringo. 'Cause if it is, he's dressed in someone else's bib-and-tucker!"

"Right, Pony, don't waste your tears on a stranger." Ringold limped back into sight, reholstering his Colt.

Their faces, Clanton's in particular, were the color of old sour-dough. They stared from Rush upon the ground to Ringold, where he stood before them minus his boots.

"Hell . . . this would'a fooled Old Nick himself, if he'd come fer you at high noon," Ike muttered, mopping at his face with a dusty bandana.

"Jest who . . . is that?" Pony waved a thumb at the dead man.

"A friend, or rather . . . someone I knew back in Texas."

"Hell of a friend." Ike looked over his shoulder. "Ain't no more, is they?"

"No. I think he was the only one. Unless some of the Earps or their crooked friends come back this way. But if they do, I'll be gone to Texas."

"Say then, I got an idee." Ike grinned his splay-toothed grin. "Pony kind'a let th' cat out'a th' bag . . . 'bout you bein' a lawman and all. So, if you're goin' back to Texas. Leavin' for good? Then why don't we up and bury that polecat and say it was John Ringo? That way there's a dead trail endin' right here. There'd be nobody else come along to try for a back shot at you, eh?"

Ringold stared at Pony, who shrugged and turned his hands upward in gesture of sheepish confession. "Didn't think it mattered now if Ike knowed who you was. And maybe he's got a good idea. This feller's a right dead ringer for you. An' if we changed your clothes, and

321

all . . . I'd bet two plugged pesos no one would ever tumble."

"But I still don't see . . ."

"Maybe Doc won't ever come back to Arizony or over to Texas, but you know Pete Spence and a couple of th' Thorne bunch are still loose. No sense in lettin' them track you down for another dry-gulch, like Ike said."

It did make some sense. He'd have enough to do back on the Ranger force without watching his coat-tails for the next few dozen years.

"All right! Get the clothes off of . . . him, and I'll switch."

"Yeah." Clanton was tugging the boots from Rush. "Somebody might come by any damned time. Let's hustle."

It was over in a matter of minutes. He'd dressed himself in Rush's travel-worn togs, retaining the Adjutant General's telegram and other papers as well as his own thin roll of bills. That money due from Wells Fargo would have to come from Jim Hume in San Francisco later.

He limped back to the oak grove to mount Jim's brown mare. He knew he'd have to leave Blackbird, and that hurt him as much as the knowledge that his boyhood friend had hated him enough to trail him to the death.

Returning he was shocked to see Rush propped up in the live oak bole, torn head tilted down upon his vest.

"What in hell are you doing with him like that?" he demanded of Pony.

"Y'see, it figgers this way, that you, *Ringo,* felt so bad about killin' pore Thorne, and shootin' up all those pore Earps . . . that you drunk yourself into a pityful state."

"And up and shot yoreself . . . thereby commitin' personal suicide," grinned Ike, now remounted upon his fat-bellied bay.

"A suicide? Damn it, I'd never do such a thing!"

"Maybe *Sergeant John Ringold* would never do such a thing . . . but pore old John Ringo, he damn-well did just that!" Pony winked slyly.

"Who in hell would believe that, you shifty little horsethief?"

"Oh, just about as many folks as I can find to tell." Pony straightened and raised a hand for silence. "Think someone's comin', probably from old Coyote's place."

Ringold looked at the slumped corpse, garbed in *Ringo's* clothing. "But you've not got him dressed right. My, ah, *his* boots are off. And . . . that cartridge belt of mine is upside down on him." He glanced at the hillside, but nothing was moving there. Yet!

"Well, you gotta sore leg on you ain't you, so you took off your boots *before you blowed off your head,*" chuckled Ike, guiding his horse over to Ringold's. "Don't you ever worry about me,

323

Sarge. Us Clantons can keep our mouths shet—when we've a mind to." He reached out and shook hands. "I'm ridin' on. Let Pony handle th' funeral *obsequees. Buenos Dios!*" And Ike, with a last wave of his ham-sized hand, was gone out of sight among the trees.

"He's right," said Pony. "Ike won't peach. He dassen't dare anyhow. I could tag him fer settin' up Stilwell to plug th' Earps."

"You mean . . . Morgan! You figured out a hell of a lot, didn't you?"

"Maybe. But I ain't gonna stay around here forever, myself. Probably go back up to visit another Doc in my young life . . . my pard Doc Middleton up in Nebrasky. Horses, y'know."

Ringold stared at the little man for a moment, and over at *himself,* sprawled there in the bole of the live oak. He reached into Jim's vest that he now wore, took out the telegram, and tore it in half, while Pony glanced at him curiously. He was about to throw it down, but put it back into the pocket along with that folded note of Doc's. "So, this is *adios*?"

"I guess so. Been one hell of a time, ain't it?" Pony turned and pointed. "Knew it. Someone's comin' over there." Several figures were sauntering down the hill from the direction of the ranch. "We ain't been spotted yet." Pony stuck out his hand. "I'll handle the funeral arrangements, like Ike said. Right there under those rocks by th' big oak would be a good place to bury *John Ringo,* eh?"

The people from the ranch were just entering the clump of trees beyond the double oak. "Well, Pony, watch your step and try to stay away from other folks' horses. Why not try punching cattle or some other game?"

"Your boots!" Pony held up Rush's worn pair.

"Give them here. I'll try them on when I get off a piece." He tied them to the mare's saddle horn. "Can't stop off in Tombstone now, so you get my stuff at the hotel and take it for a keepsake."

"Yeah. Now hit it out of here." Pony slapped the mare and Ringold rode down the river bank, pausing around a bend of the stream to listen.

"Hey, look there!" It was a stranger's voice.

Came the shrill response of Pony Deal. "Yeah, he's dead there. Just found'm myself. Musta blew his brains plumb out!"

There was an indistinct babble of shouts and calls.

He turned his horse's head toward the southwest, riding back out of the creek bottoms. The wind murmured through the trees, and the stream still rippled.

And from the fading distance came Pony's shrill tones . . . "One hell of a feller . . . never see the likes of John Ringo . . . these parts again."

He jabbed the mare with the stockinged heel of his good foot, and headed across the wastelands toward Texas—leaving a mystery that would grow into a legend.

Center Point Large Print
600 Brooks Road / PO Box 1
Thorndike, ME 04986-0001 USA

(207) 568-3717

US & Canada:
1 800 929-9108
www.centerpointlargeprint.com